JESSICA'S
new beginning
A NOVEL

JESSICA'S
new beginning
A NOVEL

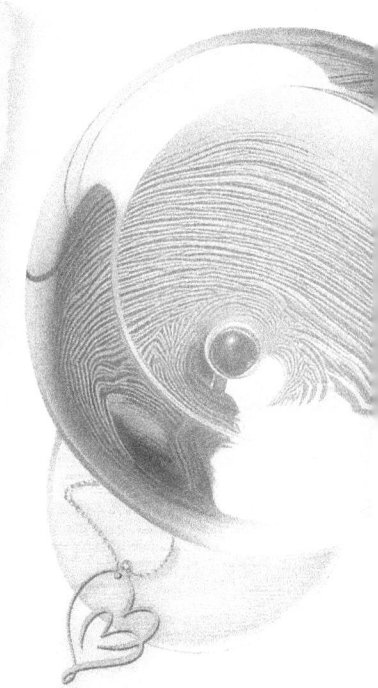

o the Woman Who Loves Him Next,

You don't know me, but I've thought about
u more than you can imagine.

ou're reading this, then it means you've
ady met Will. Maybe you've already
en for him. Perhaps you're wondering if
re strong enough to love a man who's
through tremendous loss.

e say this: if he chose you, you are.

he kind of man who remembers
saries and notices when your coffee
anges. He's the guy who will rub
 when you're sick and argue with
something doe

ANN
SCHREIBER

About the Author

Ann Schreiber is an author and lifelong book lover who lives in Minnesota with her husband and stepdaughter. She's also a proud mom to two adult children and recently became a grandmother, her favorite new title.

Also by Ann Schreiber:

Perseverance. Reinvention. (2024):
A raw and honest memoir about starting over.

The Top 10 Mistakes I Made My First Year as a Copywriter (2025):
A practical guide for aspiring writers.

Emily's Next Chapter (2025):
A heartwarming fiction debut about love, family, and second chances.
Emily's Next Chapter is book one in the *Starting Over Trilogy*.

Whether writing nonfiction or novels, Ann is drawn to stories about resilience, personal growth, and the relationships that shape who we become.

WRITE_READ_WRITE_REPEAT

For more information on what Ann is reading and writing, follow her on Instagram.

A Letter to My Readers

Dear Reader,

Thank you for picking up Jessica's New Beginning, the second book in what has become my Starting Over Trilogy. This story touches on themes that may feel deeply personal to some and unexpectedly emotional to others. So before you start reading, I want to share a few notes about the content.

This book includes familiar and beloved tropes:

- *Single dad navigating grief*
- *Slow-burn second-chance romance*
- *Found family and blended family dynamics*
- *A reluctant but big-hearted heroine rediscovering love*

It also explores sensitive and potentially triggering topics, such as:

- *The loss of a spouse*
- *The challenges of co-parenting and step-parenting*
- *Grief and emotional trauma*
- *Parental illness and loss*
- *Divorce and the long road of healing*

While this is a work of fiction, it's rooted in real emotions, and I hope that you will find moments of comfort, connection, and clarity within the pages. If you see yourself in Jessica, Will, or anyone else along the way, know you're not alone. And if you simply came for the love story, I hope it will make you smile, ache a little, and believe in beginnings.

With love and gratitude,

Ann

Copyright © 2025 by Ann Schreiber

All rights reserved. Published in the United States by Fox Pointe Publishing, LLP. No part of this book may be reproduced in any form or by any electronic or mechanical means, including information storage and retrieval systems, without permission in writing from the publisher.

This is a work of fiction. Names, places, characters, and incidents are either a product of the author's imagination or are used fictitiously. Any resemblance to actual events, places, organizations, or persons, whether living or dead, is entirely coincidental.

www.foxpointepublishing.com/author-ann-schreiber

Library of Congress Cataloging-in-Publication Data
SCHREIBER, ANN, author.
TOWN, SCOTTY, designer.
JESSICA'S NEW BEGINNING / ANN SCHREIBER. – First edition.
Summary: A heartfelt story about healing, unexpected love, and the complicated path to starting over, especially when the past isn't fully behind you.
Hardcover ISBN 978-1-955743-49-5 / Softcover ISBN 978-1-955743-50-1
[1. General – Fiction. 2. Family – Fiction. 3. Relationships – Fiction.]
Library of Congress Control Number: 2 0 2 5 9 4 2 3 8 8

First printing March 2026

Prologue

Katie

METAPLASTIC BREAST CANCER. The words hit like a freight train. No soft landings, no sugarcoating. Just cold, clinical facts delivered in a quiet room that suddenly felt too small. The doctor looked me in the eyes and told me the truth: we caught it early, but with this type of cancer, early didn't guarantee much. My five-year survival rate was 32%.

I remember nodding slowly, even as my ears buzzed and my brain tried to buffer reality. Thirty-two percent. It could have been thirty-three. I wasn't a gambler, but that didn't feel like odds I could bet on.

Will came with me to that appointment. He held my hand and asked all the questions I couldn't. That was who he was. My solid place to land. Strong. Loyal. Protective. He cried later, when we were alone in the car. I didn't. Not then. I couldn't afford to fall apart yet.

ANN SCHREIBER

Nine months later, my body told me what I already knew. Time was slipping. My joints ached constantly. I needed help just getting from the bed to the bathroom. The dizziness was nearly constant. I was exhausted. My vision blurred more days than not.

I didn't need another scan to know. The end was coming.

But I had things to do. I wasn't going to leave without a trace.

Each morning, as long as I could, I wrote letters.

To Max, my beautiful boy with his thoughtful eyes and quiet strength. There was a letter for his next birthday, for the day he got his driver's license, and for when he graduated. One for his wedding day. And one for the day after I died.

To Sophie, my gorgeous little girl, all sparkle and fight. I wrote letters for her, too. Pep talks disguised as birthday cards, advice hidden in silly stories. And one goodbye she'd open when she was ready.

I wrote two letters for Will.

The first was everything I needed him to know: how fiercely I loved him, how grateful I was to have been his wife, how I'd choose him again in every lifetime. I asked him to keep his heart open to our children. To keep talking about me, even when it hurt. I needed him to help keep me alive, at least in spirit.

But there was one more thing I needed him to hear. And it deserved its own letter.

That second letter tore something out of me. I could barely write through the tears. I wasn't ready to say it. I didn't want to. But I knew I had to. I needed Will to understand that it was okay to love again, completely. He'd never do it if he thought it was a betrayal. So I gave him permission. I gave him my blessing.

And now... There was one final letter to write. To her. The woman who would hold his heart next.

Yes, I stole the idea from Safe Haven. That Nicholas Sparks book always left me with enough tears to create a puddle, and the movie wrecked me each time I watched it. But writing this letter felt right. Even if I couldn't come back as some magical ghost to guide her, I wanted this future woman in Will's life to hear from me. I wanted her to know a few things before she stepped fully into his life.

She needed to understand what she was walking into. And she needed to know the rules.

Rule One: Love Will with everything you've got. He doesn't give his heart lightly. If he gives it to you, treasure it.

Rule Two: My kids are my soul. Max and Sophie will need your patience, your humor, and your unwavering presence. They may not make it easy. Love them anyway.

Rule Three: Be honest. Be open. Protect Will's heart as if it were your own. Because I know what it means to carry it, and I'm trusting you to carry it next.

I know you'll never truly meet me. But I hope you see me in the family you become a part of. And I hope you know how much it means to me that he found someone brave enough to love him after what he has lost.

And now it was time. Time to write my final letter.

To the Woman Who Loves Him Next,

You don't know me, but I've thought about you more than you can imagine.

If you're reading this, then it means you've already met Will. Maybe you've already fallen for him. Perhaps you're wondering if you're strong enough to love a man who's lived through tremendous loss.

Let me say this: if he chose you, you are.

Will is the kind of man who remembers anniversaries and notices when your coffee order changes. He's the guy who will rub your back when you're sick and argue with doctors if something doesn't feel right. He's a little stubborn. He overthinks things. But he will love you with everything he has.

I was lucky to be his first great love. You are fortunate to be his next.

Please don't let guilt keep you from being happy. I want you to be happy. I want him to be happy. I want you both to laugh more than you cry.

And I want you to know that I see you.

Thank you for loving him. Thank you for being brave enough to step into a life that once included me. He is yours now. Take care of him.

And if you ever doubt yourself, just remember that he deserves love. And so do you.

With peace and hope,

Katie

1

Jessica

THE STEAMY ONSCREEN KISS practically fogged up my living room television.

Lily's leggings were soft in my hands, a little too small for her now, but still in the laundry rotation because she insisted they were "super lucky." I folded them neatly and set them on the growing stack beside me, half-watching the movie playing on the TV.

Some late-night romance I'd landed on, purely by accident. Or maybe not. The chemistry between the leads had been building for the past thirty minutes. Subtle glances, hands brushing just a second too long. It was the kind of tension that sits low in your gut and dares you to ignore it. And now, it had snapped.

He pulled her to him in one quick motion, like he couldn't bear another second of space between them, and turned, pinning her gently but firmly against the wall. She gasped, but it was clearly not in protest. Her hands flew to his hair, fingers threading through like she'd done it a thousand times before and couldn't remember a single time where she didn't want more.

And then came the kiss.

It was the type of kiss where nothing was left unsaid. I imagine it was the kind that said, *I've been thinking about this since the moment I saw you, and I won't stop thinking about it after.* It was slow yet filled with hunger, a perfect mix of restraint and need. *I want you. I want you to want me.* His hand moved lower to her waist, then up to her jaw, her cheek. He was exploring, grounding, claiming. Her back arched, rounding off the wall as her body leaned into his. It was 'sexy' at its finest.

I shifted on the couch, my skin suddenly feeling too warm. That kiss. That desperate, worshipful, *where have you been all my life* kind of kiss. I remembered that kind of kiss. Barely.

I hit pause on the television. Not because I wanted to, but because I needed to.

I leaned back into the couch, letting my head drop against the cushions. The silence in my apartment pressed in from all sides. I arched my back like the woman on the screen. And practically before I started, I stopped. A blush crept onto my cheeks, and I sighed in frustration. I looked at the folded pile of Lily's laundry, Mr. Fluffles, Lily's stuffed bunny that was perched in the opposite corner of the couch, then at the empty wine glass on the coffee table, and let out a small laugh. But it wasn't one of those laughs full of joy and humor. It was more like, *Is this really my life? Am I really all alone?*

What a scene. What a life I imagined for that female character. It had been a long time since I'd been kissed like that and touched like that. Wanted like that.

Lucas used to. Back in the beginning, we couldn't keep our hands off each other. It had been hot, messy, real. And often. We used to sneak in sex before dinner reservations, after work, in the shower, against the door. Wherever, whenever. It didn't matter. But then came more responsibilities. Careers. Then Lily.

And everything shifted.

Passion was replaced with practicalities. Spontaneity got replaced by demanding work schedules. Lucas would stay up late working on architectural plans for his latest project. I would be in another room studying for an upcoming exam. As such, the nights turned into me in one room and Lucas in another. Separate television shows, but likely the same resentment. The physical stuff didn't stop right away, but it gradually faded into a routine, like it was just maintenance. Sex was something we did because we thought we should or because we knew at least that we were good at it, but not because we couldn't wait to consume one another.

I missed sex that meant something. And I missed sex that didn't. I missed being looked at like I was a fire someone wanted to burn in. I sighed and stared up at the ceiling. Was I even ready to feel that again? To want it? To want someone? I wasn't sure.

The ringtone startled me out of my thoughts. I groaned as I reached for my phone, nearly knocking over the laundry basket in the process. Mom flashed across the screen—great timing, as always.

"Hey, Mom," I answered, trying to sound casual, wishing the blush away from my cheeks.

"Well, there she is," my mother said, voice crisp and bright. "I was starting to wonder if you'd forgotten how phones worked."

I bit back a sigh, bracing myself for the lecture that I knew was to come. "It's been a busy week. I just put Lily's laundry away and was about to—"

"I haven't seen that little girl in ages," her mother cut in. "I miss her, Jessica. Maybe you could bring her up this weekend? If you're not too busy doing... whatever you do these days."

There it was. The subtle jab about whatever it is that I do these days. My mother had made plenty of comments in recent years about how nice it must be to be a half-time mother and to have half of my time available to do as I please. It was the 'you-don't-have-her-full-time-anymore' guilt trip. Carol, my mother, was a master at it. And why did it matter what I did on my own time?

"I'd love to bring her up, Mom," I said, working hard to calm my voice. "But we've got her birthday coming up, remember? And I've got a packed schedule at the clinic. I'll call you when I have a free weekend, okay?"

She gave a soft "hmm" like she didn't quite believe me. "Well, I'd hate to think she's spending all her time with Emily."

I closed my eyes. "She's not. She's with her dad. And Emily's part of the picture now, whether we like it or not." In all honesty, Emily was beginning to grow on me. She seemed good for Lucas. And dare I say it, Emily was good for Lily, too.

My mom was quiet. "I'll call you tomorrow," I added, already wanting to be off the phone.

"You always say that," she said, but her voice had softened. "Tell Lily I love her."

"I will. Night, Mom."

"Night, Jess."

I hung up and tossed the phone onto the coffee table, a little more forceful than I meant to. Trying to shove the frustration away from my thoughts, I leaned forward and grabbed the remote again. Maybe I should just finish the movie and call it a night. But as I pressed play, I let a thought take root.

I didn't want to be alone forever. Lucas was moving on. I could move on, too, right? I wanted a connection. I wanted something messy, complicated, sexy, and real. Maybe not tomorrow. But soon. Definitely soon.

2

Jessica

THE PATIO AT CAFE ASTORIA in St. Paul was still open, and I was grateful for it. The early October air had that crispness that hinted at the cooler days ahead, but the sun was still strong enough to make sitting outside pleasant, as long as you wore a light fall jacket.

I tugged my denim jacket tighter around me and sipped on my apple cider cocktail. Across the table, Liz was picking at her salad, already deep into a story about her latest client at the nonprofit where she worked.

"So then this guy tells me, dead serious, that his donation should come with naming rights for the front door. The front door, Jess. Like, 'Welcome to the Johnson Family Entrance.' Who even says that with a straight face?"

I laughed, nearly spitting out my drink. "Did you tell him no?"

"I told him he could have a commemorative doormat. He didn't laugh. But I did. And then my boss called me into her office. Again."

"You're going to get yourself fired one of these days."

"Nah," Liz said, spearing a cherry tomato with her fork. "I'm too charming. And they know no one else would put up with the crap I do."

We lapsed into an easy silence, the kind that only old friends can share without trying to figure out what to say next. I leaned back and let myself enjoy the fall sunshine and the buzz of conversation from the patrons at the other tables around us. It felt good to be out. It felt... normal. I needed more normal.

"So," Liz said, setting down her fork and leaning in slightly, eyebrows raised. "When are you going to get with it?"

I blinked. "Get with what?"

"Dating. A love life. A real, live man. Jess, it's been two years since the divorce was finalized. You're not a nun."

I rolled my eyes. "Wow, subtle."

"I'm serious! You're hot. You've got that sexy, confident, thirty-something thing going on. You're smart, funny, and you've got great hair. Seriously, people would kill for your blonde waves. You're telling me you don't want to see what's out there?"

"I mean, it's not like I haven't thought about it," I said, picking at the edge of my napkin. "But the idea of getting dressed up and going on awkward dates just makes me tired. I don't think I have the energy for that. It would be so much different than it was a decade ago."

"Ugh, not if you do it right. Dating apps, babe. You get to filter the weirdos out before you waste a Friday night on them."

I raised an eyebrow. "You've seen the guys on those apps. Half of them are posing with fish or their cars or flexing shirtless in their bathroom mirrors. It's gross. I mean, what guy thinks a girl wants to see that on their dating profile? Yuck."

"Which is why you need me. I'll do the filtering."

"Absolutely not."

Liz reached across the table, trying to grab my phone. But I was too quick for her. My reaction time had improved since becoming a mother. I yanked the phone away, laughing. "Nope. Not happening."

"Come on! Just let me make you a profile. You don't even have to swipe. I'll set you up with a decent guy who doesn't use the word 'babygirl' in texts."

"Tempting. Still no."

Liz sighed dramatically. "Fine. But promise me you'll at least think about it."

I hesitated, then nodded. "I'll think about it."

"That's all I ask."

I looked down at my drink, the ice in the cocktail starting to melt. "Okay, confession time. You know how I told you I was folding laundry the other night?"

"Yeah?"

"Well, I got sucked into this ridiculous old romance movie on TV. Like full-on, steamy, 90s hot. Shirtless construction worker falls for the sassy good girl librarian type."

Liz grinned. "Ooh, and?"

I could feel my face heat. "Let's just say it's been a long time since a movie made me feel like that. And I didn't hate it."

Liz clapped. "That's what I'm talking about! You're ready. You've got the lust, girl!"

"Good grief, Liz. The lust? Who even says that? Besides, I didn't say that. I just... maybe I'm not as closed off as I thought to starting a new relationship."

"Good. That's how it starts. A little spark."

I smiled, a real one this time. Maybe Liz was right. Perhaps I was ready for something. Or someone. It didn't have to be serious. It didn't even have to be love. But connection? A little fun? That didn't sound so bad.

As we finished our lunch and Liz launched into a new story about her own, albeit comedic, dating life, I felt lighter than I had in weeks. The October sun warmed my shoulders. Could the future be beginning to feel like less of a question mark? Maybe. I just needed to get through these next few weeks first. Lily's birthday. The holidays. Then we would see. Perhaps it really was time to move forward.

3

Liz

THE MOMENT I STEPPED OUT of Cafe Astoria, the early October breeze kissed my cheeks, and I pulled my jacket tighter around me. It wasn't quite scarf weather yet, but the air carried the kind of chill that hinted we weren't far from it. Jessica and I had taken the corner patio table, like we always did when the weather allowed, and for a moment, it almost felt like the old days.

Almost.

I paused on the sidewalk, glancing back through the glass windows where I could still see Jess sipping the last of her apple cider cocktail. She had moved inside when I left. She had that look on her face. You know the look. The look that said she was going to overthink everything we just talked about. I knew it well.

Jessica and I had been through it all together. We met in Mrs. Hammond's third-grade class, back when we both still thought boys had cooties and Lisa Frank folders were, like, totally cool.

Over the years, we traded secrets, lip gloss, hair ties, and life lessons. Crushes came and went. There were awkward middle school dances, high school heartbreaks, late-night sleepovers filled with whispered hopes followed by whispered tears. And then, real life happened.

When Jess met Lucas, she was over the moon. I remember the first time she told me about him. We were sitting in the back booth at Perkins at midnight, splitting a basket of fries like we were still seventeen. Her eyes were sparkling, and she was practically glowing just talking about him. "He listens," she'd said. "Like really listens." I knew how important it was for Jessica to have a good conversation with whoever she was dating.

And for a while, he did listen. It was like that older man thing, well, not that much older, was really working for Jess. And for a while, they were happy. But somewhere along the way, things started to crack. It was subtle, but things began to unravel. I was there for those calls, too. The quiet, late-night phone calls where her voice shook and she tried to explain how they just kept missing each other. How being in the same room started to feel lonely. It was like watching someone slowly deflate.

And then Lily came. That sweet girl was the glue that held Jess and Lucas together for a long time. But glue can only hold for so long when the foundation is crumbling; an ironic thought since Jessica was married to an architect, someone whose primary job was to build structures built to last. Yet in the case of Jess and Lucas, they held on for almost five years before it was time to call it what it was. Over. Sometimes, I wondered if they were ever meant to be. At all.

I sighed and started walking toward my car. The leaves were just beginning to change, the edges of the maples tinged with red and orange. Fall was always my favorite. The air gets crisper, the men start layering, and I'm a sucker for a guy in a long-sleeved Henley and jacket. It feels like a fresh start for both fashion and life.

Speaking of men...

Let's just say my love life doesn't look like Jess'. I believe in love, sure. But I also believe in good sex, good conversation, and knowing when it's time to move on. I don't keep a guy around just to avoid being alone. I keep a guy around if he's fun, hot, and worth my time. If he checks two of those three boxes, we're good for at least a few weeks.

I'm on a first-name basis with my nurse practitioner. I schedule my appointments like clockwork and keep my drawer stocked with the good stuff. I'm not out here catching feelings, or diseases, for that matter. I'm catching orgasms. And lots of them.

And Jess? Jess needs a little of that energy. Not necessarily the rotating roster (though I wouldn't judge), but the confidence. The reminder that she is sexy, wanted, and so damn ready for something that isn't wrapped up in play dates, PTA meetings, or her latest patients.

I mean, the girl was blushing just describing a makeout scene from some trashy romance flick the other night. "His hands were in her hair!" she'd gasped, like she hadn't felt that in decades.

Girl.

So yeah, I'm gonna help her out. She didn't hand over her phone to let me create a dating profile (yet), but that just means I have to get creative. Maybe a casual happy hour? A friendly trivia night at that new brewery where the bartenders all look like they came off an Armani commercial?

A double date.

That's what we'll do.

I'll find some non-creepy guy from the upper half of my contacts, someone with a friend who can carry on a conversation, and maybe looks decent in jeans, and we'll go out. Drinks, apps, light flirting. Nothing serious. Just enough to get her heart rate up again.

Jess has been sitting in the shallow end for too long. It was time for her to dive into the deep end. Something fun, even if it means a fast fling.

That said, she's not going to be alone forever. Not if I have anything to say about it.

4

Jessica

THE DAY BEFORE LILY'S BIRTHDAY party always felt like a mix of chaos and joy, but this year, it felt like a little more of both. I had flour streaked across my cheek, the kitchen counters were a mess, and my entire apartment smelled like chocolate and vanilla extract. The polar bear cake, her special request this year, was halfway frosted and still needed its finishing touches. Somehow, my seven-going-on-eighteen-year-old daughter had decided polar bears were her favorite animal, and when she wanted a polar bear cake, I took that request seriously.

Baking had become a ritual for me, something that started after Lily was born. In those long, late nights when I was trying to build my career as a licensed physical therapist and couldn't sleep because my mind was preoccupied, I would bake. It gave me something to do with my hands, something that made the house feel warm, and it filled the silence with purpose. Now, it had become a tradition. A tradition that made Lily's birthdays feel extra special.

I was elbow-deep in buttercream when my phone rang. I leaned over with my forearm, smudging the screen just enough to see Liz's name pop up. I smiled and wiped my hands quickly on a dish towel before answering.

"Hey, Cake Queen," Liz said, skipping over the usual pleasantries. Though let's face it, Liz is not into pleasantries to begin with.. "Tell me you're not still elbow-deep in fondant animals."

"Just buttercream today. And if you must know, the polar bear looks adorable," I said, glancing at the half-decorated cake with pride.

"Of course, you made homemade buttercream. You always go all out," Liz said, her voice softening. "Listen, I had an idea."

Uh-oh. Liz's ideas usually involved a lot of nudging and a little emotional blackmail.

"Should I be scared?"

"No more than usual. I'm thinking a double date. You, me, two guys, Friday night next week. Just drinks. Casual. No pressure."

I paused, one hand on the piping bag. "Liz, come on. Lily's party is tomorrow. I have a million things to do."

"Which is exactly why you need a break after the chaos."

"I don't know…"

"Tony's the guy I've gone out with a few times. You'd like him. And he's bringing his friend Jeremy. Software engineer. Totally normal. Not a weirdo, I swear."

I snorted. "You always say that."

"Because it's usually true. Usually. But seriously, he's smart, has a good job, and likes bookstores. That's like basically your dream man."

"You've been stalking him already?"

"Of course. It's called research. So?"

I bit my lip. My immediate reaction was to decline. I'd decline politely, of course, but something about Liz's voice told me she wasn't going to drop it. And if I had to be honest with myself, I didn't want her to.

"Alright," I said slowly. "But only drinks. And I need to see if Lucas can take Lily for the night."

"He will. He and Emily are basically super-parents now."

I rolled my eyes but smiled. "They're just dating," I reminded her. "And you're relentless."

"You love me for it. Friday night, my place at six."

We ended the call, and I returned to Lily's cake, my mind suddenly not as focused on polar bears. A date. Well, kind of. It felt weird, thinking about getting dressed up for someone who wasn't Lucas. But maybe it was time.

I tapped a few keys on my phone, pulling up my messages. Lucas would say yes. He always did when it came to Lily. And he had Emily now, someone who loved our daughter, and someone Lily clearly adored.

I took a deep breath and sent the text. Then I looked down at the polar bear cake.

"Alright, Frosty," I whispered. "Looks like your mom's getting back out there."

The bear didn't respond, but I swore he was smiling a little more than before.

5

Jessica

THE EARLY NOVEMBER SUN was already sinking as I drove toward Liz's place, golden light streaking through the bare trees that lined the familiar neighborhood. We had sold the home we had lived in together during our relationship, unfortunately, barely breaking even with the sale. Lucas had bought his current home after the divorce, and I had moved into a small two-bedroom apartment.

Seeing Liz's tree-lined streets made me feel a bit sad, thinking about what I had lost when Lucas and I had sold our home. And in truth, Lucas' new neighborhood, not our old one, felt just like the one I had always envisioned for myself. Maybe someday I would be a homeowner again. I glanced at the clock on my dashboard. There was plenty of time before our double date, though I was already feeling jittery. I wasn't sure if it was nerves or excitement. Maybe both.

As my car idled at a red light, my mind drifted back to last weekend—Lily's birthday.

We'd held the party at Lucas's house, just as we had the year before. Ten of Lily's friends from school showed up, loud and excited, stomping through the backyard trail Lucas had turned into a treasure hunt. Or, as Lily would correct me, an 'adventure trail'. The big red baskets were a hit, and the way Lily's eyes lit up every time someone found a hidden surprise. Well, it was enough to make my throat tight.

And of course, Emily was there.

I'd been bracing myself to dislike her, even though I had met Emily once before over coffee. I already knew she was someone I would like, despite my intentions. I felt like I should feel territorial or threatened. But she'd made that so damn hard. Emily was warm, thoughtful, and just the right amount of involved. She helped Lily tie her shoelaces when the kids were off on their adventure walk and passed out juice boxes like she'd done it a hundred times before. She wasn't trying to replace me, and I could see that. Still, watching the way Lily beamed up at her gave me a twinge of something I didn't like admitting. Not resentment, exactly. Jealousy, maybe.

Lucas had told me a few weeks ago that he and Emily planned to move in together. Not right away, but after the holidays, once Emily sells her house. But even with the cushion of time, the idea had stunned me.

It wasn't that I wanted him back. We'd grown apart long before our marriage ended, and I didn't miss the version of us we'd become. And I didn't regret asking Lucas to leave. I stood by my decision to end our marriage. But hearing he was building something new, something serious, with someone else so soon still hit me sideways. Our divorce was just over two years old.

I was happy for him, I really was. But part of me was beginning to wish I had someone, too.

I pulled into Liz's driveway and took a deep breath before heading up to her door. She opened it the second I knocked, already halfway into her coat.

"You ready?" she grinned. "Tony's picking us up. And I warned Jeremy you're a total knockout, so don't make a liar out of me."

"Ugh," I groaned, laughing. "You're impossible."

"You love me."

"Unfortunately."

Tony's SUV pulled up out front, and I followed behind Liz. She opened the passenger door and slid into the passenger seat next to Tony, leaving the back for me. No introduction. I was on my own, and my heart rate quickened as my nerves started to take over. Thankfully, Jeremy stepped out of the back seat. I immediately noticed his height. He was tall, lean, with a nice smile and warm eyes. Definitely attractive. He turned to me with a soft, "Hey, Jessica, nice to meet you," and extended a hand.

I shook it and felt the first flush of warmth creep up my neck. Damn. That voice. That clean, good-man smell. For a second, I remembered the movie I'd watched just a few weeks ago. The way the man had kissed the woman, pushed her against the wall, his hands threading into her hair. Her hands in his. Heat flared in my belly as I remembered arching my back against my couch, and I squirmed slightly, hoping no one noticed. I quickly made my way to the other side of the SUV to climb in.

Dinner was at a new spot downtown. It was modern, dimly lit, cozy. Perfect for conversation. We sat across from each other, and Jeremy and I started talking easily enough. He asked questions, seemed genuinely interested in my work as a physical therapist, and shared a little about his job as a software engineer for a local law firm.

He was smart. Kind. Funny in a subtle way. He was super fit, likely due to his love for hiking. And so very good-looking.

And yet... nothing. There was no spark. No butterflies. No zing. No undercurrent of chemistry pulling me toward him.

My body might have reacted at first. But that was likely because I was out of touch from being too long without a connection. And he was incredibly good-looking. But the more we talked, the clearer it became. Jeremy wasn't the one. Not even close. Not for me.

I was perplexed. There was absolutely nothing wrong with Jeremy. So why didn't I feel something? I glanced at Liz across the table, watching her laugh at something Tony said, her hand resting lightly on his arm. That was Liz. She was comfortable with light, casual affection. She could sleep with someone for fun and walk away without overthinking it.

I wasn't wired that way. I needed more than a pretty face and polite conversation. I wanted someone who made me laugh, who challenged me, who understood that my life came with an eight-year-old girl who loved polar bears and asked deep questions at bedtime.

Jeremy smiled across the table. "So, what's your favorite kind of dessert?"

I blinked. "Um, cake. Chocolate. Definitely chocolate."

"Classic. You make it yourself?"

"Actually, yeah," I said, suddenly lighting up. "I just baked one for my daughter's birthday. It had a polar bear on it. Her request."

He chuckled. "Nice. You must be a cool mom."

I smiled politely. But it felt flat. He was trying. I was trying. But sometimes trying just isn't enough.

Later that night, after the goodbyes and the polite "we should do this again sometime," I slid into the driver's seat of my car and sat there a minute. I hadn't even needed to text Liz to confirm what we both already knew. Jeremy was a good guy, just not my type.

As I started the engine and backed out of Liz's driveway, my thoughts drifted again. To Lily. To Emily. To Lucas. And to the possibility that maybe something unexpected was waiting for me out there. It had to be, right? I nodded to myself. Yes, the answer was absolutely, yes.

6

Jessica

NOVEMBER HAD CREPT IN with a chill that didn't let up, and somehow, without warning, I blinked and found myself staring down the barrel of December. The fall had been such a blur, I wasn't entirely sure how I'd made it through. Between Lily's birthday party, a handful of late nights at the hospital, and the looming holidays, I had barely had a moment to breathe.

But nothing could have prepared me for the call that had come the month before, not long before Thanksgiving.

It had been a Tuesday. My phone rang just after 8 p.m., just as I was putting away dishes from dinner. I didn't recognize the number, but something in my gut told me to answer.

"Hello?" I said cautiously.

"Hi," a woman's voice replied, hesitant but steady. "Is this Jessica?"

My stomach tightened. The voice wasn't familiar, and the uneasy tone set my nerves on edge. "Yes, this is Jessica. Who's calling?"

"My name is Janice Wilson," she said. "I... I'm not sure how to say this, but I found your phone number on a business card in Lucas' wallet."

My heart skipped a beat, and a cold knot formed in my stomach. "Excuse me?" I said, gripping the phone tighter. "Why do you have Lucas' wallet? What's going on?"

The woman hesitated, and I could hear the strain in her voice. "I'm sorry—I don't mean to alarm you. My husband and I own the property where Lucas was working today. He had an accident."

"An accident?" The word barely made it past my lips.

"Yes," Janice continued, her voice softening. "Well, he almost fell out of a tree. Thankfully, we got there—" the woman paused. "Sorry, that's not important. He was able to climb down once Richard put the ladder back in place. He seemed fine at first—but then... Well, he collapsed. We called 911 immediately, and the paramedics took him to the hospital."

I didn't realize I had been holding my breath until I felt the air rush out of my lungs. My legs wobbled, and I sat down on the kitchen barstool. "Where is he now?" I asked, my voice trembling.

"I think they were taking him to a hospital in St. Paul—the big one with the trauma center," Janice said, her voice filled with desperation. "You know, that big one along I-94? For the life of me, I can't remember the name at the moment. Anyway, I found your number and thought you might be someone close to him. Your business card was the only one in his wallet."

I didn't hear the rest of what she said. I knew which hospital. As soon as the woman had said trauma center, I knew. The phone had slipped from my hand, clattering to the floor. How could this be happening? I had thought.

In any case, I had called Mrs. Hanson, our neighbor from two doors down, and asked her to come sit with Lily. I'd barely explained what was going on when she was already grabbing her knitting bag. Five minutes later, I was in my car and speeding to the hospital, heart racing and mind spinning.

By the time I arrived at the hospital, I was shaking and pacing the hallway outside the ER doors. A nurse had come out, asked if I was Jessica, and then told me Lucas had specifically requested to see me.

That had startled me.

Not because I didn't want to see him, but because I knew he had someone else now. But in that moment, maybe he hadn't known Emily and her family were already arriving. Maybe he just needed someone familiar. Someone who'd been through all the ups and downs. Someone who would come without question.

When I entered the dimly lit hospital room, Lucas looked pale and tired, but very much himself. He managed a small grin when he saw me. "Hey," he said weakly.

"Hey, yourself," I whispered, stepping closer. I took his hand. It was still warm, still strong. I held it between both of mine.

"You scared the hell out of me," I said, trying to keep my voice light, even as my chest tightened.

"Scared myself, too," he admitted, chuckling. "Dr. Patel's already on my case about my diet. I'm guessing I won't see any more late-night pizza runs."

We'd exchanged some light banter before I told Lucas that Emily had arrived. I left the room and returned to the waiting room, letting Emily know that Lucas was asking to see her. It had felt so strange, this exchange with another woman about a man I had once loved. But I could see the relief in Emily's eyes.

Now, weeks later, I still felt that panic whenever the phone rang. But he was okay. Recovering. And from the way Emily talked about the changes at home, like new routines, new recipes, and fewer energy drinks. I was confident she'd be on his case for a long time to come.

I should have been relieved. But instead, I felt... stuck.

Liz had been hounding me on and on to set up a dating app profile. I'd nearly caved more than once, but something else got in the way every time I thought about it. Lucas' heart attack. Work. Thanksgiving. But now? I was out of excuses.

So I opened the fridge, pulled out my favorite buttery Chardonnay, poured myself a glass, and sank into the couch. I picked up my phone and started researching dating apps. After a few clicks and a little reading, I settled on a semi-respectable one.

The blank profile stared back at me.

Hidden talents? I don't know... I make a mean chocolate cake. Best quality? My hair. Long in length, wavy, and blonde. Usually in a ponytail, but when I wear it down, it looks pretty damn sexy, if I did say so myself.

Celebrity crush? Ryan Reynolds, for sure. And Rob Thomas from Matchbox Twenty. Absolutely. I typed in their names. Favorite thing to do on a Sunday morning? Sleep. Maybe brunch if I'm feeling sociable.

About 30 minutes later, I had something that resembled a decent profile. I'd even uploaded those photos Liz had taken a few weeks ago. One at the pumpkin patch sans Lily, another solo shot in my fall jacket. Not bad. I looked... dateable.

I stared at the screen. Okay, swipe right to say yes, swipe left to say no. Got it.

I grabbed the Roku remote and let Netflix load. The first recommendation in my queue was some romantic comedy that looked tame enough, so I clicked it and let it play while I started swiping.

The first few profiles were immediate passes. Shirtless selfies. Gym mirror shots. Guys holding up giant fish like that was supposed to impress me. One guy was in a tux, which might have been promising, except he'd clearly cropped out a date from the photo. I mean, her hand was still on his shoulder—hard pass.

Liz would have been cackling if she'd seen these. She loved the guys who let it all hang out. "Bare it all, baby," she always said.

Me? I wanted a little mystery. A little dignity. A guy who didn't feel the need to lead with his abs.

I finally landed on a guy named Marty. Firefighter. Clean smile. No fish photos. No ex-girlfriend's hands lingering in the frame. He seemed— normal. For the most part... Nice.

I swiped right. And just like that, it was done.

I tossed my phone on the couch, took another long sip of wine, and pulled the blanket up over my legs. The movie had shifted into a steamier scene, and I rolled my eyes at the predictable plot, but couldn't deny the tiny flicker of warmth low in my belly.

7

Jessica

I COULDN'T STOP LAUGHING.

Not the kind of laugh that bubbles up from a genuinely good time. No, this was the incredulous, exhausted, almost maniacal laugh that only came when your expectations had plummeted so far into the earth's crust they were probably being studied by geologists. My hands gripped the steering wheel as I drove the familiar route home, headlights cutting through the dark Minnesota night. The wind had picked up, stirring the leaves that danced across the road like there was music playing that no one else could hear.

God, what had just happened?

It had all started with so much promise. Marty and I had been exchanging texts for a couple of weeks, first within the app, then, once I felt safe enough, we moved to actual numbers. Our text exchanges had been... fun. Flirty. Even dirty, at times. I wasn't proud of everything

I'd typed after a glass of wine and a bubble bath, but hey, it had been a while, and it felt good to be wanted again. The way Marty talked, or typed, I guess, had made my skin tingle. He was bold, confident, and a little cocky. But in the context of our messages, it had been exciting.

And a firefighter? Come on. That had to count for something: solid career, heroic undertones, fit body. The fantasy practically wrote itself. I imagined broad shoulders, big, strong hands, the smell of smoke, and something masculine and woodsy. I should have known real life wouldn't hold a candle to that fantasy.

We finally set a date. A Friday night at a local restaurant just south of the river. Somewhere neutral, casual, a little noisy, so silence wouldn't be awkward, but not too loud that conversation was impossible. I arrived ten minutes early, nerves fluttering, so I busied myself chatting with the hostess, a girl in her early twenties with a nose ring and a welcoming laugh.

"First date?" she asked, raising her brows when I gave her my name for the reservation.

"Yup," I said with a self-conscious grin.

She giggled and leaned in. "Give me the look if you need an emergency exit. I got you."

"You're my new favorite person," I told her, and meant it.

Then Marty walked in.

He was tall, definitely, and muscular in a way that filled out his Henley. What is it with guys and Henleys? But his posture screamed cocky, not confident, and this wasn't a subtle cocky. This was full-blown rocking out with his appendage out if we could make it happen... And the moment he opened his mouth to greet me, I realized I might be in trouble.

"Hey, gorgeous," he said, swooping in for a hug that lasted two seconds too long. "You look even better than your photos. I'd say smokin', but I think I'd be hitting too close to home, huh? Firefighter humor."

Strike one.

Still, I smiled and let him guide us to the table the hostess had already set up for us. We sat, exchanged pleasantries, and ordered drinks. I went with a glass of white wine. He went with a beer, something hoppy that he described in great detail, as if I had any idea what he was talking about. I nodded politely.

We looked over the menu. I ordered the buffalo chicken wrap. Marty opted for the Cajun chicken pasta, proudly proclaiming, "Gotta keep up the protein. And I burn right through those carbs."

"Do you work out a lot?" I asked, keeping the tone light.

"Every day," he said. "Sometimes twice. You don't get quads like these from skipping leg day." He smacked his upper leg for emphasis. "And push-ups? I do 500 a day. Every day."

I smiled again, my cheeks starting to feel sore from the effort.

The first ten minutes of the conversation were fine. He talked about work, the firehouse, and how much the guys all respected him. He name-dropped a few towns, as if I should be impressed. Did he not realize I had lived in Minnesota all my life? That said, I offered up some details about my job, but whenever I tried to go deeper and talk about physical therapy, my patients, or even a recent seminar I'd attended, he brushed it off.

"I mean, that's sweet and all," he said dismissively. "Helping old ladies walk better or whatever."

Excuse me?

I blinked. "It's a bit more complex than that. I specialize in post-surgical rehab and neuro recovery."

"Right, right. Sure. But still, that's cute. You've got those nurturing vibes going on. Bet you're amazing with your hands."

Strike two.

I took a long sip of wine.

The food arrived, and I busied myself with inspecting my sandwich, but Marty kept talking, and every sentence felt like another red flag on fire. He went off on some tangent about how women these days didn't know how to treat a man anymore, something about "alpha males" being a dying breed, and women forgetting their place.

"My ex," he said, shoveling a forkful of pasta into his mouth, "was hot but mouthy. Always wanted to argue. That gets old fast. I just want a girl who knows how to make a man feel good, ya know? Keep his belly and his balls happy. Nothing sexier than a girl in the kitchen. And when you wear those short skirts and take something out of the oven? I mean, c'mon?!"

I nearly choked on my chicken sandwich. He kept going, oblivious. Or worse, thinking he was killing it.

I interjected, trying to steer the conversation somewhere safer. I asked about his favorite books. He scoffed.

"Books? Don't really read unless I have to. TV's faster."

Strike three.

Still, I kept my posture open. I'd give him another few minutes. Maybe he was nervous? Perhaps he was trying to impress me with some kind of caveman schtick? I hoped.

But then he launched into a story about how one of his firefighter buddies had "tapped this chick at a bar," and he ended it with, "She'd been giving him the eyes all night. What else did she expect?"

And that was it. I drained my wine.

He excused himself to use the restroom. The second he turned the corner, the hostess was at my side. "Do you need an out?"

I looked up at her, deadpan. "Oh, absolutely. But also... I'd like to see how much worse this gets. It's like a reality show or watching a trainwreck in real life."

She laughed, clearly trying to keep it professional but failing. "You want a refill of that wine?"

"Please."

She returned a minute later with the bottle and a sympathetic pat on the shoulder.

When Marty returned, I had my phone in hand and pretended to read a text. He sat down, oblivious. "So," he said, leaning back and letting out a satisfied sigh, "you're not like other chicks. I can tell. You're chill. I bet you know how to handle a man."

I gave him a tight-lipped smile and said nothing.

The check arrived. He didn't even reach for his wallet. Just waited.

"Should we split it?" I offered.

"You get it this time. I'll cover it next time," he returned.

There wouldn't be a next time.

I paid, signed the receipt, and walked out into the cool night air with him still yammering behind me about how "this went great."

Now, driving home, I replayed the night over and over again in my head.

This was dating now? I'd been out of the game for so long that even the red flags had looked like confetti when we were texting. The sexting? Sure, it had been racy. But there had been something playful about it. At least, I thought there was. He'd complimented me, teased me. Made me laugh with a few jokes about firefighter calendars and stripping out of gear.

But none of that had translated to a man with any actual charm.

He was crude. Rude. Sexist. And loud.

I was stunned at how disappointed I felt. Not because I had any emotional investment in Marty. But I had allowed myself to hope. To imagine the possibility that this guy could be someone worth knowing. Someone worth getting excited over. And now, here I was, driving home alone, trying to erase the last two hours of my life with loud music and an internal scream.

I pulled into my apartment complex and sat in the car for a moment, letting the engine idle.

Maybe it was time to delete the app. Maybe I just wasn't ready. Or maybe I needed Liz to screen every single date from now until the end of time.

I walked inside, kicked off my shoes, and headed straight for the kitchen. I poured a glass of wine, my third for the night, and curled up on the couch.

Tomorrow, I'd laugh about this with Liz.

But tonight? Tonight, I would rewatch that steamy '90s romance movie and let the fictional man with actual respect and a decent haircut take me away for just a little while—no sexting required.

8

Liz

THE FLUORESCENT LIGHTS of the Mall of America reflected off every shiny storefront, blinding me for a second as I rounded the corner into Nordstrom. Jessica was still chattering at my side, animated and flushed from laughter and the brisk walk from the parking ramp. We had both sworn off Black Friday crowds, but the Wednesday before Thanksgiving? That was fair game. The deals were still good, the people marginally less murderous, and it was practically tradition at this point.

I paused to tug my knit beanie down a little tighter on my head. I wasn't used to the cold quite this early in the season. Not yet, anyway, though my beanie was more of a fashion statement than a head-warmer. My leather boots clicked against the tiled floor, a sound I always found oddly satisfying. My oversized scarf wrapped around my neck like armor, another fashion statement meant to complete the look, even as my black peacoat hung open. Shopping with Jessica was like cardio, but so much more fun.

"So wait," I said, putting a hand on Jessica's arm to steady myself mid-laugh. "He actually said you looked like the kind of woman who 'knows her way around a headboard'? That was his pickup line?"

Jessica doubled over, resting her hands on her knees. "Yes! I almost spat out my drink. Who says that?"

"Marty, apparently." I straightened and wiped at my eyes. "Good lord, how are men like that still allowed to exist?"

We paused just inside the entrance of Nordstrom. All around us, other shoppers moved in swirling currents, clutching red sale flyers and bags full of early holiday gifts. I glanced over to the handbags just inside the door, momentarily distracted by a cranberry leather tote, then turned back to Jessica.

"Okay, but seriously," I said, "You should've given the hostess a hundred bucks just for sticking around. The fact that she came over while he was in the bathroom? She deserves hazard pay."

Jessica laughed again, this time with a little more weariness. "I actually told her I needed to stay. It was like watching a train crash in slow motion. I couldn't look away."

I shook my head, threading my arm through Jessica's and pulling her toward the shoe section. "Well, you're a better woman than I. I would've disappeared out the back."

We meandered past boots and sneakers, pausing to point out a pair of heels that neither of us would ever wear but both agreed were stunning. The kind of shoes you wore when you knew you wouldn't be walking further than the valet.

"So..." Jessica said, glancing sideways. "You and Tony? Is it officially over?"

I shrugged, trying to play it off. "Yep. He said he was looking for something a little more serious, which is hilarious, because he's the one who told me he wasn't into labels two months ago."

Jessica winced. "Oof. That sucks."

"Eh," I said, waving it off. "It was fun. I knew it wasn't forever. I just thought maybe we'd make it to New Year's. You know, a little holiday sparkle, champagne, one last good kiss under some twinkly lights."

Jessica gave me a sympathetic look, and I felt something tighten in my chest. Damn. I wasn't usually the type to get sentimental about flings, but this time... I kind of was. I'd liked Tony. He was smart, had that scruffy hot professor vibe, and made a killer risotto. Plus, he laughed at my jokes. That went a long way.

"I didn't realize how much I was looking forward to having someone to dress up with for the holidays," I admitted. "Now it's just me and the pile of sequined dresses in my closet that no longer have a purpose."

"We could get dressed up anyway," Jessica offered, nudging me gently. "Wine night. Matching slippers and face masks. I'll even let you pick the Hallmark movie."

I raised an eyebrow. "You hate Hallmark movies."

"Exactly," Jessica said. "That's how much I love you."

I laughed, looping my arm tighter around Jessica's. "You're a saint."

We made our way to a display of scarves, fingers running across soft textures as the energy of the mall buzzed around us. I was grateful for it. The shopping was a distraction and a chance to laugh at someone else's disastrous date for once.

But I couldn't shake the feeling that something deeper was going on with Jessica. It was more than just the bad date with Marty. It was the fact that Jessica hadn't lit up over anyone in a long time. Not really. Not since Lucas, if I was honest about it.

Jeremy had been a bust. Marty had been a walking red flag. And yet... I saw how Jessica was trying. Jess was starting to open up again. It made me protective and hopeful all at once.

After exiting Nordstrom, we grabbed coffees at a small kiosk and found a quieter bench near the rotunda, sipping our drinks while watching people wander past with bags from every imaginable store.

"So," I said carefully. "You think you'll try another date soon?"

Jessica shrugged. "I don't know. It feels like I'm forcing it. Like I'm trying to jumpstart something that's been sitting dead in the driveway for too long."

I considered that. "Maybe it's not the dating. Maybe it's the guys. I mean, we've both seen enough Hallmark movies to know the right guy never shows up in your inbox. He shows up when you least expect it. You're baking cookies for a school fundraiser, or you're running late to yoga, and then bam. The cute guy with dimples and good intentions appears."

Jessica gave me a dry look. "So I should just start living in a Hallmark movie? Got it."

"Yes, but with better shoes."

We fell into another stretch of silence, comfortable and companionable. I sipped my coffee and watched Jessica from the corner of my eye. She looked tired. Not just from work or parenting or dating disasters, but from something deeper. Like her heart had been dormant for a while and was just now starting to remember how to beat for itself again.

I remembered what that felt like.

There had been a time after college, after my own breakup with the guy I thought I was going to marry, when I'd felt the same way. Hollowed out. Like my body moved through the days while my brain kept asking, *What now? What next? Who am I without him?*

And then I'd figured it out. Not all at once, not with some grand epiphany. But slowly. Through coffee dates with friends. Through messy one-night stands that reminded me I still had fire in my veins. Through saying yes to things that scared me. Through remembering that I was enough on my own. Plus, being on my own meant I wouldn't lose someone who had become important to me. I'd already experienced enough loss in my life.

And Jessica was on that same journey now. I could feel it. But I also knew that Jessica was the type who wanted more than just a few months of fun. She was the type who, when she found the right guy, was in it to win it.

"You know what I think?" I said, standing and tossing my empty cup in the bin nearby. "I think you need a girls-only weekend. Not just a night watching Hallmark movies. Me, you, several bottles of wine, maybe a case. Face masks. No kids. No men. Just girl talk, reality TV, and some soft-porn movies."

Jessica tilted her head as her nose turned up at the thought of watching soft-porn with her best friend. Then again, why not? "That actually sounds... kind of amazing."

"Good," I said. "Because I already booked the Airbnb."

Jessica blinked. "You did not."

I grinned. "It's just for a weekend. Two nights. I knew you'd say yes. We leave in two weeks, on Friday after work. And I know that Lucas has Lily that weekend, and you don't work, so you are free with no excuses."

Jessica let out a laugh. "You're incorrigible."

"And you love me for it."

We looped our arms again and continued walking, weaving through the holiday crowds with no real destination. Just two friends, taking a break from the chaos of dating and divorce, finding their way back to joy, one laugh at a time.

9

Carol

THE SNOW STARTED FALLING just after breakfast. The flakes were thick and wet and clung to the pine trees and hushed the sound of passing cars outside the window. I stood at the sink, rinsing the last of the dishes, staring out at the backyard Ronald and I had tended for more than forty years. The garden was now long asleep, buried under a thin blanket of snow, and the patio furniture sat in hibernation beneath its weatherproof covers. Winter always arrived early in Duluth, and this one seemed to be exceptionally long.

Ronald was snoring gently in his recliner, his walker parked just within reach, the midday news mumbling in the background. I glanced over at him and smiled, feeling a combination of affection and fatigue. He hadn't fallen in nearly three weeks—a small win. Still, every time I heard him shift or try to reach for something, my heart almost stopped.

I dried my hands on a dish towel just as the front door opened. A gust of cold air blew in with Jessica, her cheeks flushed from the wind, arms loaded with a casserole dish and a grocery bag. And right behind her was Lily, bounding in like a burst of sunshine, her winter hat crooked and a wide smile on her face.

"Grandma!" Lily shouted, kicking off her boots and running into my arms.

"Well, look who it is! My favorite little snow bunny," I said, giving her a squeeze. "You're getting taller every time I see you."

Jessica laughed as she set the groceries on the counter. "I think she grew two inches last night."

"Wouldn't surprise me," I said. "She's got that Nicholau height."

Lily spun in a circle, arms out. "Guess what? I learned all the words to the song from our school play. Want to hear it?"

"After lunch," I said, smoothing her curly hair with my hand. "Let's eat first before you give your performance."

Jessica helped me unload the bags while Lily bounced between rooms, chattering away to herself. After a few minutes, I noticed that she had climbed up onto Ronald's lap and was snuggling with him in the recliner. It was a lovely sight and made my heart feel happy.

My daughter and I spent the next hour in the kitchen, reheating leftovers and setting the table with a rhythm that only came out of practice. While we worked, Jessica talked about Lily. Her excitement over Thanksgiving dinner with Lucas and Emily the day before. Her upcoming school play. And her continued obsession with polar bears.

I listened, smiling when I was supposed to, nodding at the correct times. But part of my mind wandered. Emily. Lucas' new fling.

I used to hope Jessica and Lucas would work things out. For Lily's sake. For the family. But Jessica hadn't said a single bad word about Emily. Not one. That told me all I needed to know. My daughter had moved on. And it was time I did, too. Though I knew enough about myself to understand that was easier said than done.

But Lucas seemed lighter these days from what Jessica told me. Happier. And Jessica, while still alone, didn't seem lost. Not like she had after the divorce.

Still, it was time for her to get on with her life. She had a lot to offer the world, and I couldn't stand the thought of her spending another day alone in that apartment, especially on the nights when Lily was with her father.

Later, after we ate and Lily had performed her song, complete with dramatic arm gestures, we settled in with cups of coffee and cocoa. Lily was curled up on the couch now, half-watching cartoons and half-dozing after her big show. And Ronald snored softly next to her, once again kicked back in his recliner.

"Any dates on the horizon?" I asked, topping off the coffee in our coffee mugs and settling into the breakfast nook. It had been a good day, but I was exhausted. The bit of caffeine would give me a boost.

Jessica laughed. "Oh, Mom. You have no idea."

"Try me."

So she told me. About Marty. The texts. The flirting. The trainwreck of a date.

By the time she reached the part where the hostess offered her an out, I was laughing out loud. "You're kidding. That's... horrible. But hilarious."

"It was something else," she said, shaking her head.

"Well, at least you're out there trying. More than I can say for most."

She sighed. "It's just so much work. And usually, it's disappointing."

I nodded, sipping my coffee. "It doesn't have to be perfect, Jess. Sometimes, it's just worth trying. You don't need to find a husband tomorrow, though sooner than later would be nice. But for now, just someone who brings you joy."

Jessica winced slightly at my words, but I chose to ignore it. "I'll think about it," she said.

"That's all I ask."

We sat in silence for a while, listening to the wind outside and Ronald's ongoing soft snores from the next room.

"He asks about you," I said after a moment. "Your dad. He may not say it, but he watches the clock when you're supposed to call. And when Lily's name comes up when we talk? He lights up."

"I hate that I can't get here more often."

"You've got your life. Your job. Lily. We understand," I told her. "But we miss you, and I wish you would try harder to get up here.

I can use your help from time to time, you know. Your father needs more care than he used to. And I'm no spring chicken."

Jessica nodded, her guilt obvious. I reached across the table and patted her hand.

"We're proud of you, Jess. You're doing great, even if you don't always see it."

She blinked quickly, then smiled. "Thanks, Mom."

I stood and busied myself wiping down the kitchen counter. Jessica would be back on the road before dark, but this visit, short as it was, was enough for now.

I glanced at Ronald in his chair, still dozing, still mine. Then, Jessica, who is older, wiser, and stronger than even a year ago. And at Lily, now humming to herself as she tucked a blanket around her legs. And for the first time in a while, I felt a small sense of peace.

10

Jessica

CHRISTMAS MORNING CAME far too early in our house.

"Mom, Mom, MOM! He came!"

I peeled one eye open to the glow of the hallway light and the unmistakable squeak of tiny feet dashing back and forth on the hardwood floors of the apartment. My bedroom door swung open with a thud, and Lily appeared at the side of my bed, her hair a wild halo of bedhead and excitement.

"Santa came! I saw the wrapping paper, and there's a big one, and it says my name, and I think it's the Barbie Dreamhouse!"

It was 5:31 a.m. I knew because I checked.

I rubbed my eyes with a groan, threw back the covers, and followed my daughter to the living room, where, yes, the giant pink and plastic monstrosity of every little girl's dream stood in full glory beside the twinkling lights of the Christmas tree.

Lily had clearly already gotten into the stockings. Wrapping paper was strewn across the floor, and the Barbie population had grown exponentially since last night. She was midway through redressing one of them when I finally settled onto the couch with a cup of coffee and a fuzzy throw blanket.

Ken had been exiled to the roof. Probably for something dumb. According to Lily, he "didn't understand the importance of brunch." Fair enough.

While she played, I got up and moved to the kitchen to make cinnamon rolls. Not the refrigerated kind. These were homemade, a tradition passed down to me from my mom. Warm, gooey, and perfect for a snowy morning like this. The smell helped keep me upright, because truthfully, I was exhausted. We had made another day trip to Duluth the day before to spend time with my parents. Between the long drive, hauling gifts back and forth, and trying to be cheerful through the hours of small talk, my tank was running on fumes.

Watching Lily play gave me the kind of peace that only comes in small, stolen moments. Her joy was loud and unapologetic, but it settled somewhere deep inside me like a warm hug. As I let that thought settle, images of Olaf from the film *Frozen* flooded my mind. I shook my head to clear away the thought, and refocused on Lily as she narrated her Barbies' latest wardrobe malfunction and brunch drama.

Before long, my mind began to wander again. To the texts. The matches. The letdowns.

Jeremy had been so promising. So polite. So thoughtful. But there was no spark. Not even a flicker.

And Marty... well. Marty was a walking sex drive with a man bun (okay, no man bun, but seriously) and zero respect for actual conversation. I should have seen it coming.

I picked up my phone, mostly to stop myself from spiraling out of control. I opened the app. A few new messages. A couple of new likes. One guy sent a photo of himself holding a fish. Blocked. Another wrote, "Hey babygirl." Double blocked. What was it with guys and "hey babygirl" as an opening phrase? Did guys think we actually liked that as a term of endearment? No, we do not, thank you very much.

Then I saw him. A teacher with a goofy grin and a bio full of dad jokes. He seemed sweet and grounded, precisely the kind of person who might fit into my world.

His profile photo caught me off guard. Not because he was striking or model-beautiful. He wasn't. But he looked kind. Genuinely kind. Tall, maybe 6'2" or so, judging from the way he stood beside the high school trophy case in one of his pictures. He had a light beard, the kind that said I'm casual but not careless. Brown eyes. And a smile that made me tilt my head a little. Easy. Warm. Unforced.

His name was Will. I clicked on his profile.

Bio:

"Teacher. Dad. Bad at golf, excellent at dad jokes. Seeking someone who enjoys board games, used bookstores, and spontaneous

pancake dinners. Once lost a bet and had to dress up as a banana for Halloween. (No regrets, but let your mind wander if you must). If you laugh at cheesy puns, we'll probably get along."

Okay.

I smiled, biting my lip.

More About Me:

Job: *10th-grade history teacher. Yes, I actually like high schoolers. Yes, I know that makes me weird.*

Kids: *Two. Daughter (10) and son (12). They make me laugh and occasionally make me question my sanity.*

Favorite Book: *The Book Thief.*

Guilty Pleasure: *Singing way too loudly to 90s boy bands while driving.*

What I'm Looking For: *Someone real. Someone who's been through a bit of life and still knows how to laugh.*

Something fluttered in my chest.

I scrolled through his photos. One of him standing on a hiking trail, arms outstretched like he'd conquered the world. Another holding a cake. It was badly decorated and hilariously lopsided with "Happy Birthday Max!" scrawled in blue frosting. One of him and his kids were in what looked like matching pajamas on Christmas morning, all three grinning like goofs.

My throat tightened.

Widowed. That part sat heavily on the page.

There was no elaborate explanation. Just one word. But it said enough. Enough to remind me that there was a whole chapter of his life I couldn't begin to understand. A love lost, a parenting journey shared with ghosts. It was different than divorce. Different than what I had with Lucas. This was grief.

Could I handle that? Could he handle me? Was I getting ahead of myself?

Lily launched herself into my lap, jarring me out of my thoughts. I tucked the phone under the blanket.

"Mom! Barbie wants to open a spa, but Ken says she should just be a flight attendant. Can you believe that?"

"Absolutely not," I said, kissing the top of her head. "Ken's getting demoted. Again."

She giggled and raced back to the dreamhouse, shouting, "Barbie runs her own business, thank you very much!"

I looked at her, my wild, curly-haired, spirited girl, and thought about what it would mean to bring someone into our lives. Someone who got it. Someone who had lived loss, who understood bedtime routines and hard questions. Who wouldn't get scared off by a little girl who insisted on feminist Barbies and elaborate bedtime stories?

I opened the app again and stared at Will's profile. He looked like he read books. I mean, *The Book Thief* was his favorite, and that was a good sign. Markus Zusak's novel was one of my favorites, too.

It seemed as though Will cared about the world, as though he didn't need to prove anything with shirtless selfies or talking over me at dinner.

I compared it again to what I remembered of Marty's profile—all innuendos. And suddenly, I couldn't believe I'd ever swiped right on that guy.

I took a deep breath. Then I swiped right on Will. Why not?

It was Christmas, after all. A time for hope. A time for second chances. A time for believing in something just a little bigger than ourselves. And maybe, just maybe, it was time for me to start believing in someone new.

Barbie might be running a business. But me? I was about to make a move of my own. Let's see what happens.

11

Will

CHRISTMAS MORNING had come and gone in a flurry of wrapping paper, ribbon, and soft squeals of excitement. Now, the house was quiet.

I sat at the kitchen table, slowly working through a plate of leftover pancakes and bacon. Cooper sat underneath the table, quietly hoping for scraps. I made sure a few made their way to the floor, only to be scarfed up by the fluffy pooch.

I'd gone the extra mile that morning, and I was pretty proud of myself. Strawberries with Nutella, too. It had felt right to do something a little special. I hadn't said anything to remind the kids, but it was our first Christmas without Katie, where the weight of the silence didn't feel unbearable. Not lighter, exactly, but... softer.

The chaos had settled. Max and Sophie had retreated to their rooms, their new Nintendo Switches clutched in eager hands. I had pictured the morning going differently. The two of them are on the couch together, racing Mario Kart or battling through some shared adventure. But no, Max had disappeared into Minecraft, completely immersed, and Sophie, newly fashion-obsessed, had gotten into her My Universe - Fashion Boutique game as if it were her actual job.

I couldn't fault them. They were 10 and 12. They were surviving the holidays the best way they knew how.

The rest of the gifts had gone over well, too. New clothes for both of them. Books, of course, because even though the enthusiasm was... lacking, I wasn't ready to give up on the promise I made.

Katie had been adamant about it. Even as she lay dying in her hospital bed, her body frail and wasting away from the brutality of metaplastic breast cancer, she had clung to her hopes for our kids that they would grow up to be kind. That they would love hard and read often.

"Don't let them forget books," she had whispered. "Make sure they know books are safe places. That stories can hold them together, even when we're not."

I had promised. I still carried that promise with me, tucked somewhere deep in my heart and soul.

I scraped the last bit of Nutella off my plate and stood to rinse my dish. No one had gotten me anything this year, but I didn't need anything. My kids were healthy. And they weren't yet of an age to realize that if they didn't get their dad a gift, no one would. They'd smiled and laughed and fought over bacon like nothing was missing. That was enough.

Almost.

Because what I really needed wasn't something my kids could give me. It wasn't wrapped in paper or hidden under the tree. It was a grown-up conversation. Someone to laugh with, maybe cry with, too—someone who could look at the mess of my life and still want to be part of it.

I sat back down at the table and turned on my phone, thumbing through the dating app I'd half-heartedly scrolled all week. Most profiles blurred together. I swiped left on half a dozen in a row, pausing only when a new notification popped up at the top of my screen.

You've got a match!

I tapped the alert, and my breath caught, just slightly. Jessica.

I remembered her profile well. I'd swiped on her a few days ago, charmed by the warm smile and candid bio. Blonde. Lovely. Smart.

She was a physical therapist specializing in post-surgical rehabilitation and neurorecovery. That alone had impressed me. Her job wasn't just something she did; it felt purposeful.

I tapped through her profile again.

Favorite book? *The Egypt Game*. I hadn't thought about that book since elementary school, but the moment I saw the title, the memories came rushing back. I smiled. Who picks *The Egypt Game* as a favorite? Someone who remembers how books made them feel, even years after reading them.

Celebrity crushes? Ryan Reynolds. That was predictable, but I respected it. Rob Thomas from Matchbox Twenty? That made me laugh out loud. It was the kind of answer that made her feel like she was a real person. And it couldn't be better because I had several Matchbox Twenty songs on my playlist.

She had a daughter, I remembered. Lily. I hadn't seen a photo of the little girl, but her presence was clear in Jessica's answers.

I set my phone on the table and rubbed a hand across my jaw. I wasn't new to the dating scene, but this was the first time in a while I'd felt something like anticipation.

I opened the message tab and stared at the blinking cursor. Then I started typing:

Me: *Hey Jessica. Merry Christmas! I'm sure Santa made a stop at both our houses. I hope your day's been full of good coffee and a delicious breakfast.*

I hit 'Send' before I could overthink it. Then I sat back and waited, smiling a little to myself.

12

Jessica

IT HAD BEEN A LAZY DAY. I had spent my Christmas afternoon alternating between time on the couch, taking in the latest Hallmark movies, and rooting around the living room, picking up strewn ribbons and wrapping paper from Lily's gift-opening frenzy.

It was nice to have a quiet afternoon, allowing Lily to enjoy her new gifts. The Barbie house had now become a city, spread from the living room to the hallway leading to the bedrooms. It was a mess, but Lily was content. I enjoyed watching her use her imagination, bringing her Barbie story to life. I couldn't help, however, noticing that she had pulled two more Ken dolls out of her toybox and had matched them up with Barbie dolls. It seemed that even an eight-year-old understood the significance of a relationship between two adults, even if those adults were Barbie and Ken dolls.

Now, as the sun began to dip below the trees outside the window, I stood in the kitchen, watching the air fryer as it sizzled and hummed.

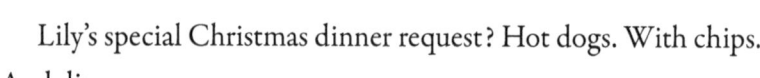

Lily's special Christmas dinner request? Hot dogs. With chips. And dip.

"Like a party," she'd explained. Who was I to deny such a simple joy?

My phone buzzed in my back pocket. I hadn't checked it in hours. I wiped my hands on a dishtowel, pulled it out, and saw the notification.

You've got a new message.

I tapped the dating app icon and blinked.

It was Will. The high school teacher. The one with the goofy grin, kind eyes, and a bio full of dad jokes. The one I'd swiped on earlier that day, half-hoping we'd match, but not really expecting anything.

We'd matched. And he'd messaged.

Will: *Hey Jessica. Merry Christmas! I'm sure Santa made a stop at both our houses. I hope your day has been full of good coffee and a delicious breakfast.*

I laughed. Out loud. The kind of laugh that surprised even me. Because this? This was sweet. Not cringey. Not sexual. Not weird. Just... charming.

I read it again, leaning back against the counter, smiling. Then I tapped out a quick response:

Me: *Merry Christmas to you, too! Santa definitely delivered. Barbie is currently hosting a fashion show for her other Barbie and Ken friends.*

I paused before making a quick addition.

Me: *Also, the cinnamon rolls, a recipe I make from scratch, were delicious. And the coffee was strong. What can be better than that? Hope your day's been just as cozy.*

I hit 'Send'.

And then, because I couldn't *not* share, I flipped over to my texts and sent a rapid-fire message to Liz.

Me: *OMG. MATCHED WITH WILL. THE HISTORY TEACHER. AND HE MESSAGED FIRST. AND IT WAS ACTUALLY CUTE.*

Seconds later, my phone started ringing. Of course.

"Hey," I answered, already smiling.

"Back it up," Liz said. "You matched *today*? He messaged already? On Christmas? Tell me everything."

I grabbed a chip from Lily's plate and wandered into the hallway, lowering my voice as I recounted the message.

"He seems pretty nice," Liz said. "And he's a teacher, right?"

"Yeah. Tenth-grade history. Widowed. Two kids. Ages 10 and 12."

"Ohhh, older kids. So it's not like you'd be wiping noses and changing diapers."

I snorted. "That is *not* my concern."

"No, but come on. This is promising, right? Cute message. Good job. Stable. Literate. Already better than Marty."

I groaned. "Don't bring up Marty."

"Okay, okay. But I want screenshots the moment he replies again."

"You're the worst."

"And you're welcome. I'm manifesting this for you. Now go eat your hot dogs and get flirty. It's Christmas."

We hung up, and I glanced toward the living room. Lily was singing to herself, narrating Barbie's latest plot twist. I walked back to the kitchen, smiling. Maybe Christmas magic didn't have to come wrapped in a bow. Sometimes, it showed up in a goofy message from a kind-eyed history teacher.

13

Liz

IF SOMEONE HAD ASKED me two weeks ago what my Christmas would look like, I'd have said champagne, sequins, and a man who smelled like cedarwood and knew how to kiss like the world might end tomorrow.

Instead, I was in leggings and a sweatshirt I'd owned since college, curled up on my couch with a half-eaten cheese plate, and watching *Love Actually* for the fourth time this season as if I was sixteen again. Not that I minded the cheese or the movie. Both were great company. But it felt weird. Quiet. Like I was waiting for something that wasn't going to happen.

That's when my phone lit up with the kind of message that made me sit up straighter:

Jessica: *OMG. MATCHED WITH WILL. THE HISTORY TEACHER. AND HE MESSAGED FIRST. AND IT WAS ACTUALLY CUTE.*

Instead of sending another text, I called her immediately.

"Back it up," Liz said. "You matched today? He messaged already? On Christmas? Tell me everything."

And she did. In typical Jessica fashion, she started with an overview of the day. The Barbie Dreamhouse. The hot dogs. The cinnamon rolls. But then, the juicy details such as the soft, subtle way his message had made her feel seen, not just acknowledged, but noticed.

I was thrilled for her. Genuinely. It felt different this time, and I could tell from her voice that it felt different to her as well. She was giddy, the way people get when they don't even realize they're smiling while they talk. And the thing was, I hadn't heard her sound like that in a long time.

Jessica had messaged with guys before. She'd sent me screenshots of witty exchanges or told me about bios that seemed promising. But this? This was the first time she texted in all caps. The first time, she couldn't wait to share the news. Which made me wonder if this Will could be someone real?

I didn't want to get too ahead of myself. Counting chickens, hatching eggs, all that. But my gut said this was a good one. Still, I'd be lying if I said I wasn't also a little jealous.

It had nothing to do with Jessica. She deserved something good. Something solid. She had been through enough and then some. But it made me realize that I had no one. No cute text from a new guy.

No date to recap or first message to overanalyze. Just me, a soft brie, and Hugh Grant doing his best Prime Minister impression.

For the past ten years, I'd always had someone during the holidays. Never the same someone, but a someone. A guy to bring to holiday parties, to sneak off with after the office happy hour, to buy a tie or a bottle of whiskey for, because we were doing "something casual." I liked casual. I liked the idea of flings that didn't require emotional gymnastics.

But this year was different. Tony had ended things a few weeks ago, which surprised me more than I cared to admit. I mean, sure, I knew it was winding down. He wasn't as funny anymore. His texts were more emoji than substance. But still... it stung.

And now I was alone. Alone with wine and cheese and my best friend's promising dating-app exchange while I sat on the sidelines, swiping on dating apps with decreasing enthusiasm. Every profile I saw looked like a clone of the last. Shirtless in a gym mirror. Holding a fish. Weird sunglasses. No, thank you.

Jessica's voice pulled me back. "I don't want to get ahead of myself," she was saying, "but... I don't know. It feels like this could actually be something."

And there it was. The part that made my heart clench in the best way. Hope. That fragile, ridiculous thing that can sneak up on you even when you think you've buried it under ten years of dating rules and one-night stands.

"You deserve that," I told her, and I meant it. "Someone who sees you. Who actually listens and asks good questions and gets why you still love The Egypt Game like it's a sacred text."

She laughed, and I smiled.

But as we hung up and I set my phone down, I found myself staring at the screen a little longer than necessary. The reflection that stared back at me from the black glass was someone I didn't recognize as easily as I used to. Someone tired. Someone may be a little lonely.

Jessica had said something earlier that stuck with me. She wanted more than just sex. She wanted a connection. Something messy and real and good. And it hit me in a way I hadn't expected. Because somewhere along the line, I'd stopped believing that I could want that, too. I had made flings my default setting. Safer. Less messy. Easier to move on from. Less likely to get hurt. But easier didn't always mean better.

Maybe I didn't need to change everything overnight. Maybe I could still enjoy the flirting, the banter, the confidence of knowing I could hold a guy's attention for an evening. And the amazing sex? Who said I couldn't still have that? But what if I wanted more, too?

The question sat with me as I blew out the last candle on my coffee table and padded off to bed, the holiday lights from my tiny tree still twinkling in the corner of the room.

I didn't have an answer. But I knew one thing: If Jessica could give a real connection a shot... maybe I could, too.

14

Jessica

MID-JANUARY IN MINNESOTA is a season all its own. The kind of cold that makes your teeth ache. The type of gray that settles into your bones. But despite the slush on the roads and the salt tracked into the clinic, there was a little spark inside me that refused to dull.

Will.

We had moved from messaging on the app to full-on texting. Morning check-ins, memes, little blurbs about our days. It felt effortless. Familiar. And somehow, not forced. Flirty, yes, but never over the top. There was a line, and Will knew how to flirt without crossing it. Not like Marty, who thought innuendo was a personality trait. Will's texts were thoughtful, clever, sometimes downright funny. The kind of flirtation that made you lean in, that made you want more.

And now... we were about to talk. Actually talk.

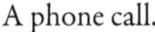

A phone call.

It had been his idea. After his profile, this time with his dog that I now knew was named Cooper, showed up on another dating app that I was going to put on hold, and I told him about it, things had shifted. Will had been horrified, forgetting that he still had that other app active. He shut it down right away.

Then, after a long exchange that veered from book recommendations to favorite breakfast foods to which decade had the best music (we both agreed on the '90s, because obviously), he said, "We should probably hear what each other sounds like at some point, don't you think?"

Cue panic.

What if we had nothing to say? What if my voice annoyed him? What if he breathed too heavily into the phone? Or worse. What if we had such good text chemistry, and the actual conversation just... fizzled?

I sat cross-legged on my couch, phone in my hand, waiting to make the call. Lily was already tucked into bed, exhausted from school and dance class. I had lit one of my favorite candles, the cinnamon vanilla one that reminded me of Christmas, even though I was trying to make a fresh start and not look back.

I glanced at the last message Will had sent: *Give me a call when you're ready. No pressure. Unless you're calling to tell me The Egypt Game isn't your actual favorite. Then, we have a problem. ;)*

God, he was charming. And then there was the heavy stuff.

A few nights ago, after the mini-fiasco with the other app had dissipated, our texts had taken a deeper turn. He had opened up about Katie. He told me about the morning she found the lump, about how she had just gotten out of the shower and called him into the bathroom, asking him to feel something on her breast. "It wasn't... sexual," he had written.

Of course not. It was fear. Panic disguised as a simple question. The lump was large. Aggressive. Metaplastic breast cancer. A diagnosis that seemed to go from whispers to sirens in a matter of weeks. A year later, she was gone.

The night he told me all of this, I had watched the "dot dot dot" on my phone for what felt like hours. Like each message he sent was a tightrope walk, he was choosing which memories to give voice to and which ones to keep close.

I had cried. Quietly, to myself. Not because I knew Katie. However, the way he told their story made it impossible not to feel the weight of their loss. The way he spoke of her... There was love there—real, lasting love.

And I wasn't jealous of it. It didn't worry me. I was honored to be trusted with it. That was the night we agreed on a call. Because if we could talk about cancer and parenting and grief through a screen, surely we could handle hearing each other's voices.

I tapped his name on my screen and took a deep breath. It rang once. Twice.

"Hey," he answered. And just like that, the nerves melted.

His voice was warm. Calming. There was a smile tucked into the edges of it. "Hey," I said, and smiled back.

We talked for two hours. About everything and nothing. Our kids. Our exes. Favorite books, again. He told me he made terrible pancakes but exceptional bacon. I laughed, reminding him that his profile had mentioned pancake dinners, to which he responded, "Well, they may be terrible, but I still make them."

I told him about the time Lily cut her own hair and said she wanted to look like a jellyfish. He laughed. Really laughed. And I laughed, too. It felt like opening a window on one of those days when the heat threatens to suffocate you.

There were pauses, but not the uncomfortable kind—just... breathing room. Like we were both learning the rhythm of this new thing, and when we finally said goodnight, I didn't feel silly for smiling.

15

Jessica

WE HAD BEEN TALKING for weeks. Texting every day. Facetiming nearly every night. I had met Cooper, Will's golden retriever, who liked to nose his way into the camera anytime we were chatting. Will had adopted him just months after Katie died, hoping a puppy might ease the loneliness in their home. Cooper was a handful, Will said, but he was theirs. And during our calls, I found myself charmed not just by Will's easy smile, but by that floppy, curious dog who clearly had no respect for personal space.

But tonight, it was happening—our first date.

I stepped out of my car and smoothed down my green blouse, palms slightly damp. I felt that weird mix of excitement and terror, the way you do before something big. Something that could go really, really well... or crash and burn.

The bistro Will had chosen was south of the river. It was quiet, cozy, tucked away behind a row of boutiques. He'd called it "unassuming but good," which seemed fitting for a guy like him. I walked in and saw him almost instantly.

"Jessica," he said, stepping forward and giving me a quick hug.

"Will," I replied, smiling back. "It's so good to finally meet you. In person."

He looked exactly like his photos and like I had imagined after seeing his face on FaceTime. A little taller, maybe a little warmer in person. His shirt was untucked, his jacket casually slung over the back of the chair he'd clearly been saving for me. We sat, ordered drinks, and within minutes, the conversation was flowing like we'd done this a dozen times before.

It wasn't awkward. Not even a little. We laughed and shared stories. Talked about work, parenting, and books. I told him more about my job, my patients, and my love for helping people relearn how to use their bodies after surgery or stroke. He listened, asked questions, and didn't look bored or distracted at any point.

Eventually, the conversation turned toward our pasts. I talked about Lucas. About how it had started passionately, then slowly shifted into something quieter. More functional than affectionate. And then it became dysfunctional before I finally decided to end things. I told Will about Lily and how much she meant to me. How much she reminded me of the parts of myself I'd buried during the last few years of my marriage.

I even told him about Emily, how I hadn't wanted to like her. It felt threatening at first. But how I'd come to see that she loved my daughter. And that mattered—more than any other emotion I might have had.

I shared a story from a few weeks ago. Lily had said something to Emily that made her freeze. From what Lucas has shared with me, Lily had asked if she would get a stepdaddy since she was getting Emily as a stepmommy. For whatever reason, the comment had unsettled Emily, and she had pulled back. I could even feel the shift, despite not being there.

Will nodded, thoughtful. "It sounds like Emily needs to hear from you that it's okay to move forward, and that Lily will be okay."

That made me pause.

"Absolutely," he said. "You're a huge part of Lily's life. If Emily knows you're on board and that you trust her with your daughter, it might help her feel more confident about her place in all this. When Katie, my wife, got sick, she wrote letters to our kids. I don't know how she found the time or energy to do it. But she had seen something in a movie or somewhere that a dying mother had written letters to her kids for all the milestones that would come in their lives—graduating from high school, going to college, getting married, and having a child. All of it. And in her first letter to the kids, she talked about how I might want to move on someday and that if and when I did, it was okay with her."

I blinked, my throat tight. He paused for a moment before moving on.

"And she wrote a very similar letter to me. Telling me that if I wanted to move on, it would be okay. That she wanted that for me. And for Max and Sophie."

I didn't know what to say. So I didn't. I just reached out and touched his hand lightly, and he gave me a small smile.

He continued. "I won't tell you that reading those first letters wasn't difficult. But it was as if she were permitting me to live my life, permitting the kids to live theirs, and supporting me in mine. It was a gift. And maybe that gift is something Emily could use from you."

It was such a simple insight, yet it carried so much weight. "You're probably right," I said softly.

He didn't say anything else, just squeezed my hand gently.

Dinner ended before I was ready for it to. There were no awkward moments. No forced goodbyes. Just two people who had shared real stories, real heartache, and a few too many fries.

As we stood outside the bistro, he looked at me, his breath visible in the crisp night air. "I'd really like to see you again," he said.

"I'd like that too," I said. And I meant it.

We didn't kiss. Not yet. But it didn't feel like a disappointment. It felt like something was building—something earned. As I drove home, I kept replaying the night in my head. And for the first time in a long time, I felt like maybe, just maybe, there was room in my life for something new.

When I got home and changed out of my blouse and skirt, I saw a message from Will pop up on my phone.

I hope you got home okay. I enjoyed our evening. You were even more beautiful in person than I imagined from FaceTime. And green is quite becoming on you. Let's go out again. Soon.

I smiled, shot him a quick text back to let him know I had indeed gotten home okay. Before pushing 'Send', I added, *I agree. Let's do it again. Soon.* And with that, I pulled my nightgown over my head and settled into bed. Tonight's dreams would be good, that I knew for sure.

16

Will

TWO WEEKS.

That's how long it had been since our first date. We texted every day, shared memes, book recommendations, voice notes, a few FaceTime chats, and even the occasional photo of Cooper getting into some ridiculous mess. But between Lily's school schedule, Jessica's clinic hours, Sophie's new dance class, and Max's wrestling meets, it had become clear that seeing each other again required more than just interest. It required intention.

And discretion. I'd been cautious. I had to be not just for myself, but for my kids. They knew I was dating, in the vaguest sense. But I hadn't introduced them to anyone since Molly, and even that had been a soft landing. A brief hello in the driveway before she stopped being part of our world entirely. Jessica deserved more than a casual introduction. And my kids deserved better than constant hellos and goodbyes.

Still, when she suggested sushi, I nearly fist-pumped in my kitchen. Katie had hated sushi. The smell. The texture. All of it. We'd tried a few places when we were dating and newly married, but she'd always wrinkled her nose and ordered teriyaki chicken. After a while, I gave up asking. But now, Jessica had texted: *Sushi? I'm in—just not sea urchin. There are lines I won't cross.*

God, she was funny.

The restaurant in Woodbury wasn't fancy. Tucked into a strip mall between a dry cleaner and a specialty pet store, the signage was a little faded, and the front windows were half-covered in photos of maki rolls and miso soup specials. But the fish was fresh, the miso hot, and the staff always remembered your name.

I got there early and took a seat at a corner table. My nerves were a low, constant hum in my stomach, but it was a different kind of nervousness than the first time I had gone on a date since Katie died. Back then, I was worried about how it would feel to sit across from someone who wasn't Katie. This time, I was worried about seeing Jessica again and not being able to stop myself from falling harder.

The door opened, and I looked up. Jessica.

She walked in like she wasn't entirely sure about the place, but didn't care. Her eyes scanned the small dining room, landing on me, and her smile lit up the whole room. Her hair was pulled back into a low bun, the kind that somehow looked both formal and effortless. A few loose strands were framing her face, and I had the ridiculous thought that I wanted to know what she looked like first thing in the morning, with that bun undone.

God, get it together, Will.

She wore a dark green sweater that brought out the warmth in her eyes, paired with black jeans and ankle boots. Casual. Confident. Sexy as hell. And I had never liked the color green until now.

I stood as she approached. "Jessica," I said, giving her a quick hug.

"Will," she replied, clearly laughing at the similarity to Christian Grey and Anastasia's typical, simple greetings at the beginning of their love story in Fifty Shades of Grey. Yes, I've read it. Who says a guy can't read smut?

Once seated, we fell into conversation as easily as we had on our first date. I ordered my usual: the spicy tuna roll, the dragon roll, and miso soup. Jessica asked the server for recommendations and settled on the rainbow roll and something called the Kiss of Fire, which made her raise an eyebrow at the name.

"Are you trying to impress me with your spice tolerance?" I teased, secretly high-fiving a higher being. A girl who loved sushi and spice? I was slowly becoming smitten.

She smirked. "I'm trying to impress myself. Also, I skipped lunch. So this could be a disaster."

She was so easy to be with. Easy to talk to. Easy to listen to. Easy to watch, even. There were little things she did like tapping her thumb against the side of her glass, tucking that stray piece of hair behind her ear, laughing with her whole body, that I knew I'd remember for a long time.

We talked about parenting again. She shared a funny story about Lily insisting on bringing a polar bear figurine to school for "emotional support" during a spelling test.

"I admire her confidence," I said.

Jessica grinned. "She's relentless. But she's also eight. So I guess that tracks."

I told her about Max's latest wrestling match, how he had pinned a kid in the first thirty seconds, and then asked me afterward if I thought he should be 'less aggressive next time.'

"Sensitive brute," she said, smiling. "That's a rare combo."

There was a pause in our conversation just long enough for the server to deliver our sushi, and I caught myself looking at her again. She caught me.

"What?" she asked, a playful smile forming on her face.

"Nothing," I said, shaking my head. "I just… you're really easy to be around."

That made her eyes soften. "You, too."

We ate. We talked. We lingered. I told her more about Katie. Not a lot. Not in a way that made the evening somber. But enough.

"She was amazing," I said quietly, after a bite of dragon roll. "And it feels strange to say this, but since our first date, I haven't felt her shadow quite so much. Like maybe she's giving me space now. Like maybe she's holding up her end of the promise she made."

Jessica nodded, and I could see something flicker behind her eyes. "What promise?"

"That it would be okay for me to move on."

Jessica reached across the table, fingers brushing mine. Just once. Just briefly. And she nodded, "I'm glad you did."

Later, as we walked to our cars, the night crisp and quiet around us, I found myself wishing the date wouldn't end. I didn't want a big gesture. I didn't want to push anything. But when we paused beside her car, I reached for her hand.

She looked up at me, her breath forming little clouds in the air between us. Was she expecting a kiss? Was it too soon? I wanted to kiss her, wanted just a small taste to see if the electricity I suspected was there, really was. "Thank you for tonight," I said. "I needed this more than I realized."

"Me, too," she replied.

And then I kissed her. Softly. Just once. No massive fireworks. No movie music. Just warmth and a slight tingle, and the certainty that I wanted more. I pulled back and she smiled at me before climbing into her car.

As I watched her drive away, I leaned back against my car and smiled to myself.

Two dates in, and somehow I already knew: this wasn't just about filling a space Katie had left. This was something different. And I wanted it. Bad.

17

Jessica

IT HAD BEEN TWO WEEKS since our sushi night, and I hadn't stopped thinking about Will. Something had shifted after that date. No, not in a dramatic, earth-shaking way, but quietly, internally. A kind of emotional implosion. Not the bad kind, not destructive. But dense, powerful. Real.

And now, we were going out again. Date number three. A big one.

We had agreed on dinner downtown at Prohibition, the speakeasy-style bar on the 27th floor of the historic Foshay Tower. I'd never been, but the photos were stunning. The decor made it feel like you were stepping into another era. It was romantic, classy, and more than a little sexy. Just like this thing with Will. Whatever this thing was becoming.

I'd just come back from visiting Mrs. Hanson two doors down. She'd helped me zip up my black cocktail dress, giving a little gasp and saying, "Oh, honey, if this man doesn't fall in love with you tonight, he doesn't have working eyes."

The compliment had made me laugh, but now, alone in my apartment, I stood in front of the full-length mirror in the hallway and twisted to see myself from every angle.

The dress clung in all the right places. Simple, black, classic. My hair was down, freshly washed and blown out, falling past my shoulders in soft, wavy strands. My makeup was light, aiming for that elusive natural look, though I'd spent a solid twenty minutes perfecting the eyeliner. And then, the final touch. My mother's cocktail ring. She had given it to me after my divorce from Lucas with the words, "Every woman needs a little bling when she's starting over." The thought reminded me that I should probably give my mom a call tomorrow.

The ring caught the light now as I checked my phone for the status of my Uber. I didn't want to drive downtown. And as much as I liked Will, I wasn't quite ready for him to pick me up. I needed this. My own space, my own pace.

And then my phone lit up with Liz's face.

"Hello?" I answered her FaceTime call, half-laughing.

"Girl," she said, without a greeting or lead-in. "You are having dinner in a fancy-ass bar in a historic hotel. In a dress? Go with it. Let it happen. Get jiggy with it."

I rolled my eyes, but couldn't help the smile. "Did you seriously just say 'get jiggy with it'?"

"I did. And I stand by it. I mean, look at you! You're stunning. I bet you smell good, too. Do you smell good?"

"I smell incredible," I said, laughing. "Vanilla and sandalwood. Soft and mysterious."

"Perfect. Like you're going to steal his heart and his wallet."

"Liz."

"I'm kidding. Sort of. But seriously. This is your night. Will is hot. He's thoughtful. He's clearly into you. You've earned a night out where someone looks at you like dessert."

"I'm nervous," I admitted. "Like... I want this to go well. Really well."

"It will. And even if it doesn't turn into some grand romance, let it be a damn good chapter. Hell, let it be a damn good paragraph."

I smiled, breathing in deep. "Thank you."

"Go. Flirt. Drink something with a stupid garnish. And if you end up back at his place or in one of those gorgeous hotel rooms at the W, I want all the details tomorrow once you get back home."

I laughed. "Goodbye, Liz."

"Bye, gorgeous."

I hung up just as the Uber notification popped up on my screen. My driver was three minutes away. I slipped on my heels, gave myself one final once-over in the mirror, grabbed my coat, and headed to the front door of my apartment complex.

Tonight felt different. Electric. Hopeful.

And this time, I was ready for whatever came next.

18

Will

THE LOBBY OF THE W HOTEL in the Foshay Tower was dimly lit and buzzing with the quiet hum of luxury. Soft jazz played from invisible speakers, and the sleek black-and-gold interior gleamed under low lights. I adjusted the cuffs of my blazer and tried to focus on anything other than the nervous energy bouncing around inside me. Why was my heart racing? It wasn't our first date. I'd known this woman for weeks. But just thinking about her made my heart rate accelerate.

Then I saw her. Jessica stepped through the revolving door, and for a moment, I forgot how to breathe.

She was wearing a black dress. It was fitted in all the right ways, hugging her curves with a kind of effortlessness that seemed to stop time. Her hair was down tonight, falling in shiny, blonde waves past her shoulders. Light makeup, glowing skin, and that cocktail ring on her right hand. Classy, feminine, confident.

And sexy. God, she looked sexy. I felt my jeans tighten around the hips and tried not to let it show. I wasn't seventeen, but the way she walked across that lobby made me feel like I had never seen a woman before. And God help me if my pants gave it away.

"Will," she said, smiling, her voice like music. She leaned in and kissed my cheek.

"Jessica," I replied, trying to keep my voice calm and measured. "You look incredible."

Her cheeks flushed, and she gave me that coy smile I was already learning to love. "Thanks. You clean up pretty well yourself."

We made our way upstairs to Prohibition, the bar at the top of the tower. Floor-to-ceiling windows framed a view of Minneapolis bathed in city lights. It was the kind of place where time slipped by without you noticing.

We were seated near a window. She ordered a lemon martini, and I went with a Manhattan. The drinks arrived quickly, and the first sip worked like truth serum. The tension melted. We laughed. Talked. Teased.

"So, what did you want to be when you were little?" she asked, swirling her glass.

"Promise you won't laugh?"

"No promises."

"A librarian," I said, grinning.

She blinked. "Seriously?"

"Yep. I liked the idea of being surrounded by books. And quiet. And being the boss of the library stamp."

She laughed. "That's adorable. I wanted to be a doctor. The kind that wore high heels and carried a clipboard."

"Not a stethoscope?"

"Nope. Just heels."

"Sounds like you became a doctor of motion."

She smirked. "Touché. And you? You kind of did become a librarian. In a way. You teach history."

"It's basically books, but louder."

We laughed again, and I realized I hadn't stopped smiling all evening. It was easy with her. I didn't have to think so hard about what to say next. The conversation came naturally, like we were continuing something we'd started long ago.

Halfway through the meal, her hand found mine across the table. Her fingers laced with mine, warm and soft. I squeezed gently, and she didn't let go.

"Jessica," I said, clearing my throat a little. "Can I ask you something?"

She raised an eyebrow. "You just did."

I smiled. "Okay, smartass. Where do you see this going? With us."

She didn't flinch. Her gaze met mine, thoughtful and inquisitive.

"I want to keep getting to know you," she said. "That sounds simple, but I mean it. You make me laugh. You make me think. I like where this is going."

There was something in her voice that hinted at more—the kind of more I wanted, too.

After we finished our meal, we drifted to the bar. It was quieter now, later in the evening. She set her drink on the counter but kept her hand on it. I reached over, sliding it gently out of her hand and moving it back further. Then I placed my hand at her waist, fingertips brushing the curve of her lower back.

She looked up at me. Her head tilted slightly. A smile teased the corner of her mouth. "Will?"

I didn't let her finish. I pulled her closer and kissed her. God. It was electric. That spark from last time was present and then some. Her lips were warm, soft, tasting faintly of lemon and something sweeter. She responded immediately, leaning into me, her hand finding its way to the back of my neck.

And I swear, the world dropped away. We kissed again. Longer this time. Deeper. When we pulled apart, she smiled—just a small, wicked smile.

"So where do we go now, Will?" she whispered. "I don't want tonight to end."

I blinked. "What?"

She repeated herself. "I don't want tonight to end."

Everything in me stirred. Not just want, but care. Desire, yes, but also the sense that this moment mattered. That it wasn't just about sex. That it was something more. I paid the tab with a shaking hand. We didn't say much as we walked down to the valet. The air outside was freezing, but I barely noticed. I held her hand the whole drive back to my place.

The kids were gone for the night. They were sleeping over at my childhood best friend's place. His kids were conveniently the same age as Max and Sophie. It felt like fate had cleared the way.

We stepped inside, and the warmth of the house wrapped around us. Jessica paused in the entryway, her fingers still looped with mine.

"This is nice," she said softly.

"It's home," I replied.

I kicked off my shoes and led her inside. She wandered to the living room, running her fingers along the back of the couch. I watched her every movement. Every curve.

She turned, and I crossed the space between us.

"Are you sure?" I asked, searching her face.

She nodded slowly. "Are you?"

I answered her with a kiss. This one was slower. Hungrier. A promise. I slipped my hands to her waist, then up her back. Her fingers slid under my shirt, pressing into my skin. She moved her hands to my chest, but she didn't push me away. I deepened the kiss, savoring the taste of her, the heat of her body. My hands found the zipper on her dress, and she didn't stop me.

Upstairs, everything was a blur of limbs, breath, and touch. We moved together like we were writing a story with our bodies. But it was a story about loss, about hope, about finding something again. When she rose above me, arching her back to feel everything I could give, emotion washed over me. How could I have found this woman? This is a real woman with a real life—a woman who felt so good.

Our sex wasn't perfect. It wasn't choreographed. But it was real. It was hot. We came together, eyes gazing at one another without breaking. When it was over, she curled into my side, her head on my chest, one hand pressed into the side of my neck, her breath slowing against my skin.

"You okay?" I asked softly.

She nodded, her voice barely a whisper. "Yeah. Better than okay. We should do this again sometime. Soon."

I laughed, kissed the top of her head, and closed my eyes. For the first time in a long time, I felt a sense of peace.

19

Jessica

LIZ HAD BROUGHT over a bottle of wine. Cabernet, her favorite. She was already pouring us each a generous glass as I rinsed off the last of the dinner dishes. Lily was in bed, finally, after a full-on debate about whether Barbie could marry a stuffed dinosaur. (She could, apparently.)

Now, with the apartment quiet, the overhead lights dimmed, and the wine working its early magic, I sat on one of the kitchen barstools and looked across the island at my best friend. Liz raised her eyebrows at me expectantly.

"Okay," I said, letting out a little breath as I picked up my glass. "So I know I already told you everything, like, twice. But... can we just go over it one more time?"

Liz grinned, taking a sip of her wine. "Jess. I've already mentally illustrated it in my head, but yes, please, go on. I want the deluxe director's cut."

I laughed and leaned in a little. "It was so good, Liz. I mean, really good. Like... we were made-for-each-other good."

She tilted her head, watching me with that best-friend-knows-you-too-well look. "Go on."

I twirled the stem of my glass between my fingers. "There were a few clumsy moments, not gonna lie. He couldn't get his socks off fast enough. He sort of did that one-legged hop thing, and then tripped over them. And I think I scratched his neck with my mom's cocktail ring, the one she gave me after the divorce. But we just... laughed. It wasn't awkward. It was real. And then it was... everything."

Liz leaned back, resting her elbow on the counter and sipping slowly. Her smile was genuine, but I caught something in her eyes. There was a flicker of wistfulness, perhaps even a hint of jealousy. But it wasn't the biting kind—more like longing.

"Jess," she said after a moment, her voice soft, "I'm so freaking happy for you. Like, I can't even pretend to be annoyed that I'm sitting here alone while you're out there getting swept off your feet by some widowed history teacher with magic hands."

I laughed. "He does have magic hands. And his mouth... God, Liz."

She groaned dramatically. "Spare me the details. Or don't. No, actually, don't. I need this."

I grinned. "Okay, well. The next morning, I woke up early. I was in his bed, everything unfamiliar and warm and quiet. And as I started to shift, like just barely, he pulled me back to him. His hands were already on me. And before I could even protest, like 'Hey, I haven't brushed my teeth yet,' he was behind me, moving against me, in me, taking his time, like he knew exactly what I needed. He didn't kiss me. He just devoured my neck, his arms around me like he couldn't get close enough."

Liz exhaled. "Jesus. Do you write erotica on the side now? Because that's hot."

I giggled and sipped my wine. "It really was. And afterward, I just lay there, completely spent. Like I could've slept another four hours. But I had to get home and clean before Lily came back."

Liz nodded, her eyes softening. "And he didn't make it weird? Morning-after stuff can get weird."

"Not even a little," I said. "He kissed my forehead, made coffee, and let me use his shower. It was... comfortable. He even drove me home, and we talked the entire way."

We sat in silence for a moment, just sipping and smiling.

"So when are you seeing him again?" Liz asked.

I sighed. "That's the only part that sucks. Not for another two weeks. Between his schedule and mine, it's the best we could do. But we've already made plans. This time it's my turn to plan the date."

"Ooh, pressure's on."

"I picked something low-key but fun. Saturday afternoon at the Museum of Natural History, then dinner at Cossetta's in St. Paul."

Liz nodded, approving. "Cute. Very you."

I looked down into my glass, swirling the wine. "It just feels... different with him. Like, I don't have to pretend. I can just be who I am, no editing."

She reached across the counter and squeezed my hand. "That's how you know it's real."

And as we sat there, together, sipping wine in the soft kitchen light, I realized I wasn't just falling into something new. I was finally rising out of something old. And it felt good. So good.

20

Will

A FEW DAYS HAD PASSED since our night at the Foshay, but the memory of it still clung to me, like the scent of her perfume on my shirt collar, or the trace of her laugh in my head. I couldn't stop thinking about her. Jessica. God, that dress. That kiss. The way she looked at me when we stood at the bar, everything else faded into the background.

I kept replaying it, that moment when I slid her drink out of her hand and pulled her closer. She had tilted her head and whispered, "Will?" and I hadn't even let her finish. I just had to kiss her. And that kiss. Jesus, it was the kind that left a scar in the best way. The kind that made you forget every failed attempt before.

And then came the drive home. I hadn't brought a woman home since Katie. Molly never made it past my front porch. That whole relationship had been built on shaky ground and ended without ceremony. I always kept my distance, even in the physical sense. We mostly met at her place, or in the rare case, in the backseat of her car, like teenagers. Looking back, that should've told me everything I needed to know.

But this? Bringing Jessica home felt different. Significant. She wasn't just crossing a threshold. She was stepping into my real life.

And what happened after... was good. Better than good. It was hot, yes, but also tender. Natural. The way we touched, laughed through the awkward bits, the way she looked at me when our bodies finally found that rhythm. It all felt... right. It was the kind of night I'd stopped letting myself hope for.

But still, I had to remind myself to slow down. We hadn't even hit the two-month mark. A lot could still happen. There were layers we hadn't uncovered. Conversations we hadn't had. Hell, she hadn't met my kids. And there was a part of me, small but loud, that worried about what that would look like, what Sophie would think, what Max would say.

Katie had told me it was okay to move on. She'd written that in the letter she left for me. That she wanted me to find happiness again. That she didn't want the kids growing up thinking their dad had to be lonely forever.

Still, that didn't mean I could ignore the reality of what blending lives might look like. I wasn't trying to replace Katie, and neither was Jessica. But there were emotions and memories layered into every corner of this house. Yet, despite all that, I was still excited.

Jessica and I had already planned our next date, her idea this time. A trip to the Minnesota History Museum followed by dinner at Cossetta's. When she told me the plan, her voice lit up with excitement.

"I've always wanted to go," she said. "I know it's kind of nerdy, but I think it'll be fun. And then we'll get pasta after!"

I'd smiled and said I couldn't wait. What I didn't tell her was that I took my tenth graders there three times a year. The exhibits were familiar, the layout etched in my brain. But that didn't matter. Not at all. Because I wasn't going for the exhibits, I was going to see her eyes light up when we walked through the giant grain elevator display. To hear her laugh when she saw the vintage schoolroom. To maybe sneak a kiss in one of the quieter corners.

This wasn't about history. It was about us making our own history.

I wanted another day with her. Not just another night. I wanted to see her in sunlight, not just candlelight. I wanted to see how she reacted when a kid screamed across the museum floor. I wanted to know what stories she'd make up about the mannequins.

And I wanted her back in my bed. Yes, but more than that, I wanted to keep getting to know her. Slowly. Honestly. So I pulled out my phone, scrolled through our recent messages, and sent her a quick text:

Me: *Counting down to Saturday. Hope you're ready to geek out with a professional history nerd.* And I added a smiley emoji to the end for good measure.

Because she was worth the wait, but before we could go much further, I needed to talk to Sophie and Max. How would they handle a woman in my life? Of course, they knew that I had dated this past year. And they knew that I had waited almost four years. Grieving and honoring her memory, being the best single parent that I could be to two children who didn't understand why their mother had been taken from them.

As much as I wanted Jessica for myself, it was time to make the next move. And that next move was all about my kids. And Lily, too.

21

Jessica

THE MINNESOTA HISTORY MUSEUM date had been, in a word, incredible. Will had seemed genuinely into it. He laughed with me at the dinosaur dioramas, leaning in to read every placard with mock seriousness, and even indulging my obsession with the vintage typewriter exhibit. But toward the end of the visit, as we strolled through the replica of a 19th-century general store, Will had chuckled softly and admitted he'd been there dozens of times.

"Wait, what?" I said, stopping mid-step.

He smiled sheepishly. "I bring my classes here every trimester. I should've said something earlier, but... You were just so excited. I didn't want to ruin that."

I'd stared at him, completely stunned for a beat, and then burst into laughter. Of course. He was a history teacher, after all. Still, he'd made it fun for me, and not once had I sensed boredom or indifference. We'd shared glances that lingered just a bit too long, stolen kisses when we thought no one was looking, and held hands like we were teenagers.

After the museum, we headed to Cossetta's in St. Paul. Pizza, wine, and a shared tiramisu later, I was officially smitten again. He'd wanted me to come back with him. I knew it, could see it in his eyes, feel it in the way his fingers had traced circles on the back of my hand. And I had wanted to. But I had an early hospital shift the next morning, and we both knew the kids were next. We needed to take that next step.

That night, we agreed: the kids would meet.

We settled on a weekend outing to Nickelodeon Universe at the Mall of America. A perfect, low-pressure setting. Bright, noisy, and distracting enough to soften any initial awkwardness.

Talking to Lily about it had been easier than I expected. We were making cookies together in our little apartment kitchen. Flour dusted every surface, and chocolate chips rolled to the floor as Lily stirred with abandon.

"Hey, Lily," I said, sitting down across from her. "What would you think about going to the Mall of America for a day of rides?"

Her eyes lit up. "Really? Can we go on the SpongeBob ride?"

"Of course," I said, smiling. "But here's the thing—it wouldn't just be you and me. There'd be a couple of other kids, too."

She looked curious. "Who? My friend, Olivia?"

"No, not Olivia," I laughed. "Remember I told you about my friend Will?"

Lily nodded slowly.

"Well, Will has a son and a daughter. Max is 12, and Sophie is 10. They like the rides, too, and we thought it might be fun for all of you to meet and hang out together. What do you think?"

Lily considered this for a moment, then shrugged. "Do they like cookies?"

I grinned. "I'm pretty sure they do."

She nodded. "Okay." And that was that.

The big day arrived, and it went better than I expected. The kids clicked quickly. Lily shadowed Sophie almost immediately, mimicking her every move. Sophie, to her credit, handled it well, even when I noticed moments of subtle irritation flicker across her face. But she didn't say anything. She didn't push Lily away. She just… adapted.

Max, meanwhile, took a more direct interest in me.

He peppered me with questions between rides: "What does it mean to be a physical therapist?" "What's neuro recovery?" "What's a stroke?" And then, more personal: "Why do you only have one kid?" "What happened to Lily's dad?" "If he didn't die, why don't you live together?"

It was a lot. But none of it felt like an interrogation. His curiosity came from a genuine place, and I answered each question as honestly and simply as I could. He listened closely, never interrupting, nodding as if cataloging every answer like a research project.

By late afternoon, we were all dragging. The unlimited ride wristbands had paid off, but the exhaustion had officially set in. Will and I looked at each other across the sea of kids, silently agreeing: it was time for food and sitting.

We steered the group toward the Rainforest Café. Max groaned. "I'm too old for that."

Will raised an eyebrow. "Sophie and Lily aren't," he grumbled. And once we got inside and the animatronic gorillas started hooting, even he cracked a smile.

Dinner was chaotic but manageable. We made small talk while the kids spilled water and giggled at the lightning effects overhead. There were no deep conversations, no emotional revelations. Just a dinner that marked a milestone.

When we finally stepped outside, the sun had long since dipped below the horizon. The temperature had dropped, and I tugged Lily's coat tighter around her as we walked to the parking ramp.

Will and I didn't kiss. We didn't hug. We just exchanged a knowing look, a soft wave. It was right, and it was what was appropriate for that outing.

Still, as Lily and I drove away, her voice from the back seat caught me off guard. "Mom?"

"Yeah, sweetheart?"

"Is Will your boyfriend now?"

I smiled but kept my eyes on the road. "He's someone I like spending time with. And we're still getting to know each other. What do you think about him?"

There was a pause. "I think he's nice. And Sophie's okay. Max asks a lot of questions."

I laughed. "That he does."

She went quiet again, then added, "I like it when you're happy."

Tears sprang to my eyes as I reached behind me to pat her leg.

"Me too, baby. Me too."

22

Sophie

I WAS LYING ON MY BED, staring at the ceiling, holding my Switch above me while it played some annoying background music from my fashion boutique game. I wasn't even playing. I was just clicking around. My fingers were moving, but my brain was somewhere else.

Yesterday had been... a lot.

Nickelodeon Universe was fun. I liked the rides, especially the SpongeBob one that goes all twisty and upside down. It was the first time I had been big enough to ride it. And it was kinda cool that we didn't have to wait in super long lines. Lily was funny. She got so excited about everything. Like, she screamed when she saw a giant Patrick walking around like it was real or something. And she wouldn't stop talking. Ever. But she wasn't awful. Actually, it was kinda nice having someone else around. At least I didn't have to hang out with Max the whole time. He's always acting like he knows everything, asking Jessica a million questions like he was her teacher or something.

Jessica. That's who I was really thinking about. Not my Switch. Not the SpongeBob ride. Not even Lily. Jessica.

She was nice. She smiled a lot and laughed when Max said weird stuff. She let me and Lily go on whatever rides we wanted and didn't complain when we wanted to go back on the same one three times. She was... fine.

But Dad looked at her weirdly. Not bad, weird. Just...

He looked at her like he used to look at Mom. Like he was seeing something amazing. Like he forgot anyone else was there. And that made my stomach feel all twisty, like I'd eaten too much cotton candy.

I rolled over and looked at the photo on my nightstand. It was my favorite one of Mom's. She had her hair then. And she was smiling, holding me when I was probably five. I don't really remember that exact day, but I remember how she felt. Her arms were soft, and she smelled like lavender. And she always hummed this one lullaby I can't remember the name of anymore. But I remember the sound.

But it's getting harder—the memories.

Most of the time when I think of her now, it's when she was sick. When she didn't have hair, she had to rest all the time. Hugging her felt like hugging a skeleton with skin. I hated that. I don't want that to be all I remember.

And now there's Jessica. Not like she's trying to be my mom or anything. She didn't say anything weird. She didn't even hug me. But she was there. And Dad looked at her like... like maybe he didn't miss Mom as much anymore. Or like maybe he was starting to forget.

And I'm not dumb. I know adults don't stay sad forever. Dad's been really good to us. He still cries sometimes when he thinks we're not watching. And he always makes sure we talk about Mom. He's not pretending she didn't exist. But still...

I rolled onto my side and hugged my pillow.

I don't know how I feel. I don't hate Jessica. But I miss my mom.

And maybe I just don't want someone new in our story. Not really.

23

Will

THE HOUSE WAS QUIET, the kind of still that only happened on a Sunday morning when the kids were too worn out to argue or slam doors. Max was curled up on the couch with a fleece blanket, half-watching some Netflix adventure movie, and mindlessly crunching a bowl of cereal. Sophie had disappeared back into her room not long after waking up. She'd come out just long enough to pour some Honey Nut Cheerios, grab her Switch, and vanish again like a ghost.

Yesterday had been a big day. Bigger than I realized until this morning.

I sat at the kitchen table, nursing a lukewarm mug of coffee and thinking about Nickelodeon Universe. The kids hadn't said much on the drive home. I hadn't expected them to. They'd been all smiles at the park, running from ride to ride like they were on a timer, but by the time they hit the car, the adrenaline had worn off, and exhaustion had taken over. They came home, had a snack, brushed their teeth, and practically put themselves to bed without complaint.

Jessica and Lily had left with a wave. No kiss, not even a hug. Just a soft smile that told me she got it. That she understood this was a big step.

And now, I found myself wondering how it had really landed with my kids, not just on the surface, but underneath.

I got up, stretched, and walked down the hall to Sophie's room. Cooper padded softly behind me. The door was half-closed, a familiar sign that meant she wasn't completely locked away but probably didn't want to be disturbed either. Still, I knocked gently. "Sophie?"

I heard a soft, almost inaudible response: "Yeah?"

I pushed the door open slowly and stepped inside. She was sitting cross-legged on her bed, her Switch resting beside her, screen dark. Her cereal bowl sat on the nightstand, half-finished. "Hey, kiddo," I said, walking over and sitting on the edge of her bed as Cooper bounded up beside us, nearly knocking over the cereal bowl as he bumped the nightstand on his way up. "You doing okay?"

She shrugged. "Yeah."

I studied her for a second. She wasn't avoiding my eyes exactly, but she wasn't meeting them either. Her fingers twisted in the hem of her pajama shirt.

"I wanted to see how you felt about yesterday," I said, keeping my voice even, open. "Did you have fun?"

Her lower lip quivered, and then, suddenly, tears sprang to her eyes.

"I miss Mom," she whispered, and then it all came out at once. "I miss her so much, and it feels like... like I'm starting to forget what she looked like. Not when she was sick. I remember that. But before. Like the way she used to braid my hair, or laugh at dumb jokes, or call me 'Sophadoodle.' I can't hear her voice in my head anymore. And I hate it."

My heart cracked right down the center. I didn't say anything right away. I couldn't. The lump in my throat was too big. Instead, I reached for her, and she folded into my arms like she had when she was five. I held her close, one hand cupping the back of her head, the other wrapped tightly around her shaking shoulders.

"I miss her too," I said, my voice thick with emotion. "Every single day."

She cried into my chest, and my own tears fell silently onto the top of her head. There were no words big enough for moments like this. No fixes. Eventually, she pulled back just a little and wiped her eyes with the sleeve of her pajama top. "Is it okay that I like Jessica? I mean, she's nice. And Lily's fun. But it feels like if I like her too much, then I'm... I don't know. Replacing Mom."

I exhaled, pressing a kiss to her forehead. "You're not replacing anyone. No one could ever replace your mom. And Jessica isn't trying to. She just... she just wants to know you. And I think your mom would want that, too. For you to be happy."

Sophie looked up at me, eyes puffy but searching. "Do you really think Mom would be okay with it?"

I nodded, certain. "Yeah. I do. She told me, remember? That letter she wrote? She said I'd probably find someone someday, and that if I did, it was okay. She wanted us to keep living. And she told that to you too, in the letter I read to you."

Sophie nodded slowly, her lips pressing into a thin line. "Okay."

I didn't press for more. Instead, I reached for the remote on her nightstand and smiled. "Want to hang out and watch something dumb together?"

She gave me a faint smile and nodded. "As long as it's not Minecraft videos. Max already claimed the TV in the living room."

"Deal."

I sat beside her and cued up something mindless, grateful for the warmth of her leaning into my side. The pain would never go away entirely. I knew that. But I also hope this new relationship with Jessica will help things in the right ways.

24

Jessica

IT HAD BEEN JUST OVER two weeks since the Nickolodeon Universe trip, and life had returned to its usual rhythm. Or something close to it. Will and I had kept talking, more than ever, actually. And tonight, I was back at his place.

He made me dinner. Pancakes and bacon, just like he'd said he would.

We stood side by side in his kitchen earlier that evening as he poured lumpy batter onto a hot skillet. He was trying to act like he knew what he was doing, but the smoke alarm had gone off once, and we'd both burst out laughing.

"I warned you," he'd said, flipping what might have been the saddest-looking pancake I'd ever seen. "The bacon will make up for it."

And it had. The bacon was crispy perfection, the kind that makes you close your eyes on the first bite. He'd also pulled out fresh strawberries and blueberries, and a small jar of Nutella. The Nutella practically saved the pancakes.

"Okay," I said, chewing a bite smothered in the decadent hazelnut spread and berries. "Not horrible."

He grinned. "I'll take that as high praise."

We were seated at his small kitchen table. It felt warm and domestic, comfortable in a way I wasn't used to. I wrapped my hands around the mug of tea he'd made me and watched him spoon more Nutella onto his plate.

"The kids are gone tonight?" I asked.

"Sleepover," he said. "Same buddy of mine. Matt. We've been friends since elementary school. His wife passed a few years before Katie, and somehow we ended up in this weird tag-team parenting setup. We take turns giving each other nights off."

"You owe him."

"I do," he said with a small smile.

After we'd cleaned our plates, we sat in a comfortable silence. But I could feel something lurking beneath it. A shift. An opening.

"Sophie asked me something after the Nickelodeon Universe trip," Will said after a while. His voice was soft. I looked over at him, my heart already bracing.

"Yeah?"

He nodded, then reached across the table to take my hand. "Well, more like... I asked her. I went into her room the next day. She'd been kind of quiet. And I asked her what she thought about everything."

I didn't say anything. Just waited.

Will took a breath. "She cried. She told me she misses her mom. That she's starting to forget the version of Katie before she got sick, and it just... broke me."

I felt my own throat tighten. "Will—"

He shook his head gently, like he didn't want comfort, just needed to share. "She said it's hard to make new memories when the old ones are starting to fade. She didn't say anything bad about you. Not one word. But I could tell it scared her. The idea of new people, new memories. It makes her feel like she's letting go."

My eyes blurred and I blinked quickly, pressing my fingers to my temple. "Of course it does. She's 10. How is anyone supposed to understand that at 10?"

"Or at forty-two," he said softly.

I let out a breath that turned into a quiet sob.

He stood and walked over to me, pulling me out of the chair and into his arms. I buried my face against his chest.

"I feel like I'm intruding sometimes," I admitted. "Even though I've only met your kids that one time. The thing is, I want to fit in, and I don't want to replace anyone. I couldn't even if I tried."

"You're not," he said. "Intruding, I mean. And I know you're not trying to replace Katie. Sophie knows it too. She just needs time."

I nodded against him. "And Max?"

"Thinks you're the best thing since dinosaurs and mac n' cheese. He told me he likes not having to entertain me all the time."

That made me laugh through the tears. "I think he feels like he has a new adult to learn from," Will added. "Which is huge for a kid like him. He likes information. And you're full of it."

"Gee, thanks."

He chuckled, then leaned back and looked down at me. "You're doing everything right, Jessica. Even when it doesn't feel like it."

My breath caught. In the kitchen, with the scent of bacon still in the air and the chill of the final days of winter pressed against the windows, his words wrapped around me. I closed my hands into a fist as though I could grab onto that feeling and keep it with me.

He tilted his head. "Come here."

He took my hand and led me down the hallway. I already knew the way. Into his bedroom, where the sheets were pulled back and his nightstand had a book resting on it. A book he'd told me he was reading again for the third time because it reminded him of his high school days.

There was no rush in the way he touched me. No push. Just warmth. Intent. A loving unfolding.

He kissed me slowly at first, then with more urgency. My fingers found their way to the back of his neck, tracing along the soft edges of his hair. It made me remember that movie when the man had the woman pressed against the wall. I moved my hands to his neck, then to the sides of his face, and then gently grasped his hair between my fingers. His hands rested lightly on my hips before they traveled up, pulling my shirt over my head.

Clothes fell away with little ceremony. There was no awkward fumbling this time. No socks getting tangled or rings leaving scratches. Just skin on skin and deep breaths and the kind of intimacy that settles into your bones.

He lay me back gently, brushing a strand of hair from my face. "You're beautiful."

"You're biased," I whispered.

"Maybe," he said. "But not wrong." He moved over me, and every kiss, every movement, felt like a conversation. It was a conversation without words, but full of meaning.

It wasn't just about pleasure. Though God, there was that. It was about being seen. Being touched like I was cherished, not just wanted. His body moved against mine, and I arched to meet him, my hands gripping his back. I felt him pause for the briefest second, forehead resting against mine.

"You okay?"

I nodded. "More than okay."

When we came together, it was like finding the exact note in a song you didn't know you'd been humming. It wasn't explosive or cinematic. It was quiet. Powerful. Real.

Afterward, we lay tangled in the sheets, our breaths slowly evening out.

He kissed my shoulder. "Still hungry?"

I laughed softly. "For pancakes or for you?"

"Dealer's choice."

I turned to look at him, brushing my hand across his chest. "I could stay like this forever."

"I wouldn't mind."

But even in that moment, I knew forever wasn't something you rushed. We had time. And tonight, we had each other. That needed to stand for something.

25

Will

LAST NIGHT WITH JESSICA had been slower, quieter, but in that stillness, something deeper had settled between us. No rush. Just us. Skin to skin. Breath to breath. It felt like something permanent had shifted, and our first time together hadn't been explosive either. But this seemed better. Something else, entirely. I didn't even know what to call it. Sacred, maybe. Intentional. Like we were saying something to each other without using any words at all.

I'd made her pancakes, which were still mediocre at best, but the bacon had earned praise. She'd laughed at the Nutella, but still slathered it on like it was magic. Her smile when she took the first bite made the disaster pancakes worth it. We'd eaten in the kitchen, side by side, and talked. Really talked.

I'd told her about my conversation with Sophie. I'd gone into her room and found her trying to distract herself with her Switch, but her eyes betrayed her. The moment I asked how she was feeling after the Mall of America trip, the tears had come.

Jessica had listened, and her own eyes had filled, not from guilt, not from fear, but from empathy. She got it. We talked through it and discussed how grief doesn't just visit once and leave. It lingers, recedes, then crashes again when you least expect it. And how hard it must be for a 10-year-old girl to make room for new people in her life when she's still grieving someone she'll always want more time with.

Jessica cried quietly. Then thanked me for telling her.

And later, upstairs, when I took her to bed, it wasn't about desire, though that was certainly there. It was about choosing her. Every kiss, every movement, said it: I want you here. And she was here. Still, and I was glad for it.

I hadn't planned on her spending the night, but there she was, curled next to me, her hand resting lightly on my chest as we slept. We were wrapped in warmth and calm, our breathing in sync, her hair fanned across the pillow beside mine.

As the early morning sun crept through the blinds, I stirred slightly, blinking against the light. I shifted just enough to feel her still beside me and smiled. I wanted to pull her close, to start the morning the same way we had before, with slow kisses, warm touches, soft whispers, and one more explosion of passion. I reached for her.

Then I heard it. The unmistakable sound of the front door creaking open. Voices. Kids. Sophie's voice. Panic hit me before I could even sit up fully. Jessica stirred beside me, confused, just as the bedroom door burst open.

"Annie got sick, so her dad brought us ba—" Sophie stopped short. Her sentence was sliced in half. She stood in the doorway like a statue, frozen in disbelief, her backpack slung over one shoulder, Max trailing behind her with a confused look.

Jessica, pulling the sheet up to cover her naked chest, immediately tried to sit up. I scrambled out of bed, yanking on the pajama pants I'd dropped hours earlier.

"Sophie. Hey, wait a sec, sweetheart—" But she was already gone. Down the hall, her bedroom door slammed shut behind her.

Max looked from me to Jessica, then said, "Uh, I guess I'll just go to my room," and disappeared as well. Jessica had pulled a t-shirt out of my nightstand and had put it on. She now sat on the edge of the bed, running both hands through her hair. Her face was pale. "Oh, God."

I sat next to her. "I didn't know they were coming home early. I swear. Matt didn't text or call."

"I know," she whispered, eyes focused on her lap. "That's not your fault."

"She's not mad at you," I said. "She's shocked. That's all. We'll talk to her. I'll talk to her."

She nodded, but I could tell her heart had dropped into her stomach. I wrapped my arm around her and pressed a kiss to the side of her head.

"Jess," I said softly. "This doesn't undo anything. It's just a bump. One we'll get through."

She nodded again, slowly. But I could feel the weight of what had just happened settle between us. It shouldn't be a deal-breaker. It wasn't a deal breaker. Was it? But one thing was for sure. This was a turning point that we hadn't reasonably anticipated so soon.

26

Sophie

IT ALL HAPPENED TOO FAST.

Annie had thrown up sometime in the middle of the night. Her dad, Mr. Matt, said it was probably something she ate, but he didn't want to take any chances. So as soon as everyone in the house was awake, he loaded all of us into his car and drove us home. Max and I were both still half-asleep when we got dropped off. My backpack felt heavy, and I was cranky. I hadn't brushed my teeth yet, and my hair was sticking out in all sorts of weird directions.

"Hey, tell your dad I'm sorry for the early drop off," Mr. Matt said as we got out of the car. "Forgot my phone. I'll text him later. Just want to be safe in case Annie has something contagious."

Max grunted something in response, already heading toward the front door and pulling out his house key. I followed slowly, clutching my hoodie around me. The sun was just coming up, and the sky looked sleepy and pale. I watched Max unlock the door, and then followed him inside.

The house was quiet. That should've been my first clue that something was not quite right.

Max went straight to the kitchen to grab cereal. I headed straight for Dad's room to tell him we were home. He probably wouldn't hear us come in otherwise, and I didn't want him to freak out if he was sleeping.

I padded quickly down the hallway to his room, the way I always did. I didn't knock. Why would I knock? I never had to before. I turned the knob and pushed the door open, rubbing my eyes, and froze.

There she was. That woman. Jessica. She was in Dad's bed. Like, in it. With him. The covers were pulled up around them, and their hair was messy, and their faces looked all sleepy and weird and... happy?

My heart dropped into my stomach. "Annie got sick, so her dad brought us—" I started, but the words died in my mouth.

Dad sat up quickly, his eyes wide. "Sophie..."

Jessica looked panicked. She was scrambling to pull the blanket higher, even though I could tell she wasn't wearing any pajamas.

I didn't know what to do. I just stared. Then I turned and ran. I didn't even know where I was running to. I ended up in my bedroom, slamming the door shut behind me. I sat down on the floor with my back to the door, clutching my stomach.

I wasn't dumb. I was 10, not five. I knew what sex was. Max had told me about it in way too much detail when I was eight. I'd seen enough shows to understand what it meant for someone to be in bed with someone else.

But it wasn't supposed to be Jessica. She was nice. Sure. She took us to Nickelodeon Universe. She bought us those giant pretzels and helped Lily tie her shoes. But she wasn't Mom. She wasn't supposed to be with Dad.

Had they had sex? Like, for real? My stomach churned. First: gross. Second: What was he thinking?

I mean, yeah, it had been a long time since Mom died. I remembered that part. I remembered how her hospital bed made our house smell different. I remembered how quiet it was at night except for the beeping from all those machines. I remembered the crying. I remembered the funeral.

But still. Moving on? With *Jessica*? I hugged my knees to my chest. I didn't hate Jessica. That was the worst part. I kind of liked her. And Lily was cute, even if she talked too much. But now that Jessica was *in my dad's bed*, I didn't know what I felt. Confused. Sad. A little bit angry. And most of all, scared.

What if Dad was forgetting Mom? What if this was him... replacing her?

There was a knock on the door. "Sophie? Can I come in?" Dad's voice. Quiet.

I didn't answer. The doorknob turned slowly and pressed in, but he must have noticed my weight against it. He stopped pushing.

"Sophie, please," he said. "I just want to talk."

I stayed quiet for a long time. Finally, I said, "You had sex with her, didn't you?"

Silence. Then he said, "Sophie... we didn't mean for you to find out this way." Which wasn't a no.

"Do you even miss Mom anymore?" I asked.

That time, he didn't answer right away. When he did, his voice sounded thick. "Every single day."

I felt tears coming, even though I didn't want them to. "It doesn't feel like it," I whispered. "You look at her the way you used to look at Mom."

There was a long pause. "I do miss Mom," he said. "So much. It hurts. But part of missing her is learning how to live again. And I think... I think she would want me to try."

That made me cry harder. Because I *knew* he was right. Mom had said stuff like that before she died. She said he needed to keep living. To laugh again. To be happy. But it still felt too soon.

I missed her. I missed having a mom. And now I was scared I would forget her altogether, as if new people were erasing her—new memories.

And Jessica? Jessica was nice. But she wasn't *mine*. I didn't know what to do with that. "Okay," I said finally, wiping my eyes. "But I don't want her in the house when we get dropped off next time."

Dad sighed. "Okay. That's fair."

I got up off the floor and opened my door a little and peeked out. He was standing there in pajama pants and a t-shirt, his face tired and worried.

"I need time," I said.

He nodded. "You'll have it. I promise." And then we both turned as we heard the front door open and close.

27

Jessica

THE SLAM OF SOPHIE'S bedroom door echoed in my ears even after the sound had faded. My body, still warm under Will's comforter, went cold. My stomach twisted, and all I could think was that I shouldn't be here.

Will was behind me, sitting up in bed, clearly just as stunned, his expression cycling between concern and guilt. But I didn't need to see his face to know what we were both thinking. This was not how we had imagined the morning going.

"I should go," I said quietly, already swinging my legs over the side of the bed, removing the t-shirt I had pulled over my chest in haste, and searching for the sweater I'd thrown over the armchair the night before.

"Jess, wait," he said, voice low, but firm.

But I couldn't wait. I couldn't breathe in that moment. I pulled on my panties and jeans, found my boots, and started searching for my socks. Where were they? My hands were shaking. "We didn't plan for them to come back so early, but that doesn't change the fact that I shouldn't have stayed over. I realize that I've stayed over before. But it was just too soon. And how will we ever know when it's the right time?"

"Don't say that," he said, standing now, pulling on a pair of pajama pants.

I turned to face him, tears pricking the back of my eyes. "Will, put yourself in Sophie's shoes? I'm thinking of this from my daughter's perspective. If Lily had walked in and found me in bed with someone new... Can you imagine that?"

He winced, and that was answer enough.

I ran my fingers through my hair, trying to calm the storm inside. "She looked devastated. I don't know what she saw or what she thinks, but I can't be the reason she feels like she's losing her mom all over again."

Will exhaled, rubbing the back of his neck. "She's been doing better lately. Opening up. I thought... I thought we were at a place where she could handle this." He paused, "Well, maybe not this."

I shook my head. "No. Maybe Max, yes. But Sophie? No. She's still figuring out her grief. I can see it in her eyes. She's still looking for her mom in the corners of every room."

He didn't argue. He just stood there, hurting. And I hated it, because I knew I was hurting him. And myself.

I sat down at the edge of the bed, seeing my socks sticking out from underneath. I grabbed them, pulled them on, trying to collect myself. "When Lily was younger and Lucas and I split, she didn't understand what was happening. She thought it was her fault. She stopped sleeping through the night. She started calling for me and her dad, alternating, as if she wasn't sure who to choose. And we were both still alive. Still there."

I looked up at Will. "Sophie doesn't get that luxury. Her mom isn't just away for the weekend. She's gone. And now I'm here. In her house. In her dad's bed. And what if, in that split second, she felt like I was replacing her mother?"

He didn't answer. He couldn't. Because he knew that's what she'd felt. We saw it in her eyes before she disappeared down the hall.

"I think," I said, standing again, sweater finally zipped, "we need to slow down."

His face fell, but he didn't argue. "I don't want to lose you."

"You're not. I'm not walking away. But I think we need some space. Not because I don't care. But because I care too much."

He stepped closer, his hands brushing mine. "What do you want me to do?"

"Be her dad," I whispered. "Help her. Talk to her. Let her cry. Let her remember. And let her forget, too, when she needs to. But don't try to fix it with me. Not yet."

He nodded, eyes glistening. "Okay."

I leaned up to kiss his cheek. It wasn't romantic. It wasn't sensual. It was sad, and soft, and full of meaning. "You know where to find me."

And with that, I watched him walk from the room and down the hall, stopping outside Sophie's bedroom door. As they began talking, the door between them, I made my way to the front door and let myself out.

The drive home was quiet, but my mind was anything but. I couldn't stop thinking about Sophie's face. The confusion. The betrayal. The heartbreak. It made me want to pull over and cry on the side of the road.

When I got home, the silence of my apartment was deafening. Lily was with Lucas for the weekend. I sat on the couch, replaying everything over and over.

My mom's words from years ago came back to me, uninvited but sharp as ever: "You've got to think about the long game, Jess. You don't just fall into a relationship when there's a kid involved. You fall into their lives."

I hadn't really understood it at the time. But I did now. Losing a parent rewires your brain. It alters the way you love, the way you trust, the way you allow joy in. And I didn't want to be someone Sophie learned to flinch around.

That afternoon, I took out a pen and started writing. Not to Will. Not to Sophie. But to myself. It was a strategy that Emily, of all people, had taught me. When she had been questioning her relationship with Lucas earlier, she had told me that she would often write letters to those she loved, even though she never intended to give them the letters.

But this letter, I knew it wasn't intended for anyone but me. And so I poured everything onto the page. My fears. My guilt. My hopes. Because even though I knew we needed to pause, I didn't want this to be the end. Not if there was still a beginning somewhere in the pause. Not if Sophie, someday, might be able to say, "I'm okay. We're okay."

And until then, I would wait.

As I finished up my letter, tucked it into an envelope, and placed it underneath all the junk that had collected in my nightstand drawer, I realized I didn't want to be alone. The apartment, though not all that big, suddenly felt vast and empty. I needed someone. So I picked up my phone and pressed down on Liz's smiling face. I needed my friend.

28

Liz

I WAS STILL IN BED when my phone lit up, the familiar vibration breaking the quiet of my lazy Sunday morning. I groaned, rolled over, and squinted at the screen. Jessica. Her name and smiling photo blinked up at me.

Weird. She never called this early. I slid my thumb across the screen. "Hey, Jess—"

Before I could even get her full name out, I heard her voice. "Can you come over? I need you."

My stomach flipped. Jessica had never called me like this before, not even when Lucas had his heart attack. Not even when she found out Lucas was getting seriously involved with Emily. Something was wrong—bad wrong.

And the only thing that came to mind was Will. What had he done? Or what had Jessica done? Was it over? Did something happen with the kids?

"On my way," I said without hesitation, already flinging the covers off as I slid out of bed.

Within seconds, I was in my bathroom, hot water blasting from the showerhead as I stepped in to wash away the sleep. My mind raced as I shampooed my hair and scrubbed the night from my skin. The thing about Jess was that she didn't ask for help unless she really needed it. And the way her voice sounded on the phone? It rattled me.

Fifteen minutes later, I was dressed in my softest, most comforting pair of black Lululemon leggings, an oversized slate gray sweatshirt, and my newest pair of tan Hey Dudes. My hair was still damp when I grabbed my keys, slung my purse over my shoulder, and headed straight for the door.

I didn't know what I was walking into. But I knew one thing for sure. I was going to be there for my best friend.

Traffic was light, thank God. The streets were still damp from an early morning rain, and the sky held that soft, pale-blue haze that only late winter mornings seemed to bring. The trees lining the road would start to bloom soon as spring rolled in. I gripped the steering wheel a little tighter as I turned onto Jessica's street. Her apartment building came into view. It was familiar and calm. But today, it felt different. Too quiet. Too still.

I parked, grabbed the latte I'd barely touched on the way over, and made my way up the stairs. I knocked lightly, then let myself in with the spare key she'd given me years ago. The lock clicked, and I stepped inside.

The apartment was still, the only sound the faint hum of the heater kicking on. Jessica was sitting at the kitchen island, wearing pajama pants and an old sweatshirt. Her hair was pulled into a messy bun, and her eyes were puffy. There was a mug of tea in front of her, steam curling up like a ghost. She looked up as I entered, and her face crumpled.

"Oh, Jess," I whispered, dropping my purse on the floor as I crossed the room and wrapped my arms around her. She leaned into me without hesitation, her body trembling with unspoken emotion.

We paused for a long moment, her head tucked against my shoulder. Eventually, I pulled back just enough to look at her. "Talk to me."

She let out a shaky breath and nodded. "It's Sophie. She... she walked in on us."

My brows rose. "Wait. Walked in?"

Jessica winced. "Yeah. She and Max were supposed to be at a sleepover. But the other dad had to bring them home early. Sophie didn't even knock. Just barged into Will's room."

"Oh my God." I sat on the stool next to her. "And she saw you...?"

"In bed. Naked. Together."

I let out a long whistle. "Yikes."

Jessica laughed weakly. "Yeah. Yikes. She ran to her room and slammed the door. And Will tried to talk to her, but she just shut down. I got dressed and left. I haven't heard from him since."

I shook my head slowly. "Poor kid."

"I know. That's just it. I keep thinking... what if we made a mistake? What if we rushed this?"

I reached for her hand. "You didn't do anything wrong, Jess. But maybe now is just... not the time for things to move forward. That doesn't mean it won't be the right time later."

She nodded, but I could see the doubt in her eyes.

"So," I said gently, "what do you need from me today?"

She looked at me, eyes glassy but resolute. "I need to not feel like the worst person in the world for falling in love with a man who has kids. Kids who lost their mom."

"You're not," I said. "You're human. And honestly? You're one of the most thoughtful, grounded humans I know."

Jessica gave a small smile and squeezed my hand.

"I just needed someone to remind me," she whispered.

"Always," I said. "That's what I'm here for."

29

Will

IT HAD BEEN SEVERAL WEEKS since that morning. I still replayed the sound of her gasp, the slam of the door, the sharp thud of her footsteps retreating down the hallway. And I still remember the look on Jessica's face as clearly as if it had just happened. She looked stunned, then guilty, then the same kind of heartbreak I'd seen in myself more times than I cared to admit.

Now, I sat on the back patio with a steaming mug of coffee, Cooper running wild through the spring grass like he didn't have a single care in the world. That dog had been one of the best decisions I'd ever made. He'd brought joy and movement back into our home after Katie passed. It wasn't a fix, but it was something. Something alive and loyal, and endlessly happy to see us.

Kristy, our therapist, had been the one to suggest it. "Grief needs space to breathe, but it also needs something hopeful to tether itself to," she'd said. Cooper became that tether for all of us.

I took a sip of coffee and looked around the yard, watching the spring sun dance between the newly green leaves. The warmth of the morning felt nice against my skin. It was beautiful out. Alive. And yet, something still felt just... not right.

I hadn't seen Jessica since that day.

We texted every day. Spoke on the phone several times a week. Sometimes our calls would last an hour, maybe longer if Lily was already in bed and the house was quiet. But something had changed. She wasn't pulling away, not entirely. But she wasn't moving forward either. It was like she'd put up a careful, invisible wall between us, trying to protect herself, or maybe me, or Sophie.

She'd told me she wasn't going anywhere. And I believed her. But even still, the space between us felt wide. Heavy. It hurt.

Kristy had been helping us, especially Sophie. Though we hadn't been seeing her as regularly before Jessica came into my life, it was clear that we weren't ready to be done. Now, it was twice a week sessions, sometimes with Max and me, sometimes all three of us. At first, Sophie had barely said a word. She'd just sit there, arms folded, legs swinging beneath her chair. But Kristy was patient. Gentle. And over time, Sophie had opened up more. We started talking about memories. About Katie. About how forgetting, or remembering less, didn't mean letting go. About how loving someone new doesn't mean you've stopped loving the person who came before.

It was progress.

And Max? That kid had handled everything better than I could've hoped. He was always the curious one, always asking questions about everything. He'd asked Jessica about her job, about Lily, about their apartment. About her past. About her divorce. He'd even asked me, when Jessica wasn't around, if I thought she made good pancakes. I had to tell him that I hadn't yet had the experience of trying her pancakes, but I hoped to. Soon.

Max missed his mom, sure. But he also had more memories of her. Good ones. Ones before she got sick. He remembered her laugh. Her terrible singing voice. The way she used to dollop chocolate chips into the pancakes on Saturdays. That foundation had given him a better grip on how to handle this shift. And he liked Jessica. He liked Lily. He told me as much. He was ready for more.

So now what? Where did we go from here?

I wanted Jessica back in my life. I wanted her in our lives. I wanted her to feel like she belonged, like she didn't have to hold back or tiptoe around us. But I also knew I couldn't force it.

Sophie had made real progress, but she still had hard days. Days when she retreated, curled up on her bed with her Switch and her books, and didn't want to talk. But those days were fewer now. She had even mentioned Jessica by name the other night. Casually. Not with warmth, not with distance. Just like she was someone she knew.

That was something.

Jessica needed to see that. She needed to know that this wasn't just grief and heartbreak and impossible hurdles. This could be a future. Not one that erased the past, but one that honored it while building something new.

I set my coffee mug down on the side table and watched Cooper flop onto the grass, panting with satisfaction. Maybe it was time to reach out again. Not just a text full of pleasantries. Not just a call to hear her voice. But something more intentional.

I had no grand gesture in mind—no speech prepared. But I did have an idea. Something simple. Something that might say: we're still here. We're still choosing this.

I pulled out my phone and opened my messages.

Me: *Hey. I was thinking about dinner this coming weekend—just you and me. No kids. No pressure. Just time.*

I stared at the screen for a moment before hitting 'Send'.

Then I leaned back in my chair, feeling the sun warming my face, and waited.

30

Jessica

THE LAST FEW WEEKS had been a blur. I'd kept myself busy, on purpose. Work was demanding, as always, and Lily kept me on my toes, but it was more than that. I'd been trying to fill every pocket of time with activity, with anything that kept me from lingering too long on that morning at Will's house.

And earlier this week, I surprised Lily with an overnight trip up to Duluth. She'd been thrilled. We hit Betty's Pies on the way up, blasted Taylor Swift in the car, and even dipped our toes along the icy shoreline of Lake Superior for all of three seconds before running back to the car laughing.

But the trip wasn't just about fun. My dad had fallen again. That made three times in less than a year. And while they lived in a single-level rambler, it became clearer with each visit that the home was no longer safe for him.

I watched the way he shuffled around the house with his walker, and the bruises on his forearms and hips from where he'd gone down. Moreover, I watched my mom. It was clear she was struggling to help him into bed, and how tired she looked even when she said she was fine.

We fought.

Mom and I rarely saw eye to eye on big things, and this was no exception. She insisted that she could manage and didn't need help. That he didn't need to move anywhere. I, on the other hand, am a physical therapist. I see what happens when people ignore the signs. I knew this wasn't sustainable.

"But I love this house," she'd snapped at one point, throwing a dishtowel on the counter. "We raised you here."

"And I love Dad," I said, more quietly than I meant to. "Which is why I can't pretend this isn't a problem."

The discussion went nowhere. I hated leaving things unresolved, but I also knew pushing harder would only create more distance. I needed to regroup. Consider bringing in some backup: her doctor, a care coordinator, someone with a badge and a title she might respect more than me.

I'd driven home feeling exhausted and heavy, wishing for the first time in a long time that I had a sibling to lend a hand. My parents had tried, I knew that. But I was it—the only one.

The day after we got back, I was unpacking Lily's things when my phone buzzed. I glanced at the screen and saw Will's name. For a second, I thought it would just be another small talk text. That had been our rhythm lately. Short updates, sharing memes, the occasional question about our kids. It was polite. Safe. Surface-level.

But this one was different.

Will: *Hey. I was thinking about dinner this coming weekend—just you and me. No kids. No pressure. Just time.*

He knew I wouldn't have Lily that weekend. And he must've figured something out with Matt to watch Max and Sophie.

My heart thumped a little harder. I hadn't seen Will in person since that morning. Since Sophie had walked in, wide-eyed and hurt and confused. We hadn't even FaceTimed since then, both of us silently agreeing that maybe some space was necessary. In the time that had passed, winter had moved on, and the Minnesota spring had set in.

And now, here he was. Reaching out and suggesting something more than just texting. Could I do this?

I missed him. I missed the way his eyes crinkled when he laughed, the calmness of his voice, and the way he looked at me, as if he really saw me. And I believed him when he said Sophie was doing better. Their family therapist was helping them, especially Sophie.

And Lily, sweet Lily, kept asking when we'd do something again with "her new friends". She mentioned the zoo, Como Town, paddleboats, and even the beach, although it certainly wasn't warm enough for that yet. Lily hadn't forgotten about Sophie and Max, or Will, for that matter. Not even a little.

I sat on the edge of the bed, staring at Will's message for another few seconds. Then I picked up my phone.

Me: *Dinner sounds perfect. Name the time. I'll be there.*

31

Carol

I STOOD AT THE KITCHEN SINK had my hands submerged in warm, soapy water, though the breakfast dishes had long been washed, rinsed, and dried. I had a perfectly good dishwasher sitting quietly a few feet away, but I'd always preferred the rhythm of handwashing. It gave me time to think. Time to remember. And this morning, there was a lot on my mind.

The clink of a plate meeting the drying rack was a familiar sound, but it couldn't drown out the voice in my head: Jessica's voice. My daughter had barely pulled out of the driveway before I started replaying our conversation. Or argument, really. Jessica had meant well, I knew that. But suggesting that Ronald and I consider moving? Into one of those senior living communities? I had thrown the dishtowel on the counter so hard it startled even me.

Who did Jessica think she was? This house was our home. Ronald and I had poured ourselves into every inch of it, from the cedar deck to the wallpaper in the laundry room. We'd built it with our own hands. Or at least, we had hired the architect and managed the entire project. And Ronald had helped with the framing. And more than that, the house was paid off. Free and clear. A rarity these days, from what I heard. The very idea of leaving it made me feel like I couldn't breathe.

Yes, Ronald had fallen. Three times. And maybe I had to admit the last fall had shaken me. But we didn't need to move. What we needed was maybe a little extra help. A nurse, perhaps. Someone to come by a few times a week. Not a whole new life. Not a boxy apartment with handrails and vinyl floors and people I didn't know calling me "sweetie" like I was a child.

I reached for the empty fruit bowl on the counter, dunking it into the dishwater and scrubbing a little harder than necessary. The headache that had been coming and going for the past couple of weeks pulsed behind my right eye again. It had flared up just after Jessica had started in about "planning for the future."

I sighed. Jessica was only trying to help. That was always her way. Even as a little girl, she'd been a worrier. After school, she'd check the calendar on the fridge to make sure I didn't miss a dental appointment. She'd lay out her own clothes for school every night without being asked. Mature beyond her years, even when she was young.

I remembered holding Jessica for the first time. After the miscarriage before her, I had been so afraid to hope. Then came Jessica. And then, heartbreak again. Three more losses. After that, Ronald and I had stopped trying. Jessica was our miracle. Our only.

I thought of the sleepovers, how the house had once been full of giggles and whispers and the sound of socked feet running down the hall. All those kids in the house had helped to ease the sadness that had come from our ability to only conceive and bring one child to term.

I used to make cookies when Jessica was young and planning to have friends over. Always from scratch. And the cakes we baked together for school parties or birthdays? Well, those were some of my fondest memories. Jessica had always loved baking. I had been tickled when Jessica made cinnamon rolls this morning before she and Lily left to return to the Cities. Perfectly soft, just the right amount of cinnamon. I hadn't said it then, but they were better than mine. And my cinnamon rolls were excellent. Ronald had once told me I should open a breakfast cafe to sell my baked goods. But I wasn't interested. I had plenty to keep me busy while Ronald worked long hours.

The memory made me smile, even as the headache pressed harder. Jessica and Lily's visit had started so sweetly. I loved watching Lily pad around the kitchen, asking questions and offering to help. A sweet girl. Sharp, too. But things soured after breakfast this morning. Jessica had broached the topic of Ronald's health and "making smart choices".

I had gone quiet. It was the silence that had caused Jessica to keep going, I realized—trying to fill the space. However, I hadn't wanted to discuss it. I hadn't wanted to think about what it might mean.

My hand gripped the counter now, the fruit bowl forgotten. This was our home. This was where Jessica grew up, where Ronald taught Jessica how to ride a bike, where she learned to drive, and where she cried on the couch after her first heartbreak. We had hosted her bridal shower in the backyard, with those blue hydrangeas blooming in the corner garden. This place was stitched into every part of my motherhood.

Was it really so hard for Jessica to see that?

The water turned cold, and I let it drain from the sink, staring into the emptying basin as though it held answers. The truth was, I was scared. Not just of change, but of what that change meant. Letting go. Admitting I couldn't handle everything anymore. That I couldn't protect Ronald from everything either.

But I wasn't ready. Not yet.

I turned and looked around my kitchen—the linoleum floor with its tiny cracks. The sun shining through the gingham curtains. The scent of cinnamon still lingering from the rolls Jessica had baked. It was more than a house. It was a life. Our life.

And I wasn't going to give that up. Not yet. Not ever, if I had my way.

32

Jessica

IT HAD BEEN ALMOST four weeks now since I last saw Will.

Not that we hadn't communicated. We'd exchanged text messages with short updates, emojis, and the occasional sarcastic comment that reminded me of why I liked him so much. But still, I missed him. Missed the sound of his laugh in person. Missed how his presence grounded me when my thoughts ran off in a hundred different directions. Missed how his arms could quiet a storm I hadn't even realized was brewing inside me.

I needed him. And maybe that was okay to admit.

Will had reassured me that we could work through things with Sophie. That we didn't have to rush. That taking it slow was the best way forward. And honestly? We were doing a damn good job at taking it slow. Between work and life and everything in between, our pace had felt... appropriate. But appropriate didn't always mean easy.

Work had been hectic. One of the other physical therapists at the clinic had gone out on maternity leave earlier than expected, and I had picked up several of her patients. The extra hours left me drained most days, but it also gave me something to focus on. Something other than the awkward goodbye with Will last month, or the memory of Sophie's cold stare, or the way Will's jaw had tensed when I'd said I should probably go.

I thought about the woman on maternity leave sometimes. Not because we were particularly close, but because the idea of her, of someone my age holding a newborn, made me pause.

Did I want another child?

It wasn't something I'd given serious thought to in years. Lucas and I had never talked about more than one because it had been such a struggle to conceive Lily. Yet, we could have tried. We just didn't. We had Lily, and we had just… stopped at one. Maybe because our marriage had started unraveling before we ever made it to those conversations. Maybe because neither of us wanted to poke at something we both sensed was already fragile. And our marriage might not have survived as long as it had, had we struggled with fertility issues again.

But now, in a new relationship, the thought surfaced. I was still young enough. I wasn't yet forty, so I wasn't ancient. Over ten years younger than Lucas. A few years younger than Will. If the timing were right and if the partner were right, maybe it could happen. Perhaps I could want it.

Then again, maybe not.

I wasn't rushing toward anything. Not a baby. Not a wedding. Not a picture-perfect future. Right now, I just wanted to make dinner for a man I was growing to care deeply for. I wanted him to see my home, not because it was perfect, but because it was mine.

After all this time, it was strange to realize Will had never even set foot in my apartment. We'd always met somewhere else. Restaurants, coffee shops, a visit to the Mall of America, and a couple of short hikes along the river bluffs. The times we'd been intimate were always at his place, and even then, it felt like I was borrowing a space and borrowing a piece of his past.

Katie had lived in that house. Katie had died in that house.

Maybe it was time to let Will into mine.

I'd told him to name the place for dinner this time, but after I texted it, I had changed my mind. I called him the next day and asked if he wanted to come over instead. I offered to cook. His voice had softened when he said, 'Yes.' I could hear the smile behind it.

"About time you let me see where you live," he'd joked. He wasn't wrong.

I looked around my apartment and felt an odd mix of pride and anxiety. It wasn't a palace, but it was nice. Clean. Comfortable. Ours. Lily had her own room and bathroom, which she'd decorated in polar bears and ice scapes and whatever Target had been selling in the "Elsa and Olaf" aisle that month. My bedroom was simple.

White comforter, a few framed prints on the wall, and a nightstand cluttered with books I'd half-started. A copy of The Women by Kristin Hannah sat at the bottom of the stack. It was the only book I'd finished in recent months.

The kitchen was my favorite space. I'd splurged on a few gourmet tools when I first moved in, including a gorgeous set of copper pans I never used but liked to look at. I'd picked this place because it had a real balcony and a 6-burner gas range, and because I didn't want to deal with a lawn or snow shoveling or leaking gutters. I'd dealt with all of that in the house with Lucas. And when something broke, I didn't want to have to call him anymore.

Now, I call the landlord. Or better yet, email him.

I opened the fridge and checked on the chicken breasts I'd been marinating. Garlic, lemon, and rosemary. Those were my go-to flavor combinations when I wanted something that smelled fancy but took minimal effort. I'd already chopped the vegetables and set the table. Two plates. Two wine glasses. I'd even lit a candle. And I had double-checked that I had flour, vanilla, eggs, sugar, and a few other items on hand. Bacon. After all, who knew what I might need if things were to last the night?

All said, it was strange to feel nervous. Will and I had been dating for a few months now, if you counted back to those initial exchanges on Christmas Day. We'd seen each other at our best and, in a few cases, our worst. But this felt different. This felt like showing a part of myself I hadn't before.

Lily was staying with Lucas for the weekend, and I was grateful for the time alone. Not because I didn't want her here, but because I wanted this to be just Will and me. I wanted to show him the life I'd built for myself. For me and Lily.

A knock at the door pulled me from my thoughts.

I opened it to find Will, slightly windblown, holding a bottle of wine and a bouquet of tulips.

"You brought flowers," I said, already smiling.

"Wasn't sure if it was too much," he said, stepping inside.

"Not too much at all," I replied. "They're perfect."

So was he, in a worn way. His hair needed a trim, and his beard looked a bit scruffier than usual, but he still looked good. Comfortable. Real.

I showed him around the apartment. He paused in the kitchen to admire the backsplash, of all things. And then we sat down for dinner. The conversation flowed easily. We talked about work, and about Lily's newfound obsession with making slime. Will shared with me that Sophie had gone through the same obsession a couple of years back, promising me that it wouldn't last.

And then, as the plates cleared and the wine settled, we sat on the couch, close but not touching.

"I missed this," I said quietly.

"Me too," he said, looking over at me.

I moved closer. He leaned toward me, and we kissed. Soft at first, then deeper. And when I pulled back, I felt it. That shift. The one where something moves from casual to something else. Something more permanent. Like maybe I wasn't just showing him my apartment.

Maybe I was showing him the door to something new.

I stood quickly and climbed onto his lap, taking his wine glass from his hand and placing it on the end table. I pushed his hands to his sides as he tried to put them on my hips. I rolled my pelvis forward as I leaned down and trailed my tongue below his ear and along his neck.

This wasn't the house where Katie had lived. This was my home. My rules. My chapter. And tonight, I was going to take charge.

33

Will

THE LATE SPRING SUN WAS HIGH and warm, blanketing the backyard in a golden light that made everything feel just a bit more relaxed, except for Cooper, who had a mad case of the zoomies. The dog bolted across the muddy yard, which was par for the course in Minnesota this time of year, circled back, and launched himself after the tennis ball I'd just lobbed toward the fence. His legs kicked out in every direction, as if he were made of some sort of spring, not bone and muscle. I couldn't help but laugh.

"You're out of your mind today," I called after him. "Must've had a good night, too."

The kids were inside. Sophie, with her earbuds in, was probably sketching or scrolling, and Max was playing a game online with his friends. They were content. Happy, even. The overnight at Matt's had gone well, and when I picked them up this morning, there was none of the usual reluctance or sibling squabbling. It helped me to breathe a little easier, that was for sure.

And I needed that peace today. I needed space to think.

Last night with Jessica was something else.

Not just the sex, though, yes, the sex had been fantastic. Best yet, no question. She'd taken control in a way that surprised me, turned me on, left me breathless. One minute, we were sipping wine and letting our meals settle, and the next, she was straddling me on the couch, her voice low and sultry. There was no hesitation in her. No question about what she wanted. And what she wanted was me. Right there. Right then.

It had been fast, rough in the best way, and yet thoroughly grounded. I didn't feel like a bystander in it. No, we were in it together, even though she had pinned my arms down to my sides. But she led. And I let her, starting with when she straddled me on the living room couch. I'd never look at that couch the same way again.

It wasn't about proving anything, I don't think. She wasn't trying to erase the past or one-up what we'd shared before. It felt more like she was finally comfortable enough to show me another part of herself. And that trust? That fire? I welcomed it. Every second of it. And in every part of my body. And to be honest, with every part of her body.

I felt the heat rise in my cheeks as I remembered her standing up, leaving me on the couch. She'd placed her fingers to her lips, telling me to stay put and quiet. Slowly, she'd started removing the layers of her clothing. Underneath her long-sleeved blouse and dress slacks had been some of the sexiest underwear I had ever seen. Black silk and lace. Sheer. Though it wasn't like I got to enjoy her in those pieces for very long, as before I knew what was happening, she was fully undressed, I had no pants on, and she had straddled me again.

Later, when we moved to her bedroom, things slowed down. I made love to her in a way I hadn't made love to anyone in a long time. I loved her body with care, with attention, with reverence, as if she were something rare—someone I wanted to know inside and out.

And afterward, we'd just talked. Nothing serious. No evident stream-of-consciousness kind of stuff. We chatted about what kind of cereal we hated as kids. I hated Wheaties and Life, and she hated Malt-o-Meal. Which movies have we seen too many times? We had both said Die Hard in unison, which gave us a fun laugh. I told her about the treehouse I helped Max build in the backyard, and she told me about how Lily had tried to convince her to get a guinea pig by putting together a full-on presentation built with construction paper, lots of cellophane tape, crayons, and some beautifully misspelled words. We'd laughed—a lot.

But underneath the laughter, there was comfort. Ease. And something else. Something quiet and creeping that settled into my chest as I drifted off to sleep beside her.

I was falling in love with Jessica. I hadn't said the words out loud. At least not to her, and not even to myself, until this morning when it hit me. The feeling really struck me while pouring coffee at my kitchen counter. But it was there. Undeniable.

And maybe I should've seen it coming.

From the first moment I met her, I knew there was something different about her. Something reliable, something smart, something that didn't try too hard to be what she wasn't. She didn't play games. She didn't act like someone who needed to be saved. She was just...real.

And now I'd seen even more of her. The woman who took what she wanted in the living room. The woman who melted into me in her bedroom. The woman who let me into her space, her home, her quiet.

I tossed the ball again, and Cooper launched after it like a maniac.

The thing was, I didn't know exactly what to do with all this. Sophie was still adjusting. She liked Jessica, I could tell. But she also liked keeping her guard up. Understandable, given everything. She still clung to memories of her mom in ways I hadn't entirely expected. And Jessica wasn't trying to replace Katie. Thank God. But she was here now. A part of my life. Of our lives.

And I wasn't in a rush to define things. I just wanted to let them grow.

But still... I was falling. And for the first time in a long time, I wasn't afraid of the fall.

"Okay, Cooper," I said, catching the slobbery ball he dropped at my feet again. "That's it, buddy. We're calling it. You're gonna give yourself a heart attack."

I wiped my hands on my jeans and glanced back at the house.

It felt good to be home. But I had to admit, being at Jessica's place last night, hearing her laugh echo off her apartment walls, indulging in her pancakes and bacon for breakfast. Wow. I could do this. This could become something real. And my arms were wide open.

34

Carol

IT HAD BEEN SEVERAL WEEKS since Jessica and Lily's last visit, but I couldn't stop replaying it in my mind. That goodbye was so sharp. It felt unfinished. And it lingered more than I liked to admit. Jessica had called since, of course. She always did—at least once a week, sometimes more. But lately, something had changed. Her tone felt clipped, rushed, like she was checking a box and not asking how we were really doing. Just verifying we were still breathing.

I wasn't sure what bothered me more: the fact that she'd suggested we move, or the fact that she might've meant it.

I looked out the kitchen window, watching the wind shuffle the leaves on the back maple tree. Ronald and I had planted that tree over 30 years ago. And every time I looked out the window, my heart smiled a bit, knowing we had built this home together.

I looked back at the counter, saw the breakfast dishes stacked neatly by the sink, waiting. The dishwasher sat empty, but I rolled

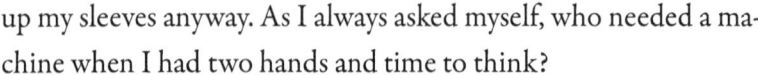

up my sleeves anyway. As I always asked myself, who needed a machine when I had two hands and time to think?

"Move," I muttered under my breath, rinsing a plate. "This is our home."

And my mind took me back. Again. We built this house, board by board. Ronald had helped with every stud, every joist. I painted every wall, picked every tile. We brought Jessica home from the hospital to this house. I remembered her pink cheeks, quiet cries, and how she was such a miracle after what we'd been through. The miscarriage before her nearly broke me. And the three that followed nearly broke Ronald. But Jessica. She was ours. The only one we got to keep.

She grew up in this house. Sleepovers and giggles from her bedroom. Cookie dough on every surface of the kitchen. Her teenage door slamming when we told her no, and her quiet apology the morning after. This house has seen every chapter of our lives.

And now she wants us to just… leave?

I scrubbed a bit too hard on a glass and cracked it at the rim. I stared at the jagged edge for a second longer than I should have, then sighed and tossed it in the trash. I pressed my fingertips to my forehead, staving off the headache that was beginning to loom.

It's not that I don't see what she's seeing. Ronald's had three falls now. Well, four, but we hadn't told Jessica about the most recent one. And yes, even small tasks are getting harder for him. I've started doing more around the house, laying out his socks and pajamas, and making sure his toiletries are within easy reach. It's tiring, sure. I've been more tired lately than I care to admit.

But we're not helpless. We don't need to downsize into one of those sterile senior communities. Not yet. Not while I can still manage things. I'm strong. I've handled worse.

The phone rang in the living room, but I didn't rush to answer it. It was probably someone wanting to sell us something, or maybe Jessica again. And I needed a moment. So, I ignored it.

I dried my hands, folded the dishtowel over the sink, and leaned against the counter. The light was fading outside. Ronald was in his recliner, half-dozing through a rerun of something we'd seen a dozen times. I watched him for a long time. I sighed with relief as I saw his chest rising and falling slowly, his head nodding slightly with each breath.

God, I love that man. We've been through so much. And even if his memory slips sometimes, or he forgets what day it is, he's still here—still mine.

And there it was. That headache I've been battling off and on all month came crawling back again, sharp and pulsing behind my eyes. I pressed my fingers to my temples again and exhaled.

"Alright, sweetheart," I said softly, touching Ronald's arm. "Let's head to bed."

He stirred, blinked at me, and nodded. I helped him up, one step at a time, guiding him gently down the hall to our room. We didn't speak much. It had become part of our routine, this quiet shuffle to the end of the day.

Once he was settled under the covers, I went to the bathroom to wash my face. The reflection staring back at me looked older than I felt. I looked at the lines I don't remember earning and eyes that betrayed the ache in my head.

Back in the bedroom, I climbed into bed beside Ronald. The house was still. The ache in my head had bloomed into a pulsating throb. I reached for the bottle of aspirin on my nightstand, thought against it, and lay back instead.

I turned toward him, watching his profile in the dark, and let out a breath I didn't realize I'd been holding.

Jessica thinks she knows what's best for us. Maybe someday she will. But not yet. Not tonight. I closed my eyes and let the headache pull me down into a deep, deep slumber.

35

Jessica

I WAS IN MY KITCHEN, hard at work on my grocery list. Lily had clearly been going through a growth spurt, sometimes asking for four or five small meals a day. And as such, the contents of the refrigerator and cupboard were getting a bit bare.

As I worked on the list, I found myself distracted by thoughts that alternated between the last evening with Will and my parents. The sex with Will had been phenomenal. And where had that part of me been hiding? I couldn't remember the last time that I had taken charge in the bedroom. Or in the living room. Yikes. Surely, I had done that with Lucas, hadn't I? And men liked it when women took charge, right? But with Will. Well, with Will, it had been different. I closed my eyes for a moment, allowing myself to remember the feel of him as I had straddled him on the couch.

Shaking off my thoughts, I refocused on the bigger issue at hand: my parents. It had been several weeks since our last visit. My mom's words still rang in my head, the tension in her voice, the way she had thrown the dish towel down and dismissed my suggestion like it was some kind of insult. I hadn't meant it that way. I just... I just wanted to help.

Since then, I've done some research. Quietly, between patient visits and late nights when Lily was asleep. I'd found a handful of senior living communities. There was one right there in Duluth and a few more in the Twin Cities. I wasn't talking about some depressing nursing home. These places were beautiful. They had private apartments with full kitchens, oversized windows, and access to shared dining rooms if you didn't feel like cooking. Some even had little gardens out back and walking paths. And book clubs. Baking clubs. Movie nights.

My mom would never admit it, but she would love something like that. It would give her something to do beyond managing my dad's meds and doing dishes. She could be Carol again. A wife. Her own person. Not just a caregiver.

But convincing her? That was the part that left me stuck. She didn't want help. She didn't want to change. She wanted everything exactly the way it had always been. Even when it was apparent she was tired. Even when she got confused, even when she looked pale the last time I saw her, and had rubbed her temple like a headache was settling in and wouldn't leave.

I'd finally worked up the courage to call last night. I had been nervous. My hands had been sweating, and I had found myself pacing the kitchen like a teenager waiting for a date to text back. It rang five times before it went to voicemail. I left a short message. "Hey

Mom, it's me. Can you give me a call when you get a chance? Just want to check in." I didn't mention housing, nurses, or plans—just a simple message. But I still hadn't heard back.

I sighed and picked up my grocery list again. It mainly was scribbles—milk, eggs, apples, cereal. And none of it felt particularly urgent anymore. I just needed to get out of my own head.

I pushed back from the counter and grabbed my sneakers. I slid one on, then reached for the other. That's when my phone rang.

I froze. That same flutter in my chest hit like it always did when my parents' number popped up on the screen.

"Hello, Mom?" I said as I picked up. But it wasn't her.

"Jessica," my father said. His voice was trembling. "Something has happened."

I dropped my shoe to the floor and sank onto the nearest kitchen chair. "Dad," I said slowly, already bracing myself. "What is it?"

36

Will

I WAS IN MY HOME OFFICE, working on lesson plans to take me through the rest of the school year. I always liked this time of year when we focused on Minnesota history. And the students were always pleasantly surprised to find out that Minnesota had its own share of cool stories.

We kicked things off with statehood, May 11, 1858, when Minnesota officially became the 32nd state in the union. Most kids had no clue we'd been around that long. And then there was the discovery of the source of the Mississippi River at Lake Itasca. That always blew their minds. To think that one of the most iconic rivers in the country began right here in our backyard.

But what they really loved and what always got their attention were the celebrities. I had a slide dedicated to Prince, of course, and another to Jessica Lange and Richard Dean Anderson. I always saved Anderson for last. The second I mentioned he was MacGyver, hands would shoot up, eyes would widen, and the room would come alive. How could kids in this era know MacGyver? But they did. So, for fun, I'd show an old episode every year. It was tradition.

And then there were the sports legends. Herb Brooks and John Mariucci always got nods from the hockey fans. Tommy Gibbons? A bit of a history lesson there, but I always appreciated the nod to boxing. I'd thrown in Lindsay Whalen and Joe Mauer in past years, depending on the class. It was fun to watch the kids connect the dots, realizing that greatness didn't always come from somewhere else.

As I worked through my lesson plan, I thought back to the visit that Jessica and I had made to the Natural History Museum. A totally different line of thinking, but I couldn't help but remember how beautiful she was that day. And the effort that she had put into planning something she thought I would love. Any woman who put that kind of thought into something was a keeper.

I watched Cooper saunter into my office, a bone in his mouth. This dog loved trying to hide his bone, as though the kids and I would try to steal it from him. The problem was, his hiding skills weren't as good as he thought they were. He seemed to think he could hide something in plain sight and we wouldn't be the wiser. It made me chuckle.

Cooper finally decided to hide his bone at the foot of my desk. I shook my head and laughed to myself. I thought about how Jessica might find this amusing. It was a great opportunity and excuse for a quick FaceTime call.

I grabbed my phone and hit her contact, letting it ring a few times as I waited for her to answer. No response. I tried once more, just in case she'd missed it. Still nothing. Figuring she was probably busy, maybe at the clinic or out running errands, I set the phone back on my desk and headed down the hall.

I knocked on Max's door. "Hey buddy, want to come toss the ball around with me and Cooper?"

Max cracked open his door and gave me a quick thumbs-up. "Let me put on shoes," he said, already moving toward his closet.

"Meet me out back," I said, grabbing Cooper's leash just in case we decided to walk down to the park after a few throws.

We stepped out onto the deck. My phone was completely forgotten in the house. The sun was shining, and the breeze felt good on my skin. Cooper ran ahead, tail wagging, ready for the first toss. Max joined me a moment later, and the three of us fell into an easy rhythm. Throw, chase, return. Throw, chase, return.

Just ten minutes after we stepped outside, my phone lit up on the desk inside. Jessica was calling back. But I wasn't there to see it. I didn't hear it ring over the laughter and barking in the backyard.

And so, it went unanswered.

37

Ronald

SLEEP NEVER CAME EASILY ANYMORE.

I could drift off in my recliner without a second thought, the hum of the television or the soft rattle of the newspaper from the light breeze of the ceiling fan often lulling me into a doze. But in bed? In bed, it was like my mind refused to shut down, and my body joined the protest with a chorus of aches and complaints.

The pain was constant now. My knees throbbed, my back ached, and sometimes, it felt like even my fingers were tired. Age had snuck up on me in a slow, merciless crawl, and the falls this past year hadn't helped. Four of them. Four stupid, unexpected moments where my legs simply gave out. Not a slip on ice or a trip over something. Just... gone. It was as if someone had yanked the cord out and powered me down.

Carol had been after me to use a walker ever since. She meant well, I knew that. But damn it, I was a man. I didn't need a walker. Not yet. I could get stronger again. I just needed a plan. A routine.

Something to work toward. I could feel it in me somewhere. These spark plugs could still fire. I knew it.

But convincing her of that? Different story.

Carol was so sure she knew what was best for both of us—always had been. Stubborn as the day is long. And lately, she'd been pushing ideas about downsizing, maybe even moving into one of those retirement places with the little apartments and scheduled activities. She thought she was being practical. And it was ironic that she had proposed such an idea to me when I had overheard her chastising Jessica that we would never leave our home.

And Carol was right. At least what she had said to Jessica was right. This was our home. We built it with our own hands. Every floorboard and cabinet had a story. This place was paid for. Ours. And I loved it here.

Still, I had to admit, I wasn't making things easier for her. I knew she was tired. I could see it in the way she rubbed her temples when she thought I wasn't looking. Hear it in the sighs she let out when helping me out of a chair or fetching my slippers for the hundredth time. And my body just wasn't cooperating like I wanted it to.

Carol wanted help. Professional help. Someone who could take the load off. And maybe... maybe she was right. That thought alone was enough to keep me staring at the ceiling.

My mind drifted to the past. It always did this late at night, back to when we met. Carol had been radiant, full of fire and life and opinions. God, she'd challenged me on everything in the beginning. That woman had never let me win a single argument without earning it. That's what pulled me in.

Jessica had come along not long after we were married. Our miracle baby, we used to say. Because the pain that followed her arrival nearly tore us apart.

Four pregnancies. One before Jessica. Three after. None of them made it past the first trimester.

Carol had been devastated. Each time, she retreated further into herself, and I hadn't known how to help her. I tried. I held her when she cried. I fixed things around the house. I went back to work and brought home her favorite ice cream, hoping it would make the day a little easier. However, the truth was that I didn't know what to say. What could I say that wouldn't feel empty or useless?

I had wanted a son. I won't lie about that. Someone to toss the football with in the yard. To go fishing. To teach how to drive a nail without smashing his thumb. I had these visions in my head, and with every baby not meant to be ours, I buried them deeper, a shovel full at a time.

Jessica had been enough, though. More than enough. She was bright and bold, just like her mother. And God, I was proud of the woman she had become. Still, some nights, I found myself mourning the family we might have had, wondering what kind of dad I could've been to a house full of kids.

I turned my head slightly to look at Carol, lying next to me in the dark. Even now, after all these years, she took my breath away. Her hair was thinner, her shoulders more sloped, but she was still her. Still, the woman who baked cookies with Jessica on snow days, who knew every word to her favorite hymns, who sang along even when her voice cracked.

I loved her. I never stopped. And she was being foolish. Not about loving this home, or standing by me, or insisting she could still carry the weight of both our lives. But in thinking she could do it all herself. She couldn't. I could see that now.

Maybe it was time to get some help. A therapist. The physical kind, the ones who made you do those weird stretches and leg lifts. A physical therapist, just like my daughter. They could help me rebuild my strength, allowing me to walk without the fear of collapsing. If I could just stand on my own again, I could take care of Carol. Be her husband again, not just a burden.

I'd talk to her about it in the morning, I decided, settling deeper into the mattress. The decision brought me a little peace. My eyes grew heavy. My body finally gave in.

Sleep took me.

The light filtering through the curtains told me it was morning.

I blinked into the stillness of our bedroom, the comforter tugged high over my chest, my joints already beginning their morning protest. I stretched slowly, wincing as my muscles ached, and turned my head.

Carol was still there, lying beside me. That was odd.

She was always up before me. Had been for years. Her routine was clockwork: up with the sun, coffee brewing, slippers shuffling across the kitchen floor as she put away dishes after she'd washed and dried them, or tidied up before I ever swung my legs over the edge of the bed.

But this morning, she was still. Still as a stone. "Carol?"

I reached out, placing my hand on her arm. The touch sent a jolt through me. She was cold. Too cold. And unmoving.

I pulled my hand back like I'd touched a hot stove, my chest tight, my breath caught halfway in my throat. My brain scrambled, trying to deny what my body already knew.

"Carol?" I said again, louder this time, my voice cracking.

But there was no answer. No twitch of her lips. No rise and fall of her chest. Nothing. I reached for her hand, took it between both of mine, and felt the final confirmation. She was gone.

My Carol. My wife of nearly fifty years. The woman who had stood beside me, held my hand through triumph and tragedy, baked pies in the summer, and shoveled the damn driveway in the winter when I couldn't. Gone.

Tears welled up, sharp and fast, and I let them come. I wasn't ready. I would never be prepared. I turned toward her one last time, placing a trembling kiss on her forehead.

"I'm so sorry," I whispered. "I should've done more. I should've seen it coming." But of course, I hadn't. And now, I was alone.

38

Lucas

THE LAST THING I HAD EXPECTED this morning was the phone call from Jessica. But how do you ever prepare for a call like this? The call of all calls. The call that tells you that someone you loved dearly is gone. Of course, Carol was technically no longer my mother-in-law. But she was Lily's grandmother. And I would always hold a special place in my heart for Carol and Ronald.

Jessica had been hysterical. "Lucas," she had started, and several seconds had passed before she spoke again. I had almost wondered if we had been disconnected.

"It's my mom," she said.

"What about your mom, Jessica? Are you okay? Is your mom okay?" Emily had overheard the sounds of exasperation creeping into my voice and had joined me in the kitchen, where I had been pouring myself my third cup of coffee for the morning. The architectural plans for a treehouse I was building for one of my favorite clients were laid out before me. We'd received building permits quickly and had been fortunate enough to break ground on the project with two complete crews working at all hours of the day. A grand opening had been planned to coincide with the Fourth of July holiday. However, I still couldn't help but triple and quadruple-check that all the artist renderings and final blueprints aligned with my vision. The project was moving faster than I could have imagined, so I wanted to make sure nothing got missed along the way.

Jessica was silent. I could hear her deep breathing on the other end of the line. Emily looked at me with wide eyes. I pulled the phone away from my ear and pointed to the screen so that Emily could see who was on the other end. She raised her eyebrows in concern.

"Jessica," I repeated. "What's going on?"

Finally, the words I had feared were spoken aloud. "My mom died, Lucas." Another pause. "And I don't know what to do."

I had ended the call with Jessica shortly after, telling her that I would be over to her apartment as soon as possible to pick her up, and we would make the drive to Duluth together. We had agreed that Lily would stay with Emily for the time being. Jessica hadn't even questioned the suggestion. And Emily hadn't thought twice about me taking a drive with Jessica. My ex-wife. To her parents' home, nearly three hours away.

I was packed and out the door in under ten minutes. The overnight bag I always kept half-stocked came in handy for moments like this, though I'd never anticipated needing it. I threw in an extra shirt, a pair of jeans, a hoodie, and my shaving kit before heading to the living room to talk to Lily.

She was sitting on the rug, her legs crossed, flipping through a book she'd already read three times this week. Emily was perched on the armrest of the couch, keeping a quiet eye on her, understanding the weight of what I was about to say.

"Hey, Lil," I said, crouching down in front of her. "I have to go help Mommy and Grandpa for a little bit, okay?"

Lily looked up, her brow furrowed in curiosity. "Why?"

"They need some help at their house. Grandpa especially. So I'm going to go be there for them, and you're going to stay here with Emily for a day or two."

She didn't ask more than that. She just nodded. I knew she was used to her parents managing things in bits and pieces and used to goodbyes that didn't come with full explanations. Maybe she was too used to it. But how could she know what I wasn't telling her? That the grandmother who had taught her how to play Go Fish, who had sent her birthday cards with glitter pens and little notes inside, was gone. That she wouldn't be making another visit to Grandma and Grandpa's house, at least not with her grandmother waiting for her in the kitchen.

Emily stood and walked over, offering a soft smile and a hand on my shoulder as I stood back up. "We'll be okay," she said.

I believed her. She was good with Lily. Patient in a way I admired.

In the car, I hit the highway with my hands tightly gripped on the steering wheel and my thoughts running in too many directions to count. Jessica hadn't had much information when she called, just that her father had woken to find Carol still lying beside him in bed. Still. Cold. Gone.

It seemed that Carol had died in her sleep.

That was the phrase Jessica had used. As if saying it plainly might make it easier to believe. But it wasn't easy. None of it was. Carol had always seemed so sturdy, so full of life, the type of woman who didn't just fade. And yet, that's precisely what had happened. It made me think of the loss of my own mother, who had died nearly two decades ago, to breast cancer. I still missed my mom today, and reminiscing about my own loss made me that much more sympathetic to what Jessica was experiencing.

When I'd asked Jessica what had happened, she had just said, "I don't know, Lucas. Dad called 911. The ambulance is at the house. They're waiting for the coroner. She didn't wake up."

I'd asked if she had reached Will. That's when she told me about the call to his phone ringing through to voicemail. I didn't comment. Not my place, really. But the fact that she had called me instead said enough.

"I didn't know what to do," she'd whispered. So I did what I always did. I stepped in.

Now, with the road stretching in front of me and three hours of drive time ahead, I couldn't help but think about Carol. About the early years, when she and Ronald welcomed me into their home with a mixture of curiosity and skepticism. About how she had always kept a tidy kitchen and how she'd sneak Lily cookies behind Jessica's back. How she had this special laugh. It was low, warm, and scratchy at the end, like someone out of an old black-and-white movie. If I didn't know better, I would have thought Carol had been a smoker back in her day—that deep scratchy laugh. But I did know better. Carol ate healthily. Didn't drink. Didn't smoke. She was as good as they came, despite her uncanny ability to sometimes push Jessica when Jessica didn't want to be pushed.

I shook those thoughts away. I remembered the holiday dinners, the card games, the advice she'd given me when I didn't know how to talk to Jessica after we first separated. She had loved her daughter fiercely. And she had made it clear that she wouldn't take sides, but that didn't mean she wouldn't keep me in line when I needed it.

What would Ronald do now?

The question sat like a stone in my chest. Jessica had told me he sounded shaken on the phone. Understandably so. A man like Ronald was proud and independent, aging with all the stubborn dignity that came with it. But what would he do without Carol, the woman who had kept his world upright for decades? I knew his own health had been in a rapid state of decline in recent years. And Jessica had mentioned that he had fallen a few times in the recent months.

I had to be strong for Jessica. But I also knew I'd have to be strong for Ronald, too. And that was something I hadn't prepared for.

My phone buzzed in the cupholder with a message from Emily: *Lily's doing great. Made pancakes. Please let me know when you arrive.*

I glanced at the screen for a brief second, grateful. Then put the phone back and let my focus return to the road. I didn't know what we were walking into when we got to Duluth. I didn't know if the funeral home had been called, if Jessica would need to make arrangements, or if we'd just be there to sit with Ronald and try to hold him up through it.

But I knew one thing for sure: I would be there. No questions. No hesitation. I would be there for Jessica and for Ronald. For Carol.

That much, I could do.

39

Jessica

THE HIGHWAY BLURRED past my window, streaks of gray and white, and evergreens barely registering in my peripheral vision. Lucas drove fast. Faster than I was comfortable with, but I didn't say anything. What right did I have? I was the one who called him, after all.

I stared down at my hands, fingers clenched tightly in my lap. I couldn't remember the last time I'd sat beside Lucas like this, just the two of us. Not as parents swapping drop-offs or coordinating holiday schedules. Not as the people we once were. Just... Jessica and Lucas are in a car. Heading to Duluth. Except this time, my mother was dead.

I swallowed hard and turned toward the window again. The warm late-morning sun filtered through the glass, but it didn't reach the cold that was settling deep in my chest.

"I'm fine to drive the rest of the way," Lucas said suddenly, breaking the silence. "In case you were wondering."

"I wasn't," I lied.

He gave a soft, breathy laugh. "Sure you weren't."

I sighed and leaned my head against the passenger side window. "I shouldn't have called you."

"Probably not," he said. "But I'm glad you did."

I looked over at him, the corner of his mouth lifting slightly. His hands were firm on the wheel, knuckles relaxed, but I knew better. He was pushing the speed limit, probably on instinct, probably because he knew I was breaking apart inside. And he wanted to get me there before I unraveled completely.

"Are you okay?" I asked, even though I already knew the answer.

"Heart-wise? I'm good," he said, eyes fixed on the road. "Cardiologist says I'm boring, which is apparently a good thing."

"That's a relief."

He nodded.

I wrapped my arms tighter around myself, wishing the seat heater could reach the kind of cold that had taken hold inside me. "Liz is out of town," I said, almost to myself. "And Will... I didn't even think he'd be able to come. Not with the kids. Not with work."

Lucas said nothing, but his silence wasn't judgmental. It was the kind that said, I get it.

I bit my lip. "I just felt... alone. And when Will didn't answer. Well..."

He reached over and turned the heat up one notch. "You're not alone, Jess."

That did it.

I blinked quickly, eyes stinging. "I know I should be thinking about my mom. But all I keep replaying is that morning Will and I were in bed, and Sophie walked in."

Lucas let out the smallest, surprised cough, like I'd just hit him with a conversational left hook. I could practically feel his eyes darting sideways, unsure if this was a trap or just a detour into way-too-personal territory.

"We weren't doing anything," I added quickly. "Just... waking up. But she looked at me like I'd just stolen her puppy and eaten it for breakfast."

Still no response from the driver's seat, though I was pretty sure I saw his knuckles tighten slightly on the wheel.

"I don't even know why I said that out loud," I muttered, rubbing my temple. "You're definitely not the person I should be unpacking this with."

Lucas finally let out a low chuckle. "Nope. But I'm honored you chose me anyway."

I stared at the dashboard. The time blinked back at me. It was only 11:42 a.m., but the sun was already high, casting that soft, golden glow that made everything outside look deceptively peaceful. Late spring in northern Minnesota had a way of pretending everything was fine. "I don't know how bad my dad is," I said quietly. "She always downplayed it. I don't know if that was because she didn't want me to worry or if she was in denial. Or maybe both."

Lucas nodded. "Want me to stay up there a day or two? Just to help you get things sorted?"

"No," I said, too fast. "No. Thank you. But... no. Emily's waiting for you."

His fingers flexed against the wheel. "She understands."

That surprised me. "Really?"

"She does," he said simply. "She was the one who told me to go when I told her what happened. She said if it were her ex, she'd want to know she could count on him, too. Her ex hurt her, but she still believes that he will stand up when needed."

I exhaled slowly. "That's... mature."

"She's kind of the grown-up in the relationship," he said, his smile faint but genuine.

I managed a smile, too. "I like her."

"I know."

And for a moment, we weren't exes with baggage or parents juggling life from two homes. We were just two people who once cared for each other deeply and still shared something that went beyond co-parenting.

I turned my attention back to the trees. I had always enjoyed the drive up to Duluth. The pine trees and the open road. It was the kind of quiet drive that muffled everything else. But today, it amplified the grief, confusion, and regret.

"I'm going to have to help my dad move," I said. "Eventually. The house is too big, too much. Especially without her."

"Do you think he'd come down to the Cities?"

"I don't know. He's so rooted in Duluth. The neighbors, his routine. But he can't stay there forever."

We were both quiet again.

I thought about the funeral. About how I'd have to sit down and pick out a casket. Or cremation. Music. Flowers. Would I speak? Could I? My mother had been a complicated woman, sharp-edged and strong-willed. And I'd loved her. But how did you sum up a lifetime in a eulogy?

Lucas adjusted the rearview mirror. "Lily's with Emily tonight," he said gently. "If I know her, she'll make a fort and declare it a no-grownups zone, unless it's for snack deliveries."

That brought a ghost of a smile to my lips. "Sounds about right."

"Lily made Emily one of those little polar bear drawings again. Said it was for comfort."

I looked over at him. "She's a good kid."

"She has a good mom."

That nearly broke me. I looked down at my lap and blinked hard.

"Thank you," I whispered.

We were about twenty minutes outside Duluth when I finally spoke again. "What if I'm not ready for all of this?"

"All of what?"

"Losing her. Taking care of my dad. Sorting through a lifetime of their memories and deciding what to keep, what to box up, what to throw away."

Lucas reached over and squeezed my hand. Just for a second. Just enough. "You don't have to be ready," he said. "You just have to keep going."

I let out a shaky breath. "That sounds like something you'd put on a mug."

"Hallmark wisdom," he said with a smirk. "But still true."

We drove the rest of the way in silence. But it wasn't empty. It was the kind of silence that felt like a weighted blanket. It was heavy, yes. But it was grounding. And that was what I needed right now.

As we pulled off the freeway and onto the familiar side streets of Duluth, my chest tightened again. The neighborhood hadn't changed. The lawns were green and baking in the June sun. A few daffodils peeked out near mailboxes. I noticed the crooked mailbox at the end of the street. My mom had always said they'd fix it, but they never did.

Lucas pulled into the driveway and shifted into Park. The porch light was on, despite the daylight. My dad must've turned it on for us. I didn't move.

Lucas looked over at me. "You want me to walk you in?"

I shook my head. "I need to do this."

He nodded but didn't move right away.

I'll go check into the Hampton Inn down in Canal Park," he said. "Drop my stuff, get settled. I'll come back in a few hours and see where I can help. We'll figure out what tomorrow looks like from there."

"Okay," I said, grateful he wasn't pushing, but that he would be there if I needed him.

"Text me if you need anything," he added. "Seriously. Anything."

I opened the door and stepped out into the warm air. The breeze carried the smell of damp earth. I didn't need my jacket, but I zipped it halfway out of habit, more for armor than warmth.

Lucas rolled down the window. "Jess?"

I turned.

"You're not alone."

I nodded. "I know."

I didn't know what exactly was waiting for me inside, just that it would be hard. And heavy. And far from over. As I stepped toward the house and heard the screen door creak open before I could even knock, one thing settled in my chest like a weight. This wasn't something I could fix. It was just something I had to get through.

40

Will

I COULDN'T REMEMBER the last time I'd spent an afternoon completely unplugged.

It had started with a game of catch in the backyard with Cooper. Max had grabbed his glove, tossed mine to me, and Cooper trotted between us in the yard like the self-appointed referee he was. Sophie had followed us out and perched herself in the shade with her Switch, legs tucked under her and nose buried deep. But eventually, even she had wandered over, tossing a few lazy throws and laughing when Max made dramatic diving catches worthy of an ESPN highlight reel.

After about thirty minutes of chasing down balls and arguing over the rules of backyard baseball, Max had said the magic words: "We should get pizza."

And somehow, that turned into a late lunch at Cossetta's.

We drove with the windows down, with Max and Sophie arguing over music choices. The moment we walked into the Italian market, the familiar scent of marinara and fresh-baked crust enveloped us. The kids made a beeline upstairs to find a table.

I ordered the usual. Two slices of pepperoni for Max, one slice of cheese for Sophie, and a meatball sandwich for me. And afterward, like always, we wandered into the attached pasticceria. The kids bounced from case to case, agonizing over whether they wanted pistachio or stracciatella gelato, or if they should just skip it and go straight for the cannoli and sfogliatelle.

In the end, they picked both.

We sat upstairs in the restaurant, tucked into our usual table by the window. The late afternoon sun filtered through the glass, casting a golden glow over the worn wood and bustling scene below. Sophie had a streak of gelato on her cheek. Max was telling some exaggerated story about a kid in his gym class who had allegedly thrown up mid-dodgeball. I half-listened, half-watched the slow trickle of people moving through the street below. It was the kind of afternoon that felt suspended in time. Simple, good, fleeting.

It wasn't until I shifted in my seat and reached for my back pocket that I realized something was missing. My phone. I patted both back pockets, then the front. Checked my jacket. Nothing. My stomach dipped. I never left the house without my phone. Especially not when I had the kids. What if there had been an emergency? What if something had happened?

"Everything okay?" Max asked, licking the last of his gelato from the spoon.

"Yeah," I said, forcing a smile. "Just realized I left my phone at home."

"Whoa," Sophie said. "You? Mr. Responsible?"

I laughed. "I know. It's a rare moment."

Max grinned. "Maybe it's a sign. Like, we were supposed to actually have fun today."

He wasn't wrong.

We finished our pastries and piled back into the car. The kids sang along to some ridiculous pop song as we wound our way back through St. Paul, windows down again. It was only once we got home that I started to feel that low hum of unease again.

The kids ran off to their rooms after dropping off the boxed pastries and leftover pizza slices on the kitchen counter. I shook my head, moving the boxes to the refrigerator before letting Cooper out into the backyard, then headed into my office. The phone was right there on the desk, screen dark.

When I picked it up, the notifications lit up all at once. Two missed calls from Jessica. Three missed calls from an unknown number. One voicemail.

My heart stuttered. I tapped on the voicemail, hit speaker, and held the phone in my trembling hand as the robotic voice read it aloud:

"Hey Will, it's Lucas. Sorry to call out of the blue. I'm with Jessica right now. She... her mom passed away this morning. She tried calling you earlier, but I think your phone was off. We're in Duluth. She didn't know who else to call—just wanted to let you know. I'm staying the night up here and helping her get settled. You can call me back at this number. I got your number from a school directory printout Jessica had tucked in her bag."

I froze. Lucas? Duluth? Her mom passed away? I sat down hard in my desk chair, staring at the phone like it might offer some kind of clarification.

Jessica had tried calling me—more than once. And I... I had been off eating gelato with the kids, not even realizing I'd left the most important device in my life sitting on my desk while someone I cared about was facing the worst kind of day.

I felt sick. I called her immediately, straight to voicemail. I tried again—same result.

I pulled up Lucas' number from the voicemail transcript and called him instead. It rang. Once. Twice. Then: "Hey, Will?" His voice was quiet. Tired.

"Yeah. Lucas. Thanks for calling. I just got the message. I didn't have my phone with me. Is she okay?"

A pause. "She's... not good. I dropped her off at her parents' house a couple of hours ago. I'm giving them some space. Figured I'd head back in a bit, see how I can help."

I rubbed a hand over my jaw. "Damn. I should be there."

"She didn't expect you to drop everything. She just didn't know who else to call. Liz is out of town. I was the only one who picked up."

My chest ached. "I'll call her again. Or text."

"Yeah. Just... maybe keep it light. She's... pretty wrecked."

"Thanks, man," I said quietly. "For being there."

"Of course."

We hung up. I sat there for a long moment, staring out the office window as Cooper barked at a squirrel outside. The sun was still shining, casting dappled shadows across the lawn. It felt wrong, somehow, for the day to be so beautiful.

I opened my messages and typed:

Me: *Just saw your missed calls. I'm so sorry, Jess. I left my phone at home and didn't realize until a little while ago. I'm here if you want to talk, or not talk. Whatever you need.*

I stared at the blinking cursor, then added:

Me: *I wish I could be there.*

I hit 'Send' and waited. No response. I walked back into the kitchen and poured myself a glass of water. Took a sip. Set it down. Feeling restless, I poured the rest down the kitchen sink.

How do you sit with something like this? How do you balance the good parts of your day with someone else's grief? I'd spent the afternoon with my kids, happy and whole and laughing, while Jessica's life had been quietly falling apart.

I didn't know her mom well. I'd never met her, actually. But I knew how complicated that relationship was. Jessica had mentioned it in bits and pieces. The guilt. The expectations. The distance. And underneath all of that, the deep, unshakeable love that only a daughter could carry for someone who drove her crazy. Now her mother was gone.

And I hadn't answered when the woman I love had needed me. I retreated to the living room, sat down on the couch, and leaned forward, elbows on knees, staring at my phone on the coffee table like it might light up with a message any second.

Please text me, Jess. Let me be there for you. Let me try to get this right.

41

Jessica

THE MOMENT THE FRONT DOOR shut behind me, the quiet overcame me. No clinking dishes. No smell of coffee, fresh muffins, or cinnamon rolls. No low hum of the television playing her morning shows. Just the still air of a house that suddenly felt unfamiliar.

I stepped out of my shoes and walked into the living room.

There was my dad, sitting in his recliner. Not reclined. Not reading. Just sitting. The newspaper was still rolled tightly on the coffee table, rubber band clinging to it like a tourniquet. The TV was dark. The only sound was the tick of the wall clock and the soft groan of the floor under my feet.

"Daddy?"

He didn't look up. Just blinked slowly, like I'd spoken through water. I rushed to him and dropped to my knees in front of his chair. I grabbed his hands. Cold. Still. And for a moment, every fear coursed through my veins. Not him, too. But slowly, he turned to me.

"Daddy, what happened?"

For a long moment, he just stared at me, and I thought maybe he wouldn't answer. Then his jaw moved, like it took effort to remember how to speak. "I woke up... and she was still in bed," he said, voice hoarse. "That never happens. She always gets up before me. Starts the coffee. Turns on the television." He paused and shook his head. "I reached for her. Just to... You know, make sure she was okay. Her shoulder was cold. Not just cool. Cold. Still."

I bit down on my lip to keep from crying.

He went on. "I got myself up. Walked around the bed. Her face... she looked peaceful. Like she was just sleeping. But I knew." He shifted in the chair and picked something off the armrest. His reading glasses. He turned them over in his fingers, as if he wasn't sure what they were for. "Phone was on her side. I got myself out of bed and called 911. Paramedics came. Then the coroner. Said she'd been gone for hours already." His hand fumbled in his pocket. He pulled out a plain white business card and handed it to me. It shook between his fingers. "Funeral home. They were in touch with the morgue. Want to know if they should... should pick her up."

My throat burned as I took the card. "Did they say anything else? About what happened?"

He nodded, jaw clenching. "I told them about her headaches. The coroner said it was likely a stroke. In her sleep. Said she wouldn't have felt anything if that's what it was. The coroner said no autopsy was necessary. No foul play. Nothing suspicious. Just... natural." He looked at me then, really looked at me. Eyes red-rimmed, wet. "Doesn't matter what it was. She's gone, damn it."

The anger cracked in his voice, sharp and aching. His hands curled into fists on the armrests, and his shoulders shook. The tears came then, silent but in full force, cutting through the creases in his face.

I stood and leaned into him, wrapping my arms around his shoulders, holding him as tightly as I could.

"I'm here, Daddy," I whispered, burying my face into his shoulder. "We'll get through this. Together." His breath hitched against my ear. And then he let go, finally, into me.

42

Liz

THE AIRPORT HAD SMELLED like overpriced coffee and missed connections. And when I say missed connections, I mean sweat. A lot of it. Did people totally forget to bathe before they traveled? Gross.

I had stood in line to board, clutching a paper cup of coffee that had long gone cold. My phone buzzed again in my coat pocket, probably another update from the conference group chat. I didn't care. The conference was over for me the second Lucas called.

Jessica's mom. Gone.

I'd barely said two words before Lucas gave me the rundown. Jessica had called him, of all people. And he'd gone. Of course, he had. I hated that it hadn't been me. But I was two time zones away and I had been sitting on a panel about expanding financial literacy access in low-income communities while my best friend's life was falling apart.

I called my boss on the walk back to the hotel. I explained the situation quickly, promised to catch up on everything remotely, and then took the elevator to my floor. I was already on the phone with Delta as I packed, phone tucked between my shoulder and ear, stuffing clothes haphazardly into my carry-on.

Red-eye. Middle seat. Didn't care.

Now, bleary-eyed and slightly stale from hours on a plane, I stood at Will's doorstep at 7 a.m., Minneapolis drizzle clinging to my hair and coat. I knocked, the sound echoing in the quiet morning. Cooper barked inside.

The door creaked open. Will blinked at me, clearly trying to place who the hell I was and why I was on his porch.

"Hi. You must be Will. I'm Liz. Jessica's friend. The one she's always talking about? The one who can't sit still and refuses to date anyone longer than a movie runtime?"

Recognition dawned in his tired eyes. "Right. Liz. Yeah. Wow. Okay. Uh, come in."

The house smelled a bit like dog, covered up by some sort of room freshener. Cozy. Lived-in. Slightly chaotic.

Will rubbed at the back of his neck. He looked like he hadn't slept. "She hasn't called me back or texted. I tried. Multiple times."

I nodded, peeling off my damp coat. "She's overwhelmed. You know how she gets. It's a lot. Her mom, her dad, Duluth. She's the only one left to deal with everything."

He sighed. "I feel like I should be doing something."

"You should," I said, already scanning the room like I was about to reorganize it. "Pack a bag. Get up there."

He blinked. "The kids—"

"That's why I'm here." I smiled. "Do you have someone who can stay with them for a day or two? Someone who can get them to school? Friend, neighbor, family? Someone you trust?"

He hesitated. "Matt. He's my buddy from elementary school and we went to college together.. Lives a few blocks over. His kids are in school with Sophie and Max. I guess I could call him."

"Great. Call him."

Will stared at me for a second, probably still trying to catch up. Then he nodded and grabbed his phone.

By 8:15, Matt was at the door. The kids had overnight bags packed, school backpacks ready to go, and leftover pastries boxed up. They were chattering with excitement like this was a sleepover instead of a temporary life disruption.

When Matt stepped inside, I felt it. Just a second of something. A shift. A pause.

He was tall, with warm eyes and that worn-in, dad-next-door kind of look. Not trying too hard. Just... there. Solid. Cute. Really cute.

"Hey," he said, offering a polite nod. "You must be Liz."

I opened my mouth and absolutely forgot what my name was for a full second. "Uh. Yeah. Hi. Liz. Yep." Brilliant. I needed to get a grip. But seriously, why hadn't Jessica told me about this guy? And then I remembered. He had kids. I wasn't against kids. I wanted kids. But it wasn't in the cards for me. I had my reasons.

Will glanced between Matt and me, eyebrows slightly raised, but said nothing.

Matt smiled, easy and genuine. "You're helping out too?"

I cleared my throat. "Trying to. You're a lifesaver for grabbing the kids."

He waved it off like it was nothing. "Max and my son are practically inseparable anyway. It's no trouble. And the kids love Cooper, so he'll be spoiled rotten."

I nodded and stepped back as he wrangled overnight bags and got the kids and Cooper into his SUV. Once Matt drove away, Will turned to me.

"Okay. I'm packed. You sure about this?"

"She needs you, Will. Even if she doesn't know how to ask."

He looked toward the door, then back at me.

"Okay," he said. "Let's go."

43

Will

I WASN'T SURE WHAT TO THINK when I opened the door this morning to see an unfamiliar woman standing on the front step. But as soon as she started talking, and before she even said her name, I realized who it was. Liz. Jessica's best friend. And she had flown overnight to be here for her best friend.

I felt like a schmuck. Do people even say schmuck anymore? I wanted to say I felt like an asshole, and it was true. But letting myself go there just brought more anger to the surface. Here I was, Jess' boyfriend, and I had spent the night in the comfort of my own home, while the woman I love was suffering up in Duluth. And who was there to offer her comfort? Her ex-husband, Lucas.

It wasn't like I had any ill will toward Lucas. Jessica had only good things to say. He was a good father, but they had lost their spark as a couple. And she had shared with me that she wasn't sure they had really had that true of a connection to begin with.

That all said, as Liz had directed me around my own home, I found myself questioning my lack of action. Why hadn't I called Matt to watch the kids? I should have thought of it myself. That man was the best friend a guy could have. He's been through his own loss when his wife, Alexa, died in a car accident shortly after the birth of their second child.

The loss had been devastating, to say the least. One moment, Alexa had been home, giving Owen a bottle. The next minute, she was telling Matt she needed to head to the convenience store to grab more formula. An hour later, Matt had opened his front door to two police officers, asking if they could come inside.

Owen had been just eight months old. His older sister, Annie, had been just about to turn three. And there he was. A single dad. Just like that. But despite his pain and having to start over again, Matt was always there for everybody else. He had been by my side during Katie's illness. During her last days. And every day that I had needed him since Katie's death.

I needed to take a big life lesson from Matt. I should have called him immediately after that call from Lucas. I should have dropped the kids off with Matt and headed north to be with Jessica.

The whole situation had my mind spinning, and I found myself wondering about the status of our relationship. It was good, yes. I'd say it was even great. But was it going to go somewhere? I guess I wasn't sure. Even though I had felt myself falling in love with Jessica, we really hadn't talked about the future. And now, her future had changed overnight.

I turned my attention back to Liz, who was driving my car. Not sure how that happened. Something about how Lucas had driven Jessica in his car, and it would be better for me to have my own car up there. She'd made some additional comment about me needing to get it together, and before I knew it, I was in the passenger seat.

"Earth to Will," Liz said, snapping a finger in my left ear.

I turned toward her, shaken out of my thoughts. "Sorry. Zoned out."

"Yeah, no kidding." She glanced sideways at me, then back at the road. "You looked like you were trying to solve world peace in your head."

"Something like that."

She softened a little. "It's a lot. For everyone. You, her, me. I mean, her mom's gone. That's... It's just a huge shift. You think you have time, and then you don't."

I nodded. "She hasn't answered my calls or texts. I feel like I failed her."

Liz reached over and gave my arm a quick squeeze. "You didn't fail her. You'll be there soon. That's what matters."

"I should've been there yesterday."

"Yeah, well, hindsight's a bitch. Look, she called Lucas because she knew he'd answer. That's not a dig at you. It was a moment-of-need thing. But now she's going to need you in a different way."

I let that sit for a second. "She's probably drowning in stuff right now. Funeral planning. Her dad. She told me that he's not in the best of health. Jess always made it sound like her mom would live forever. So I'm not sure how to feel about this turn of events."

"Well, Ronald's a strong old bugger. I think he's probably stronger than Jess realizes. Carol was just the type to take over when she thought it was needed. And neither Carol nor Jessica is the type to ask for help, not really. So, now, you show up. You don't wait for the invitation."

"I want to. I just... I don't know what she wants from me in the long term. We haven't really talked about it."

Liz snorted. "Of course you haven't. You guys are emotionally constipated. But let's fix that after the funeral, okay?"

I laughed, despite myself. "Emotionally constipated?"

She grinned. "You're welcome. That one's on the house."

Then she got quiet for a moment. "So... your friend Matt. He seems like a decent guy."

I eyed her. "You mean the guy who showed up this morning and took my kids with zero questions asked?"

"Yeah. That one."

I raised an eyebrow. "Why?"

She shrugged like it was nothing. "Just curious. Is he single?"

"He is."

"How old are his kids again?"

"Annie is Max's age. Owen is Sophie's age." I paused for a moment as Liz turned to stare at me blankly. Encouraging her to put her eyes back on the road, I clarified. "Annie and Max are 12, and Owen and Sophie are 10."

"Is he dating anyone?"

"Nope."

She tapped the steering wheel with a little nod, eyes forward. "And his wife passed away?'"

"Yeah. It's been quite a while now. She died in a car accident when Owen was just a baby."

"Hmm."

"Hmm?" I repeated, glancing sideways.

She smiled, but didn't look at me. "Nothing. Just asking questions. You know. Girl stuff."

"Twenty-five questions is more like it."

"Please. That was barely ten. I'm pacing myself."

But something had shifted in her expression. She'd gone from snarky to thoughtful, and I couldn't help but notice that she'd gone a little quieter, her fingers still drumming that light rhythm on the steering wheel.

"I thought Jess told me you weren't the settling-down type," I said after a beat.

She turned and gave me a sharp look. "Hey, now. I said I'm not a boring type. Doesn't mean I'm not observant. And no one said anything about settling down."

I chuckled. "So you're saying Matt's not boring?"

She gave a noncommittal shrug, but I didn't miss the faint pink in her cheeks.

Before either of us could say more, she hit the blinker. I hadn't even noticed that she had turned off the freeway. I needed to get it together. She turned onto a residential street, and I recognized it as the Kenwood neighborhood. The houses were older, well-kept, and lined with towering pines. It took just a few more turns before we pulled into the driveway of a sprawling rambler tucked beneath the trees. It was huge. Far bigger than I had imagined.

"Wow," I said, stepping out and staring at the house. "This is where she grew up?"

Liz nodded, getting out and slamming the door behind her. "Yeah. Big house. Big memories."

I followed her up the path, nerves suddenly tightening in my chest.

44

Jessica

THE KITCHEN TABLE was covered in papers. Legal-sized documents, pamphlets from the funeral home, and a yellowed folder labeled Wills & Important Docs in my mother's curling script. It looked like a mess, but somehow, each piece was part of something bigger. It was my mother's goodbye.

My dad sat beside me, his reading glasses sliding down his nose as he reread a paragraph in the pre-planning guide for the third time. I had to give him credit. He was doing his best. But the faraway look in his eyes told me he was barely holding on. The house was too quiet. No TV, no classical music playing from the little speaker my mom kept tucked near the sink. Just an occasional rustle of paper and sighs here and there from my father.

We'd agreed on the casket. It would be a beautiful cherry wood design with polished handles and a soft cream lining. It had been one of the first decisions, surprisingly easy, all things considered. My mom had taste, even in death, and something about the warm wood had felt right. Then came the flowers. Pink roses, just like the ones she used to grow in the front garden every summer. She'd always said they were temperamental and too much work, especially with the Duluth climate, but she adored them anyway. Typical Mom. Choosing beauty even if it came with thorns.

The funeral director had stopped by earlier, a kind man named Brad whose gentleness made the whole ordeal bearable. He'd left us with the paperwork, talked us through the major decisions, and assured us we didn't need to leave the house if we weren't up for it. Dad, for one, definitely wasn't.

So here we were, sitting in the kitchen where my mom used to make potato pancakes on Sunday mornings. And we're planning her funeral.

I blinked down at the obituary draft we were working on. "Carol Elaine Miller passed away peacefully in her sleep..." My chest tightened at the word "peacefully." It was meant to be a comfort, but there was nothing peaceful about this. This was the kind of pain that was the worst.

"She'd hate this picture," I muttered, thumbing through the stack of older prints we'd pulled out of the photo albums. My dad gave a grunt that might have been agreement, but he didn't look up.

I rubbed the heel of my hand into my temple, trying to push away the dull ache that had been lingering all morning. I hadn't eaten and hadn't showered, had barely slept. But none of it mattered.

There was a to-do list, and the only person left to do it with me was sitting beside me, looking like a ghost of himself.

The front door opened with a soft click. My breath caught. My first thought was that Lucas had come back, but he'd already said his goodbye this morning before heading back to the Cities. He promised he'd bring Lily to the service. He was good like that.

Then footsteps, lighter than Lucas'. And another pair behind them. A woman's. I stood and made it to the living room just as Liz was pulling off a light summer jacket and setting it on the bench near the door.

My eyes filled instantly. "You came."

Liz opened her arms, and I walked straight into them. We stood there in a long, wordless hug. I felt her hand run up and down my back in that familiar way, the one that used to calm me down after college finals or breakup meltdowns. This time, it didn't calm me. But it helped. And I clung to her tighter than I expected to.

She pulled back just enough to look at me. "I wasn't missing this, Jess. I'm here for you. Always."

I nodded, swallowing hard. And then, just beyond her, I saw him. Will. He looked exhausted. His hair was a bit more unkempt than usual, his eyes rimmed with what I could only guess was guilt. But he was here. "You came," I said, my voice catching.

"I should have come yesterday." His voice was quiet. "I'm sorry."

I didn't know what to say to that. Yesterday had already happened. But today. Well, today, he was here. Instead of saying anything, I stepped forward and wrapped my arms around him. He hugged me back immediately, arms tightening around my shoulders like he didn't want to let go. And for a second, I let myself rest there, against someone who wasn't asking me to make any decisions. And I knew coming here hadn't been easy. He'd had to arrange care for his kids and for Cooper. And I wasn't quite sure how happy he'd be to have a substitute teacher stand in for him this close to the end of the school year.

I stepped back before the tears could start again. "Dad's in the kitchen," I said. "We're going over everything. Do you want to come in?"

Will nodded, and Liz was already kicking off her shoes. "I'll make another pot of coffee," she said, disappearing toward the kitchen like she'd lived here all her life.

I followed them in and rejoined my dad at the table. He looked up at the new arrivals, blinking like he was seeing them through a fog.

"Dad, you remember Liz," I said gently. "And this is Will."

My dad gave a slight nod. "You folks hungry?"

"No, but thank you," Will said, pulling out a chair and sitting beside me.

I gestured to the pile of papers. "We're just finishing the obituary. The funeral home's going to take care of placing it."

"Did you pick a date?" Liz asked, pouring water into the coffee maker without even asking where anything was. She was busying herself replenishing the coffee pot, likely realizing we'd already been through the first one.

"We're thinking Saturday," I said. "End of this week. That gives people time to plan. The garden club, some of the folks from church. And Mom's cousins."

Liz nodded. "That makes sense."

Will sat quietly for a moment, then asked softly, "How are you holding up?"

I hesitated. "I don't know. There's just... so much to do. I keep thinking I'll feel it later, you know? Like, really feel it."

He reached across the table and brushed his fingers against mine. Just once. "It's okay if you don't know."

I nodded again, eyes pricking with fresh tears.

"We found her will," I said, trying to change the subject before I completely fell apart. "She actually wrote down most of what she wanted. That helps."

My dad finally spoke again, voice gruff. "She planned everything but didn't say a word about it. Just tucked it away like some sort of secret." I couldn't help but notice the anger in his voice. I knew that my mom had closed herself off throughout the years. I assumed it had been her way of trying to be strong, even though I knew she could have benefited from more support.

The edge in his voice. Well, it hurt. I didn't know what to say, so I just reached for his hand and squeezed it. "She wanted the service at the Lutheran church," I added. "And to be buried at Calvary."

Liz turned from the counter. "We'll help with anything you need. Seriously. Anything."

I nodded, overwhelmed again, but grateful.

"Will," my dad said suddenly, turning to him. "You got kids, right?"

Will nodded. "Yeah. Two. Sophie and Max."

"You tell 'em you love 'em every day?"

Will blinked. "I do. Every single day."

"Good." He leaned back slowly. "That's what matters. The rest of this... It's all noise."

The room grew quiet again, the only sound the burble of the coffee pot as it finished its cycle.

I looked around at the table—Will, Liz, and my dad. The cluttered stack of loss spread out before us. It still didn't feel real. But for the first time in twenty-four hours, I didn't feel entirely alone. Will was here. And I needed him.

45

Will

WALKING INTO JESSICA'S home felt like stepping into a photo album that had been cracked open and left on display. There were pictures everywhere. On the walls, on the bookshelves, and even along the credenza, photos were tucked into little decorative frames. And it wasn't just the volume of photos. It was the history in them. The story of a life lived here, in this iconic port city, framed in snapshots.

There was one of what I assumed was Jessica as a baby with her mother, both of them bundled in oversized coats against what I could only assume was a brutal Duluth winter. I recognized Enger Tower in the background. Another, tucked on the corner of the coffee table, showed a much younger Jessica on a bike, grinning so wide her cheeks nearly swallowed her eyes.

But the one that stopped me cold was on a high shelf situated at the entry of the kitchen. A photo, maybe twenty-five years old, of a flour-dusted Jessica and her mom, both mid-laugh, caught in the joy of baking something together. It was messy and unposed and absolutely perfect.

That's when Jessica saw me. Really saw me. She stepped away from Liz, her eyes red-rimmed but focused.

"You came," she said simply.

There wasn't any edge to it. No trace of anger or disappointment. Just quiet surprise. And in that second, I could feel my chest tighten, not with guilt, although that still lingered, but with something else. Relief. Gratitude. Love.

I crossed the room, and she stepped into my arms without hesitation. She held me tightly. Her arms wrapped around my back like she meant to anchor herself there. And I did the same. I didn't want to let go. Honestly, I could've stayed like that all day.

But she pulled back after a moment, blinking fast, trying not to cry. I let her go, even though I didn't want to, and followed her into the kitchen.

She introduced me to her dad, Ronald, who was seated at the kitchen table, surrounded by paperwork and a half-drunk cup of cold coffee. He nodded at me in greeting, his voice raspy when he said hello. The exhaustion on his face, echoed by his sagging shoulders, was evident.

Jessica walked me through everything they'd managed so far: the casket, the pink rose spray, and the location for the service. The obituary was nearly finished. She spoke quietly but clearly, her voice stronger than I expected, given everything she was carrying.

Then her dad looked up at me and asked, "You got kids, right?"

I nodded. "Yeah. Two. Sophie and Max."

He tilted his head slightly, squinting. "You tell 'em you love 'em every day?"

The question knocked the wind out of me in a way I didn't expect. But I answered without pause. "I do. Every single day."

Ronald gave a slight nod and leaned back again, as if that settled something.

But it didn't settle anything for me. If anything, it stirred up more because I could still remember Katie saying something nearly identical in those final days.

Love is felt, but hearing those words can mend so many things, she told me once, her voice weak but certain. *Say it even when they already know. Especially then.*

So I did. I made that promise to her before she died. And I've kept it. Every day. With Max. With Sophie.

And now, sitting in this kitchen filled with memories and grief and pink rose plans, I wondered when I'd get the chance to say it again. This time to someone new. Someone who already meant so much.

I loved Jessica. I'd felt it earlier, and I was now more sure than ever as I rode in the car with Liz, now, somewhere between Hinckley and Duluth. And seeing her now, the weight of it hit me again. There was no maybe about it. I loved her.

But how do you say that to someone who's wading through such fresh grief? It hardly seemed fair. Or timed right. But the feeling was there, undeniable.

Maybe that was what Katie meant. Especially then.

Still, I would have to keep it to myself for now. There would be time. There had to be. Telling her now wouldn't feel right. Words of that type need to be said for the first time at just the right moment.

For now, I stayed at that kitchen table and helped them finish the obituary. I kept my hand near Jessica's, close enough to feel her presence, but not demanding anything more.

And I told myself that when the moment was right, when the dust settled and the flowers were put away to dry out into a keepsake, and her heart had room again, I'd tell her. Not just in the way I looked at her or showed up for her. I'd say the words. Because hearing them matters. And my love for her was stronger than I had ever expected.

46

Liz

THE LOWER-LEVEL BEDROOM smelled the same as it always had. There were hints of cedar and that old-house mix of laundry soap and time. I dropped my overnight bag at the foot of the twin bed and took in the familiar surroundings. I had spent plenty of nights in this house over the years. Sure, it's been a while, but it still feels oddly like stepping into a time capsule.

Jessica and her dad insisted I stay. No hotel room in downtown Duluth for me. And why not? I've been coming here since grade school. Back then, we'd ride our bikes between our neighborhoods for hours. Back when no one worried about kids disappearing for an entire afternoon.

Jessica's neighborhood always seemed a bit more polished, more put-together than mine, but none of that mattered to us. Not when we were kids. Not when we were sneaking Popsicles from the garage freezer and daring each other to ride up to the Enger Park Tower or down to Canal Park. I can still remember how our thighs would burn from the hilly Duluth streets.

But tonight, the house was quiet. It was heavy. The sadness and loss were thick.

I sat down on the edge of the bed and let the silence settle around me. Today had been a lot. A lot for Jessica. A lot for Ronald. And maybe, in a quieter way, a lot for me, too. It had been years since I lost my parents. Both of them were gone in a flash thanks to a drunk driver on a weekend trip to Two Harbors. You never fully recover from something like that. You just learn how to carry it differently.

Jessica was still in the early hours of her grief, but I would be here. For however long Jess needed. With Lucas back down in the Cities, Jess would need help with the practical things. Final arrangements, the funeral, and figuring out what came next for Ronald. He was clearly not as steady as he used to be. It was a lot to manage.

And then there was Will.

I hadn't been sure what to expect when I knocked on his door this morning, but the more time I spent around him, the more I understood what Jessica saw in him. He was kind. Thoughtful. But I had made up my mind. I wasn't just going to take Jess' word for it. I needed to see it for myself. I needed to see if Will was the man who would truly stand by Jessica, even when things got hard, especially when things got hard, because this was the epitome of hard. Right now. Today, tomorrow, and in the weeks and months to come. None of this would be easy.

And if I happened to find myself in a deeper conversation with Will... well, I wouldn't mind asking a few more questions about that Matt character. There was something about him. Not that I typically went for the calm and capable. But he was a little rough around the edges, too. I could just see it when I looked at him, even in the few minutes we were in the same room. That had piqued my curiosity more than I wanted to admit. And seriously, that guy was hot. I could totally fall for a hot dad.

I pulled back the quilt on the bed and settled in. I switched off the lamp on the bedside table. Tomorrow would be another full day. But I was here. Jessica wasn't alone. And whatever came next, we'd face it together.

47

Jessica

I STARED AT THE CEILING above my childhood bed. The nightlight my mom had always kept in each of the bedrooms provided just enough light for me to see. I had thought of flipping it off, but couldn't bring myself to do so.

The once-familiar bumps and tiny spider-veined cracks had somehow shifted over the years, or maybe I had. Either way, sleep had stayed just out of reach. I'd dozed off once or twice, but nothing restful. Just brief patches of numb before waking again to the sounds of the CPAP humming from the next room and the weight of reality sitting square on my chest.

Will, wrapped in the thin blue quilt beside me, breathed deeply and evenly. His body was warm against mine in the cramped full-sized bed, his arm curled protectively around my waist. Sometime after midnight, we'd stopped talking. Or maybe I had just run out of words. Grief had a way of stealing your vocabulary, flattening your sentences until all that remained were sighs and tears and nods that said, *I know. I'm still here.*

Today I'd have to talk to my dad. Really talk to him. The idea of it sent a flutter of anxiety through me. Not because I was afraid of his reaction, but because I wasn't sure how to start. My dad had never been one for long, meandering conversations. He was a man of few words, firm handshakes, and slow nods. He fixed things instead of talking about them. Grief didn't lend itself to fixing.

And yet here we were.

I blinked up at the ceiling, trying not to let the image of my mother's handwriting on those final documents haunt me. A funeral. At the Lutheran church. Burial at Calvary. A casket. Cherry wood, just like the dining room hutch she adored. Pink roses, of course. All the decisions she'd made years ago, tucked into a folder that my dad had found in the back of a file cabinet behind some old tax returns. As if she had known she wouldn't get the chance to talk to us about it.

And our last conversation? An argument. About this house. About how they shouldn't be trying to keep it up anymore. I'd pushed, she'd pushed back harder, and I had left frustrated, convinced there would always be time to smooth it over later.

There wasn't. The tears came silently, sliding down my temple and into the pillow.

Will stirred beside me, his arm tightening around my waist. "You okay?" he mumbled.

I nodded, and faintly said 'yes'. I didn't want to wake him fully. Not yet. He had been there for everything yesterday, quietly showing up in every way that mattered. And today, there would be more. He shifted and kissed the top of my head. "I'm here."

"I know," I whispered.

Later that morning, the house stirred with quiet activity. Liz had made coffee, scrambled some eggs, and fried up some bacon, filling the kitchen with a sense of normalcy that felt borrowed from someone else's life. Will showered while I sat at the table with my dad and reviewed the final schedule the funeral director had dropped off after our morning meeting.

Saturday, 11 a.m. service. Visitation one hour prior.

The obituary will be published in the paper today and run tomorrow, with a digital version available online by mid-afternoon. The floral arrangements had been ordered. The church had confirmed the organist.

It was happening. There was no pause button—just a series of boxes to check, things to sign, and decisions to make.

But now, sitting beside my father as he quietly chewed his turkey sandwich and sipped iced tea, the day felt frozen again. Like I had finally arrived at the moment I'd been dreading since waking up.

He was in his recliner, one of those oversized La-Z-Boy styles with a cracked leather arm and a woven afghan draped over the back. He looked smaller in it than I remembered. Smaller than yesterday. Smaller than he had ever looked in my entire life. And how could that be? Yesterday, I couldn't have imagined that today would be so much worse.

"Dad?" I said quietly.

He glanced at me and nodded.

"We need to talk about... after."

He grunted acknowledgment, the kind that meant he was listening but reserving judgment. I folded my hands in my lap.

"I know everything's still fresh. And I'm not trying to rush anything. However, I return to work in another week. Lily will need me. And you..."

"I'll be fine," he said, not unkindly.

I nodded. "I know you can be. But should you be? Here, alone?"

He didn't answer.

"I just... this house is a lot, Dad. I know it's a rambler, and everything you really need is on the main level, which is a plus. But it's still a big place to manage on your own. Even with the yardwork and upkeep, it's a lot. I know you and Mom didn't always see eye to eye on downsizing, but..."

"She wanted to move," he said, voice quiet but clear.

I blinked.

"She brought it up a few times. I didn't want to hear it." He set his sandwich down and leaned back. "It's not the house, Jess. It's what it means. Giving it up will feel like giving her up."

Tears rose again, uninvited.

"But I know." He looked around the living room. "Now it just feels empty."

"I don't want you to feel that way."

"I know." He gave me a small smile. "You're your mother's daughter. Always trying to fix everything."

I laughed, and it cracked something open in both of us. "I don't know what the answer is," he admitted. "But I know I don't want to be rattling around in here alone."

There it was. He had opened the door for me. We sat in silence for a while, the weight of that admission sinking in. "I could start looking at places," I offered. "Something nearby, or—"

"Maybe something closer to you," he said before I could finish.

My eyes widened. "You'd be okay with that?"

"I'd miss this view," he said, glancing out the window where we could see Lake Superior off in the distance. "But yeah. I think your mom would want me to."

I reached out and took his hand. "She would."

That afternoon, while Liz took a nap and Will caught up with the kids over FaceTime in the den, I sat alone on the back deck with a notebook, jotting down names of people to call and things to remember. It wasn't just funeral planning anymore. It was housing searches. Doctor transfers. Estate paperwork. My mom's garden club friends who'd want to bring food whether we asked for it or not.

A soft creak behind me made me look up. Will stepped out, coffee in hand, his eyes searching mine.

"How did it go?" he asked, settling into the chair beside me.

"Better than I thought. He said he doesn't want to stay here alone."

"That's a big deal."

"Yeah." I stared out at the blooming lilacs along the fence line. I smiled, reminiscing about my mom's gardening skills. Those lilac bushes bloomed at the end of every spring, without fail. "It feels like everything is shifting. Like nothing is going to be the same again."

He reached over and laced his fingers through mine. "That's because it won't be. But that doesn't mean it'll be bad."

I squeezed his hand. "You're really good at this."

"At what?"

"Showing up. Saying the right thing. Making space."

He shrugged. "I've had a lot of practice. Losing Katie taught me a lot about how not to show up, too. But... I didn't come the day you called. I'm still trying to forgive myself for that."

We sat in silence for a bit longer before I asked the question that had been on my mind. "Are we... dating?"

Will turned to look at me. "I hope so."

I smiled. "Me too."

"Do we need to define it right now?"

"No," I said, leaning my head on his shoulder. "I just needed to say it out loud."

"Then consider it said."

That night, as I lay back in my childhood bed once more, Will beside me and the CPAP in my dad's room on the other side of the wall now familiar in its rhythm, I stared at the ceiling with a little less dread. The conversation with my dad had gone as well as I could have hoped. Plans were in motion. There was support. There was love. There was a path forward.

And as I drifted off, one thought stayed with me. Maybe I hadn't made peace with my mom yet. But I would.

48

Will

THE HOUSE WAS QUIET. It was the kind of calm that settles after a day packed with emotions and obligations. There was an overbearing feeling of exhaustion. We were back at Jessica's dad's house after the funeral, the luncheon, and the burial. Jess, Liz, and I were sprawled out in the living room, all of us sitting in silence, emotionally wrung out. Ronald had retreated to his bedroom not long after we got home, saying little more than that he was going to lie down for the night. The day had clearly taken a lot out of him.

I looked at Jessica, sitting curled up in the corner of the sectional, a blanket thrown over her legs, and her eyes glassy from crying. Liz sat opposite, feet tucked beneath her, hands folded in her lap.

It had been a day. A hard one. And despite everything, I hoped I'd been what Jessica needed.

That morning had started quite a bit differently than I would have predicted. I'd woken to her hand between my legs, her fingers stroking me gently. It had taken me a moment to register what was happening. Her touch was soft yet deliberate. Before I could say anything, she had climbed on top of me, straddling me, pressing her body to mine.

"Jess," I whispered, trying to slow her, to stop her. Today was her mom's funeral, for God's sake, but she silenced me with a soft "I need this."

And so I let her. I held her close. It wasn't hurried or heated. It was slow and quiet, like the two of us just trying to breathe in the same rhythm for a while. She moved against me as if trying to regain her balance, and I did everything I could to steady her. We stayed that way for a long time after, tangled up, not speaking, just existing. Eventually, we showered. She cried a little, and I wiped the tears from her cheeks as the water ran over us.

Afterward, we dressed. She went to check on her dad, and I went to the kitchen to help Liz make breakfast. We'd kept it simple with toast, scrambled eggs, some sausage patties, and fruit. No one had much of an appetite, but we all needed something in our stomachs.

Then I drove us all to the church.

Ronald rode shotgun, silent for most of the ride. Jess and Liz were in the back, whispering occasionally, but even their voices were subdued. I caught Jessica's eyes in the rearview mirror once. She gave me the faintest nod. I wasn't sure what it meant. Was it gratitude, maybe, or reassurance? Whatever it was, I took it.

The service was beautiful. Thoughtful. Everything Jessica had said her mom would've wanted. The organist played "On Eagle's Wings" near the end, and that's when Jess broke. Her shoulders started shaking, and Liz reached for one hand while Ronald reached for the other. I stood a few feet back as they followed the casket out. The air outside was warm, the sky cloudless. Almost unfairly beautiful for a day like this.

The luncheon afterward was a blur. People came up to Jessica in waves. Some hugged her. Some cried. Some asked about Lily, about Lucas. That part was strange; watching people assume Jess and Lucas were still together. I guess most of them didn't know they'd divorced. Lucas had driven up that morning with Emily and Lily. They stayed for the service but left quietly afterward. Lily had been overwhelmed, clinging to her dad and clearly unsure of what was happening. She didn't fully grasp that her grandmother was gone. And me? I was just... present. Supportive. Quietly there.

A few retired teachers approached me, as well as some women from Carol's garden club and book club. They were kind, telling stories about Carol's patience, her wit, the way she always brought lemon bars to their meetings. One of them pressed a recipe card into my hand and whispered, "She gave me this last summer. Said it was her favorite." I thanked her, even though I didn't know what I'd do with it. I just nodded and said "thank you."

At the burial, Jess didn't let go of me once. She clung to my arm as the casket was lowered. Liz and Ronald each tossed a rose onto the top, and Jess followed, her hand trembling. I wrapped my arm around her waist as the reverend said a final prayer. And then we drove home.

Now, the silence in the living room was deafening.

I cleared my throat. "Tomorrow," I said, glancing between the two women. "How can I help?"

Jess didn't answer at first. She was still staring at the coffee table like it might offer a solution to everything. But then she blinked and turned to me.

"Tomorrow," she echoed, her voice low. "The estate sale rep is coming. And the real estate agent."

Liz sat up a little straighter. "Do you want us there for that? Or should we give you space?"

"I don't know." Jess sighed. "I haven't figured that out yet."

"You don't have to decide now," I said gently. "We'll take it one step at a time."

She nodded. "They think the house will go fast. It's in good shape. Good neighborhood. Single-level living."

"Those listings don't stay on the market long," Liz added.

Jess' eyes flicked toward the hallway where her dad had disappeared earlier. "I'm not even sure he realizes we're talking about selling it." She paused. "I mean, he told me he was ready and that he wanted my help finding a place in the cities, but I'm not sure if he has put two and two together yet."

Liz gave her a sad smile. "He'll understand. Maybe not right away. But eventually."

"We haven't even started sorting through Mom's things," Jess said. "There's just so much... stuff. And memories."

I reached for her hand. "We'll do it together."

She squeezed my hand, and her voice cracked when she whispered, "Thank you."

We all sat that way for a while. Quiet, but not uncomfortable. Just tired. Worn out.

Eventually, Liz stood and stretched. "I'm going to head to bed. Tomorrow's going to be another big day."

She leaned down and kissed the top of Jess' head, gave me a soft smile, and disappeared down the hallway toward the stairs that would take her to the basement guest room.

Jessica and I stayed where we were. "I'm scared," she said suddenly.

I looked at her. "Of what?"

"Everything," she said. "Losing her was hard enough. But now there's just... so much left to do. So many decisions. And I feel like I'm supposed to be the one holding it all together."

"You don't have to hold it all together alone," I said. "You've got people. You've got Liz. You've got me."

She scooted closer to me and leaned her head on my shoulder. "I know. I just… it feels like my whole life is shifting. And I'm not sure what any of it will look like after this."

"We'll figure it out," I said. "One piece at a time."

We sat like that for a long time. Eventually, we headed to bed, her fingers curled around mine the whole way down the hallway. Tomorrow, Jessica's next chapter would start. But tonight, we rested.

49

Jessica

THE ROOM FELT FOREIGN NOW.

My childhood bedroom, once painted a sunny yellow and cluttered with posters, books, and the usual relics of teenage life, now sat bare. The bed was gone. The closet was empty. The only thing left behind was the faint outline of furniture on the carpet. The memories were still there, however. In my head. In my heart.

The past five days had been a blur. The estate team and real estate crew had moved with remarkable speed, packing, labeling, sorting, and coordinating what would stay with my dad and me in the cities, what would go, and what would be donated. It was a logistical miracle. Somehow, amid the exhaustion and emotion, everything had fallen into place.

Everything my dad and I wanted to keep had been carefully boxed up and loaded onto the moving truck. His recliner. The photo of Mom in her garden. The clock from the mantle that had been given to them as a gift on their wedding day by his parents. The cross-stitched sampler from Grandma that hung above the kitchen doorway. All of it headed south to St. Paul, to his new apartment.

It was a good place. Modern, bright, quiet. Just a few blocks from Liz's house. I'd taken the virtual tour a couple of days ago with Will before he left to relieve Matt and get time with Max and Sophie. The space was clean and manageable. A little too beige for my taste, but it had big windows and a small patio. Dad would like that. And better yet, it was a senior living facility, which meant someone would check on him three times a day. He could have his meals delivered to his apartment or eat in the cafeteria. He had options, and I liked that.

Everything else from the house? Well, it was gone now, transported to an offsite showroom where an estate sale was already underway. They'd cut us a check in a couple of weeks. The leftovers would be donated to places Mom had specifically mentioned in her will: the women's shelter, the library, and a reading program she'd helped organize at the church. It felt like her fingerprints were still everywhere, gently guiding us even now.

I looked out the bedroom window one last time. The view hadn't changed in decades. The neighbor's crabapple tree still leaned just a little too far to the left. The driveway still curved like a question mark toward the street. The lake glimmered in the distance, a silver slash just beyond the edge of town.

And now, there was a For Sale sign on the lawn. It felt surreal. I closed the front door behind me. I locked the door and placed the key in the lock box that hung from the knob.

In the driveway, Liz was helping Dad get buckled into the front seat of Mom's old SUV. It was the car we'd used all week, roomy enough to be comfortable, familiar enough to keep him calm. I watched for a moment as Liz double-checked his seatbelt and handed him a travel mug of tea. Then she turned toward the door, saw me standing there, and caught my gaze.

Time to go.

"Everything good?" Liz asked.

I nodded. "As good as it's going to be."

Dad looked tired, but not frail. There was a distinction. He'd barely said two words all morning, but he was dressed neatly in his button-down shirt and khakis, the same pair he'd worn to Mom's service. His shoes were polished. His white hair combed back. He was ready. And I guess, so was I. We drove away slowly. I didn't look back. Not this time.

50

Will

THE QUIET WAS DIFFERENT NOW.

School was out. The halls were mostly empty, save for the occasional teacher wrapping up last-minute tasks or a custodian pushing a broom down the corridor. My classroom door stood open, the stale scent of pencils and floor wax filling the air as I stepped inside.

It was always a little strange, these last few days of June, when the noise fades and I'm left alone with the artifacts of a school year gone by.

I didn't have to pack up, thank God. I'd been in this room for over a decade, and the administration was kind enough to let me stay planted. But I still liked to do a little reset. Walk the room. Take stock.

I started at the windows, working my way around the space.

The world map above the whiteboard had curled corners. I made a mental note to tack them down better before fall. My bulletin board was still covered with timeline projects from my 10th graders, half historical, half hilariously off-base. I'd keep a few of the funnier ones to show next year's class. I wrote them down in my notebook and then wiped the board clean.

The bookshelves were dusty but intact. A few volumes were stacked unevenly, the result of rushed returns during the last week of school. I aligned them out of habit, fingers brushing the spines. *Night, To Kill a Mockingbird, The Book Thief.* The heavy hitters.

I moved next to my desk, opening drawers and sorting through stray papers: permission slips, orphaned Post-it notes, and mismatched Expo markers. Then, as I reached the back of the bottom drawer, something slid forward.

A green envelope.

I froze—Katie's handwriting. My heart jumped, stalled, then restarted in a kind of stuttered rhythm. I stared at the envelope, as if it might vanish if I blinked. How had this gotten here?

I reached in and realized it must have slipped out of an old manila folder underneath. A warped and overstuffed thing I hadn't touched in years. I tugged it free, placed the green envelope on the desk, and opened the folder.

Inside was a stack of colored envelopes.

Green. Blue. Pink. I swallowed hard. Letters.

I remembered them now. Katie had written us letters after the diagnosis. She kept them in the drawer of her nightstand, one for each of us to open the day after she passed. I remembered reading mine, how she permitted me to move forward, how she said she wanted me to live fully again.

But these... these letters were different. Surely I had known about them, right? Could I have forgotten that Katie had written letters to our children, preparing for monumental occasions in their lives?

Each envelope had a name in her handwriting, each scrawled with instructions.

"To Max, on his 16th birthday."

"To Sophie, on her wedding day."

"To Max, when he gets his driver's license."

"To Sophie, on her first broken heart."

They were color-coded—blue for Max and pink for Sophie. My own were green. Katie's favorite color had been orange, a bright, soft kind of tangerine. I always said it matched her laugh.

My hands shook as I opened the green one addressed to me. This one wasn't about moving forward. It was about us.

She wrote about how we met. How she thought I was too serious at first. How I made her laugh when I didn't even mean to. About our first date, when we got caught in the rain and I gave her my sweatshirt. She wrote about how I always made the coffee too strong and how she secretly liked it that way. She wrote about the way I held her hand when the doctor told us the news, how I didn't flinch, how I stood beside her.

She told me what she loved about me. Not just the partner or the father, but the man. By the end, I was crying. I didn't even try to stop the tears. It felt like her voice had come through time just to wrap itself around me.

I sat in the silence of my classroom for a long time after that, the envelope resting in my lap. Eventually, I wiped my eyes and gathered the rest of the letters. They needed to come home with me. I wanted them somewhere safe. Somewhere close. And I was puzzled as to how the letters had ended up here, in my classroom desk, and not in my desk at home.

I picked up the stack and slid it gently back into the folder. But something blocked the papers from settling into place. I tilted the folder forward and reached inside. Another envelope slid out. Smaller than the rest. A soft, pale orange. My pulse stuttered again.

I turned it over slowly, my thumb brushing the surface. Katie's handwriting, blurred in places, like the ink had been smudged. Maybe from tears. Maybe from time. It read: *To the woman who loves him next.* I stared at the words, unable to move. Katie had written her a letter—the woman who would come after Katie.

The woman who might love me—*would* love me someday. The woman who would sit beside me and share my life, raise our children, walk into my house knowing it had once belonged to someone else's dream. She'd written *her* a letter.

Katie, who had known how hard it would be for me to let go. Katie, who had known I'd need a nudge. And she'd gone a step further. She'd thought of her, too.

I closed my hand gently around the envelope. I didn't open it. Not yet. This wasn't a moment I wanted to rush. And the letter wasn't written to me. I placed the envelope on my desk, next to the green letter. I sat back in my chair, surrounded by the quiet remnants of another school year, and let the weight of the envelope settle into my chest.

Katie believed I would love again. And I believed she was right.

51

Jessica

THERE WAS SOMETHING ODDLY comforting about fluorescent lights and the quiet hum of a busy clinic. After the whirlwind of the past month, grief, decisions, and goodbyes, it had felt good to be back. Not because everything was back to normal, because I didn't even know what normal was anymore. But because helping others helped me. Always had.

Today had been my first day back, and while my energy was definitely lower than usual, it had gone well. A post-op ACL patient was finally walking without crutches. Another had mastered stairs again after a nasty fall. These little victories, small though they may seem, were reminders of movement. Forward, calm, healing.

Just like I needed.

I'd picked Lily up from Lucas' on the way home, and now we were officially on our week together. Lucas had graciously kept Lily for most of June as I had dealt with things up in Duluth. I hadn't realized how much I'd missed her until she came running into my arms. That little body curled against mine, and I had to blink away tears. She smelled like shampoo and summer. For the next several days, she'd be with me. Daycamp at the Y while I worked, and then all the evenings and weekend hours I could soak up.

We had a plan.

Tonight was build-your-own-pizza night. Lily had insisted on pineapple and black olives, a combination I never quite understood, while I kept it fancy with mushrooms, onions, and arugula. We'd lined the counter with ingredients like contestants on a cooking show and spent way too long "perfecting" our pizzas.

"Mine's a masterpiece," she'd said, grinning at me, pizza sauce smudged near her nose. I didn't argue.

We'd eaten at the table, just the two of us, with our glasses. Apple juice for her, a healthy-sized pour of white wine for me, clinking together like we were celebrating something. Maybe we were.

After dinner, Lily wanted to read another couple of chapters of her Diary of a Wimpy Kid series. We were on book five, and who was I to say no? She fell asleep not long after that, curled around her favorite stuffed polar bear. And Mr. Fluffles was sticking out from under the pillow. I lingered in her doorway for a minute, watching the slow rise and fall of her chest. The apartment was quiet. Peaceful. And that was exactly what I needed.

Back in the living room, I sank into the couch with a throw blanket and let out a sigh I hadn't even known I'd been holding.

The last few days and weeks had been a blur. Returning to the Cities, getting Dad settled into his new apartment, catching up on laundry and groceries, scheduling a plumber, and rescheduling a dentist appointment.

I'd spoken to Will last night while folding towels. He'd asked how I was. I didn't know how to answer, not really. He didn't push. He just listened. And now, tonight, he hadn't called. But he had texted earlier.

Will: *Hope the first day back went okay. I'm around if you want to talk. Or not talk. Either way.*

It made me smile. He had this way of knowing what I needed before I even said it—and giving me space without making me feel alone.

I'd replied:

Me: *Pizza night with Lily. Couch now. Exhausted but okay. Thank you for being patient with me.*

His response had been simple.

Will: *Always.*

That was it. Always.

I ran my fingers over the fabric of the couch cushion and let myself imagine what the weekend might feel like. Lily had surprised me earlier, asking if we could do something with Will and Sophie.

"Like a friend date," she'd said, brushing her hair behind her ears like she'd thought long and hard about it.

I hadn't expected it. I mean, yes, Lily loved Sophie. But it hadn't occurred to me that she'd ask for time with her. That she'd want to see Will again so soon. It made my heart ache in the softest, most hopeful way.

So I'd texted him:

Me: *Lily wants to do something with you, Max, and Sophie this weekend. Maybe the zoo?*

Will: *We're in. Saturday morning sounds okay?*

And just like that, it was a plan.

The Minnesota Zoo. The girls could roam the tropics trail or feed goats at the farm exhibit. We could walk the loop and get ice cream afterward. It was something to look forward to. And I especially wanted to walk the new treetop trail that had gone in where the old monorail used to be. I was looking forward to a day that didn't involve grief or hard decisions or signing paperwork on behalf of someone else's life.

Going to the zoo was something happy. I needed that. God, did I need that.

And I realized I was starting to miss Will more now, not in a way that overwhelmed me, but in a way that whispered 'You're ready.' Ready to keep going. Ready to reconnect. Ready for the light that started to peek through after a long, hard winter. Or in this case, a long few weeks. I reached for my phone one more time and typed:

Me: *Looking forward to Saturday. I've missed you.*

It was the truth.

I curled up against the armrest, blanket pulled to my chin, and closed my eyes. I didn't cry tonight. That felt like progress.

The pizza pans still needed to be cleaned, and I'd have to rewash the wine glass in the morning, but for now, everything in my world felt... settled. Tomorrow, Lily would go to camp. I'd head back to the clinic. And maybe this new version of normal wouldn't feel so unfamiliar after all.

52

Sophie

MY DAD HAD TOLD ME what happened. Jessica's mom died. And she was sad.

I understood this kind of sadness. Losing your mom. It's not supposed to happen. Ever. Well, I guess it's supposed to happen since your parents are older than you. But when my mom died, it wasn't fair. My mom would never see me graduate from high school, go on my first date, or attend my first school dance. She wouldn't be there for any of those big events. She didn't even get to see me start Kindergarten. It made me feel like crying.

And then I thought of Jessica. I didn't know how old people were when they died. Or at least not when they're supposed to die. But I got the idea from my dad that Jessica's mom hadn't been that old. So it wasn't fair for her, either.

I lay on my bed and stared at the ceiling. My room was dark, except for the soft glow from the pink lamp on my nightstand. My mom bought it for me when I was little. I don't remember how old I was.

I rolled over and opened my nightstand drawer. The pink envelope was still there, just like I'd left it. A little bent at the corners now, because I'd opened it so many times.

The day after Mom died, Dad had sat Max and me down on the couch. He was still in the clothes from the hospital. His eyes looked tired, and his voice was scratchy like he'd been crying but didn't want us to know.

He handed us each an envelope. Mine was pink. Max's was blue.

"This is from Mom," he said. "She wrote them before..." He didn't finish the sentence. But he didn't have to. And then he read them to us. We'd been too young to read them ourselves. And at the time, I hadn't understood much of what my mom had written. Max and I had been so young.

But I do remember holding my envelope as if it were made of glass. Like if I breathed too hard, it would disappear. It would shatter. Just go away like my mom had, never to be seen again.

Now, I slid it out carefully and opened it. Again.

The paper was soft, like the pages of my favorite books. My mom's handwriting wasn't perfect. She always said she had a doctor's scrawl, but I could read every word. I now knew most of the words by heart. But tonight, I wanted to feel her again, as if she were here.

Dear Sophie,

If you're reading this, it means I'm not there anymore. And that makes me very sad. But I want you to know something right away. Mommy loves you. So much. More than you will ever know.

I know you're probably feeling confused and mad and maybe even a little scared. It's okay to feel all of those things. I wish I could be there to talk through it all with you. However, I wrote this letter to share a few things I hope you will carry with you. Forever.

Choose kindness even when it's hard, even when someone else is mean first. Kindness is your superpower. It will open doors that nothing else can.

Choose love. Love is what makes life complete. It doesn't always mean big things. Sometimes love is helping someone carry their books. Or sitting next to the new kid at lunch.

Choose to make a friend. Sometimes it feels scary to say hello first. But you are brave. You are the kind of girl who can make someone else feel welcome.

Choose to be the one who reaches out when something feels broken. People aren't perfect. We all mess up sometimes. But saying "I'm sorry" or "let's talk" is powerful. You can fix more than you know with just a few words.

Take the high road. (Ask Daddy what that means. He'll explain it better than I can in a letter. And I promise you'll understand this more when you're older.) But it means doing the right thing, even when it's not the easy thing. And you, my beautiful girl, are capable of that.

And above all... live your life. Laugh so hard your belly hurts. Dance in the kitchen. Eat ice cream even when it's snowing. Make mistakes and learn from them. And know that I am proud of you. Always.

I love you more than any words can ever say. You will feel my love when it rains, when it snows, when the wind blows, and when the sun shines down on your face.

Love, Mommy

I wiped at my eyes with the sleeve of my pajama shirt. I wasn't sobbing. But I wasn't not crying, either. Her words made me feel like she was hugging me. Like her arms were still wrapped around me, telling me everything would be okay.

But I couldn't help but draw my eyes back toward a certain section of the letter. Choose to be the one who reaches out when something feels broken. Did Jessica know anyone else who had lost her mom? I knew what it felt like. Maybe I could help her.

I folded the letter carefully and slid it back into the envelope, pressing it to my chest before tucking it away.

I thought about Jessica again. I liked her. I did. But sometimes I felt weird around her. Like, I didn't know what I was allowed to feel. Was it okay to like her? Was it okay to wish she came around more? Was it okay to look forward to seeing her at the zoo this weekend?

Dad had said Jessica had been through a lot. That she might be sad for a while, I got that. I really did.

I could be kind, like Mom said. Maybe I could make her feel like she belonged. Like we could be something new. I didn't know what we were yet. She wasn't my mom. And I wasn't ready for another mom. But maybe... maybe we could be something else. Perhaps I would be the one who reaches out to help her put her pieces together again.

53

Jessica

SATURDAY MORNING HAD ARRIVED before I knew it. Lily had raced into my bedroom at 8 a.m. on the nose, dressed and ready to go. Why did kids have to get up so early? Didn't they understand that the weekends were for sleeping in? Besides, we didn't need to meet Will and the kids until 11:00 am.

I dragged myself out of bed, pulled Lily in for a hug, and then sent her to the bathroom to brush her hair and her teeth. I headed to the bathroom attached to my bedroom and turned on the shower. Hot. I needed a wake-me-up.

Yes, of course, I was excited to see Will. But my emotions had been really wearing me down this past week. Though work had kept me busy, my every-other-day visits to spend time with my dad before work, and then racing to get Lily from day camp each night before closing time had taken about all I had.

Still, I rallied. I pulled on jeans and a flowy T-shirt, tied my hair up in a loose ponytail, and headed to the kitchen.

Lily was already sitting at the table with two stuffed polar bears in her lap.

"Sweetheart, you can only bring one today. Just one. I know they're best friends, but your backpack won't fit both of them. And I don't want to end up carrying them."

She frowned like I'd asked her to choose between breathing and blinking. But after a long sigh and an extra squeeze, she settled on the one with the crooked ear.

"Only Snowball comes today. Snowflake will wait at home and hang out with Mr. Fluffles."

"Thank you," I said, kissing the top of her head. "Now let's talk about footwear. Please wear your tennis shoes."

"But my Crocs are easier," she whined.

"You always complain about your feet hurting after five minutes. We're going to be walking a lot."

She crossed her arms but stomped off toward her bedroom to change shoes. Victory.

By the time she returned, grumbling under her breath, I'd plated two homemade cinnamon rolls, ones I'd made from scratch earlier in the week when I couldn't sleep. I warmed them in the oven and poured two glasses of orange juice.

"Breakfast first, zookeeper later," I said, sliding her plate in front of her.

She beamed when she saw the cinnamon rolls and dug in. Sugar was always a good motivator.

And just like that, we were out the door and on our way to the Minnesota Zoo.

We met Will, Max, and Sophie by the entrance. Lily ran straight to Sophie and hugged her. Sophie accepted it stiffly but didn't pull away. Max gave me a polite "hi" and smiled before reaching for Lily's backpack and slinging it over one shoulder like it was no big deal. Will stepped up beside me, pulling me in for a quick side hug and pressing a kiss to the top of my head when the kids weren't looking. It made me laugh, because clearly we were beyond the kiss-the-top-of-the-head-and-side-hug thing, but I appreciated his discretion nonetheless.

We let the kids lead the way. "Penguins first!" Lily shouted.

"Penguins it is," Will said.

Thankfully, Sophie and Max were both game. Max was so easygoing. He seemed content just to be out and about, happy to walk alongside his sister and listen to Lily narrate facts about every animal she'd ever seen in a book.

Sophie was harder to read.

She was polite. Friendly. But... distant. She talked when asked questions—responded with a smile. But there was a wall up. And I didn't blame her. Our last run-in hadn't exactly been easy for either of us.

After the penguins, we made our way through the tropics trail, where we paused to watch monkeys swing from ropes and tropical birds that looked too colorful to be real.

Then it was outside again, this time toward the bears, and then finally onto the otters.

Lily pressed herself against the thick plexiglass wall, eyes wide as the two otters chased each other in circles and then batted around a floating red ball. Max stood close, pointing things out to her and making jokes that had her laughing louder than zoo etiquette probably allowed. But I loved her squeals of laughter and couldn't bear to quiet her or ask her to lower her voice.

Will had excused himself a few minutes earlier to use the restroom, and I sat on a nearby bench, letting myself rest for a moment in the quiet of the otter cave.

That's when I noticed Sophie look over her shoulder. She hesitated, then turned fully and walked toward me. She sat beside me. Her body was rigid, hands folded tight in her lap.

I offered a small smile. "Are you having fun, Sophie?"

She looked at her lap, then up at me. Her voice was soft, quiet. "I'm sorry your mom died. My mom died, too."

My heart twisted. I hadn't expected her to say anything, let alone that. I nodded, not sure what to say. "Thank you," I said quietly.

Sophie took a shaky breath. "When my mom died," she said, stumbling over the past tense, "it was unfair. I was only five years old. I had just turned five years old."

I turned my body a little more toward her, giving her my full attention.

"I'm starting to forget her," she said. "And I don't want to. I remember her smell. She used to wear this lotion that smelled like oranges. And she had a song she made up for me. But I can't remember the whole thing anymore." She looked me straight in the eye then, and I could see the pain in her gaze, raw and unhidden.

"I'm sorry," she repeated. "If you ever want to talk about your mom, I would like to listen."

I blinked, swallowing the lump in my throat. This girl. This is an incredible, brave little girl. My heart cracked open.

"Thank you, Sophie," I said, my voice just above a whisper. "That means a lot to me."

She nodded. And then, without another word, she got up and walked back toward the otters.

Will returned a few minutes later, and we wandered through the rest of the exhibits, eventually ending our day at the zoo café with overpriced popcorn, chicken nuggets, and lemonade.

But Sophie's words stayed with me. The way she looked at me. The way she opened her heart.

I wasn't sure what we were to each other yet. But there was definitely something beginning to grow. My heart was grateful.

54

Will

I RETURNED FROM THE RESTROOM and saw Sophie sitting next to Jessica on the bench. I wasn't sure what that was about. What was Sophie saying? I knew Sophie liked Jessica, but she was still reserved about her thoughts. I worried that Sophie was saying something I wouldn't want her to say. But the look on Jessica's face told me that wasn't the case.

She was listening, really listening, the way someone listens when what's being said is fragile and important. I could see emotion in her eyes. But it wasn't overwhelming or frustrating like I'd seen from her a few times in the last few weeks. These were softer. Sad, yes, but there was something else. Comfort? Understanding? That deep emotional recognition when someone's pain mirrors your own.

Sophie was speaking from that place, I could tell. And Jessica wasn't just hearing her. She was honoring her words with silence, with stillness, and with presence.

Then Sophie stood and walked calmly back to the plexiglass wall, resuming her post beside Max and Lily as they watched the two otters twist and somersault in the water. She slipped in right between them, and Max adjusted without even blinking. Lily handed her the ball of crumpled zoo map she'd been clutching, and Sophie smoothed it out, starting to trace the paths with her finger.

I quickly backtracked the few steps I'd taken, not wanting to interrupt the moment or let them know I'd been watching. After a ten-count, ten slow, even breaths, I casually made my way back into the otter cave, like I hadn't just been frozen with awe watching the two of them share something sacred.

Jessica didn't look up when I sat down beside her, so I scooted just a little closer until our hips bumped. She looked over and giggled softly, shaking her head.

"What?" I asked with mock innocence.

"You," she said, her voice low but warm. "You're always just there."

I leaned in and brushed a soft kiss against her lips. She accepted it without hesitation and then leaned her forehead against mine. We sat that way for a moment, forehead to forehead, breathing the same air.

"You okay?" I asked, still holding her gaze.

She pulled back, just far enough to see me clearly, and nodded. "I think I am, actually."

It was the way she said it, calm, surprised even, like she was realizing it just then. Like it hadn't occurred to her until now that peace might actually be settling in again.

"Whatever she said to you..." I began.

Jessica nodded, eyes soft. "It wasn't what I expected. But it was... everything I needed." She paused. "I think Sophie and I are going to be just fine."

I didn't press, but I felt my heart swell a bit with happiness. And I knew she'd tell me more if and when she wanted. And honestly, I didn't need to know the words. I could already see the effect they had.

"She's a good kid," Jessica said after a few seconds, glancing back at Sophie. "Strong. Thoughtful."

"She is," I agreed, feeling that swell grow in my chest that I always got when someone saw my kids the way I did. "She gets that from her mom."

Jessica smiled again, but this time it was a different kind of smile. There was reverence behind it like she was holding a fragile piece of something sacred. "Katie would be proud."

"I think she already is," I said, meaning every word. "And I know I can say this to you, but the anniversary of her death is coming up. So are the kids' birthdays. It was horrible that year she died. Trying to celebrate their fifth and seventh birthdays, knowing that their mom only had weeks left." I paused. "But we've come a long way."

We sat in silence a bit longer, just watching the kids and the otters and the slow movement of Saturday families drifting past the exhibit. Eventually, we all made our way through the rest of the zoo. There were snacks, complaints about the heat, and a minor meltdown from Lily when we bypassed the stingray touch pool due to the long line. But it was a good day. A healing kind of day.

Later, as we walked toward the parking lot, Jessica let her hand fall into mine. I laced our fingers together without saying a word. Sophie and Lily had started skipping ahead, Max lagging behind just enough to play the cool, responsible kid role he wore so well. Though I did hear him mutter, "gross."

"You think it's always going to feel like this?" she asked, her voice barely above a whisper.

"Like what?"

"Like I'm balancing on the edge of something," she said. "Like I could fall either way, into sadness or back into real life."

I gave her hand a gentle squeeze. "I think that's what grief is. Not a straight line. Just this back-and-forth, until one day you realize you've made it further than you thought."

She nodded slowly, taking in my words, but not answering right away.

"And I'll be here," I added. "On whichever side you land."

Jessica looked over at me, eyes soft, lashes catching the late afternoon light. "You always say the right thing, Will."

"That's because I'm terrified of saying the wrong thing," I admitted, half-laughing. "But I mean it. I'm not going anywhere."

We reached the cars and loaded up the kids. There were promises to make plans again soon and a round of hugs that were less awkward than I'd expected. Even Sophie gave Jessica a quick side hug, almost like she wasn't even thinking about it—just a reflex. And I took it for what it was. A big step forward, and something I desperately needed to see to know that I was doing the right thing. Falling in love with Jessica.

As we pulled out of the parking lot, I looked in the rearview mirror at my kids. Sophie was already texting someone, her forehead pressed to the window. Max was eating the last of the popcorn he'd begged me for at the zoo café. And I felt... good. Not perfect. Not over it. But good.

Back at home, after dinner and a round of dishes, I found myself thinking about the letter again. The orange envelope I hadn't opened yet. I didn't know if I would. It wasn't written for me. It was still sitting on the counter, right where I'd placed it the night before.

I picked it up and turned it over in my hands. The handwriting, Katie's, was faint, worn in spots. I thought of the blurred words and wondered what might have been going on in Katie's heart and mind as she wrote that letter.

To the woman who loves him next.

I stared at those words, wondering how she'd known, how she'd known that I'd need this. That Jessica might need it, too.

This last thought startled me. When I had discovered the letter earlier in the week, I hadn't necessarily processed that the letter was for Jessica. But as I sat myself down at the kitchen counter and reflected, I realized that it was definitely for Jessica. It was the letter that Jessica would need. Maybe not right now. But sometime in the future. Sometime soon.

I brought the letter into my office and placed it in the top drawer of my desk with the folder of other letters I had found in my desk at work before returning to the kitchen to pour myself a glass of water. I was now deep in thought, thinking about the bench at the otter tank, about Jessica's face when she turned toward Sophie, and the soft smile she gave me afterward.

Maybe we were all just finding our way back. One word. One gesture. One Saturday at a time.

55

Jessica

FRIDAY NIGHT.

It had only been six days since our zoo outing, but somehow it felt longer. Maybe it was the emotional weight of the last few weeks finally settling into the edges of my life, or perhaps it was just that I missed him. Missed *us*. Since my mom passed, life has been a constant juggle. My dad's transition, getting Lily back on a regular summer schedule, returning to work, and trying to sleep again.

But tonight, the chaos paused.

Lily was with Lucas for the weekend. Will had told me earlier in the week that he was thinking of leaving the kids at home for a few hours. Max was about to turn thirteen, mature for his age and probably more responsible than some adults I knew. Will had checked in with other parents, done his research, and even asked Max directly. And tonight was the test. Max was excited for the challenge. Sophie, apparently, had made a snack schedule. I wasn't even surprised that she had done so. It was so Sophie.

So it was date night.

Real, grown-up, no-kids, no-curfew, no-shared-zoo-pretzels kind of date night.

Will had offered to pick me up, which I appreciated more than I expected. I'd almost forgotten what it felt like to be picked up for a date, like we were in our twenties again. He texted when he was in the parking lot, and I met him downstairs, heart fluttering in a way it hadn't in years. He looked so good. A button-down shirt, sleeves rolled, clean-shaven, with a dimple in his cheek showing as he smiled.

"You clean up well," I said, slipping into the passenger seat.

He grinned. "You always look amazing. But tonight... wow."

The restaurant was a small American grill between our two neighborhoods, only fifteen minutes from either of our places. Casual. Candles on the tables, light rock humming from speakers, waitstaff who knew when to hover and when to disappear.

I was halfway through my glass of Chardonnay when Will reached across the table and took my hand.

"Jessica," he said, his voice soft but steady, "do you remember when I asked you before, where do you see this going?"

My smile was immediate. "Of course I remember."

It had been during one of our early dates. That lounge at the W, the city lit up below us, the beginnings of something already stirring.

That had been before so much, before we'd tangled up our lives and emotions, before the kids were introduced, before my mom died.

Before life had flipped everything upside down.

I studied his face now. Serious. Gentle. Open. "Are we having this conversation?" I asked, my tone light, maybe too light.

His expression faltered slightly, and I immediately realized how it had landed.

"Wait, I didn't mean it like that," I said quickly. "I meant... are you thinking this isn't going the way you want it to?"

His eyes widened. "No. God, no. Jessica, I think this is going exactly the way I want it to."

Relief softened my shoulders, and he went on.

"I feel alive when I'm with you," he said. "Like I've been in some kind of half-life and didn't even know it until you showed up. I love how we talk. I love how you look at the world. I love how you listen to my kids, even when they don't realize you are. I love us."

He paused, and something flickered behind his eyes. Hesitation. Vulnerability.

I didn't wait. "I love you," I said. My voice surprised even me with how sure it sounded.

And in the same breath, he echoed, "I love you."

We both stopped, blinked at each other, shy smiles creeping up our faces.

"I am in love with you," I said again, more firmly this time. "I don't know when it happened, but it did. And it's real. You've become this... reliable, grounding, hopeful part of my life. It's more than chemistry or timing. It's you, Will."

His hand squeezed mine, and his gaze was warm.

"I've felt this way before," he said quietly. "With Katie. And I won't pretend I didn't. But after she died, I thought that part of my life was over. I didn't think I'd ever feel this again. But I do. I really do."

My heart twisted at the mention of Katie, but it wasn't painful. It was honest. It was true. It was part of him, and I didn't want to pretend it wasn't.

I stood from my seat and leaned across the small table, brushing my lips against his in a soft, lingering kiss. When I pulled back, I held his gaze. I could tell he wanted more. And I did, too.

"I think this is going exactly where we want it to go, Will."

His thumb brushed over my hand, slow and deliberate.

"I want more of this," he said. "More nights like this. More Saturdays at the zoo. Mornings where we fight over who gets to make the coffee."

"You think we'd fight over that?" I asked with a laugh. "Trust me, you can make the coffee."

He shrugged. "Only if you keep insisting on using that fancy oat milk creamer."

I raised a brow. "It's vanilla bean. Don't knock it until you try it."

He grinned. "Noted."

Dinner went on, lighter after that. We talked about work and the kids. He told me Max was obsessed with an idea to build a Lego model of the Colosseum. Sophie was still obsessed with her Switch games, though she had been falling asleep at night with a book tucked in beside her. We talked about their upcoming birthdays. Max was having a bunch of friends over for a basketball tournament in the backyard. And Sophie's party would be at a trampoline and inflatable park in Woodbury. We talked about Lily's growing love of puzzles and how she still refused to wear matching socks. We discussed how Mr. Fluffles seemed to be in the picture, no matter whose house she was at.

It was normal. Domestic. A glimpse into something lasting. Was I ready for that?

When we stepped outside into the cool night air, he reached for my hand again. I leaned into his shoulder as we walked toward the car, a content sigh slipping out before I could stop it. When we got to his car, he leaned down to open the car door for me, but then seemed to rethink his strategy. Before I knew what was happening, he pressed me against his car, his body warming me from the slight evening chill.

His hands found the sides of my face and took me in for a deep kiss. Our tongues searched desperately for one another. I tasted him—that taste of his single glass of bourbon lingering on his tongue.

"Take me home, Will," I moaned into his kiss. I could feel his erection against my stomach.

He hesitated. "The kids," he said.

"Take me to my home," I responded.

56

Will

WE ENTER JESSICA'S APARTMENT, and she tosses her purse down on the kitchen counter. I swing her door shut with my foot and reach behind me to lock the latch. A glance at my watch tells me it is only 8:30 p.m. Still time before I need to get home to the kids.

Jessica leans against the kitchen counter and turns to me. I grab her by the waist and lift her onto the counter. She wraps her legs around me, pulling me close. I take her mouth for a kiss, ravaging her with my tongue.

She reaches down between my legs and runs her hand over my crotch, firmly enough that my body shudders softly in response. Seeming satisfied, she starts to unbutton my shirt as my tongue runs down her neck, around her ear, and to her chest. I lift her with one arm as her legs stay wrapped around me, the lift just enough to remove the problem of gravity keeping that dress on her body.

She pauses from unbuttoning my shirt to raise her arms. I slide her dress off over her head. I breathe in a deep sigh of relief and lust as the dress comes off easily. Underneath, she is wearing a thin pair of yellow panties. No bra. Instead, she has these little flowers stuck over her nipples. I lean down and gently grab one with my teeth, tugging to release her breast in full.

I grinned as she peeled off the second petal and let it fall to the floor. Her eyes held mine. Playful, confident, completely in control. "Those were… unexpected," I murmured, letting my hands roam up her back as I stepped closer.

"Thought I'd surprise you," she whispered, brushing her lips along my jaw. "Judging by your reaction, I'd say it worked."

"Oh, it definitely worked."

I lifted her off the counter again, and this time, I didn't stop until I'd carried her all the way down the hall. She laughed softly in my ear as her bare legs wrapped tighter around me, her skin warm against my chest where my shirt hung open. I kicked open the bedroom door and pressed her gently against the wall, bracing her weight with one arm as I traced kisses down her collarbone.

"God, Jess," I murmured against her skin. "You drive me crazy."

"Good," she whispered. "That's exactly what I was going for."

I took her mouth again, this time more slowly. I wanted to savor the feel of her, every sigh, every shiver, every quiet moan that passed between us. Her fingers found their way into my hair as I pressed deeper, her hips rising to meet mine in a rhythm that made my blood pound.

She was so open, so present with me, not just in body, but in every way that mattered. I didn't realize how much I'd missed this until now. And it wasn't just the intimacy, but the deep connection. The trust. The love.

I carried her the rest of the way to the bed, laying her down gently before stripping off my shirt and climbing in beside her. Above her. Entering her. There was no rush. Not at first. Just the pull of desire and the intimate knowledge that we were exactly where we were meant to be. But with every thrust, her body tightened against me more and more.

I lost control, fighting to prioritize her pleasure while indulging in my own. I called out her name when I came inside her. Seconds later, she responded in kind, and I could feel her body clenching in ecstasy.

It was by far the best sex I had ever had. The lust and the love had been something that had been building, piece by piece, between grief and healing, over dinners and shared glances, whispered phone calls and late-night tears.

As our breathing calmed, she curled into my side, one leg thrown over mine and her fingers drawing slow circles against my chest.

"I meant what I said earlier," she murmured. "I love you, Will."

I turned my head and kissed the top of hers, this time without hesitation, regardless of who was watching or not.

"I love you too, Jess. And I'm not going anywhere," I paused, looking at the old-fashioned alarm clock on her bedside table. "Except home," I laughed. "I guess I need to go home."

57

Liz

JESSICA HAD BEEN AT MY PLACE for over an hour, and we were deep into our second glasses of wine, the sun dropping behind my neighbor's rooftop while cicadas buzzed somewhere in the distance. Lily was with her dad for a few more days, and Jess needed a night out of the house. I was happy to oblige.

We'd already caught up on all things Ronald. Jess had received a generous offer on her parents' house that morning and planned to accept it the following day. If everything went according to plan, closing would happen on August 1. She told me the estate sale had gone surprisingly well, too. I shouldn't have been surprised when she added that her dad, good old Ronald, had told her to take the profits and put them into a trust for Lily's college education. Between his social security checks and pension, he had enough to cover the costs of his new senior living apartment.

"'It's just money. I can't take it with me,'" Jess said, mimicking her dad's gruff but lovable tone before bursting into laughter.

"Classic Ronald," I said, raising my glass. "Generous to a fault."

We clinked and sipped, and now that all the logistics were out of the way, I leaned forward with a grin. "Okay. Now tell me what's up with Will."

And just like that, I saw it. That look. That little twitch of the smile, the subtle light in her eyes. She was gone. That girl was in love.

"Well, I'll be damned."

Jess had told me once, years ago, maybe right after the divorce, that she thought she was destined to be alone. But here she was, looking completely and entirely like a woman who had fallen hard. And now it was time to dig a little deeper.

"Jessica," I said, shifting in my chair. "What do you want with Will?"

She blinked at me. "What do I want?"

I gave her a look. "Don't play dumb. You've been dating this guy for, what, over seven months now? And you're almost forty. Dating at our age isn't like it was in our twenties. You don't need to date for five years to know where it's going."

She held up her hand, stopping me. "Liz, I'm not ready to get married again. At least not yet."

That gave me pause. "Really?" I said. "That's not what I expected you to say."

She shrugged, a little apologetic. "Lucas is getting remarried. I'm happy for him. I like Emily. Lily likes Emily. But I'm not Lucas. I don't know that I want to get married again. And with Will... there are so many other things to think about."

She took another sip of wine and looked down at her glass. "His kids lost their mom just five years ago. And then there's something else."

"What?" I asked.

She hesitated. "I think I might want another baby."

My eyebrows shot up. "Another baby? Really?"

She nodded slowly. "I didn't think I did. I hadn't even said that out loud until just now. But I think... yeah. Maybe. And if things progress with Will, what would that mean for Sophie and Max? How would they feel about a new sibling? Would they feel like their dad was starting a new life without their mom? And what about Lily? She's eight. She's had me to herself for a long time. Would she even want that kind of change?"

I didn't answer right away. Jess wasn't looking for answers. She was sorting her thoughts aloud.

"What do you want?" I asked again.

She stared off for a moment before answering. "I like how things are. I like my independence. I love my one-on-one time with Lily. And I love that I can pick up the phone or FaceTime Will whenever I want. It feels like the best of both worlds."

She paused, then looked at me with something soft in her eyes. "But there's more, too. Sophie talked to me at the zoo."

"Oh?"

"She sat next to me and told me she was sorry about my mom. And then she told me about losing hers. She said she was starting to forget her. She was five when Katie passed. And her brother was seven. Katie died right after their birthday. Can you imagine?"

My heart ached at the thought. I knew too well what it was like to lose parents at a young age. I hadn't been that young. I'd been in my early 20s, off at college, when I got the call from my neighbor that there were police officers at the door of my house. I shrugged off the memory, not something I wanted to relive in that moment.

"She said she'd listen if I ever wanted to talk about my mom. Liz, she's only ten. And she said it with more grace and maturity than most adults I know. But still... I'm not sure I can be someone's second mom. I don't know what my role would even be. There's no manual for this kind of thing."

I stood and moved from the loveseat to the couch next to her. "You need to talk to Will about all of this."

"I know," she said quietly.

"You're not wrong for having questions, Jess. This is a big deal. You're not just dating anymore. You're building something. And it's okay if that something doesn't look like a wedding or a white picket fence. But Will deserves to know where your head is at."

She nodded slowly, and I could tell she was taking it in. We fell into a comfortable silence after that. I leaned forward with my glass of wine and clinked it to hers.

58

Will

THE SUMMER PASSED IN A BLUR.

I barely had time to blink between drop-offs, pick-ups, and the endless meal planning that came with having two growing kids in constant motion. Sophie had begged to attend a summer dance intensive. Five days a week, all day. And I couldn't say no, especially if it meant getting her away from the television and her devices. Dance had become her world. It gave her something to focus on, to move through, to sweat into. Max, on the other hand, had committed himself to dryland hockey training, pick-up basketball games, and his usual two weeks of wrestling camp. My calendar looked like a patchwork quilt stitched together by a madman. Additionally, we had hosted their birthday parties in early August. It was convenient and not so convenient that their birthdays were just three weeks apart.

In the middle of it all, I had gone back to school. Not as a teacher. This time as a learner.

It felt strange even to say that out loud, back to school at 42. But I'd started a master's program in teaching. I had enrolled years ago, before Katie got sick, but had hit pause when life took its turn. Since then, the idea of going back had always been there. Silent and persistent. But easy to ignore. This summer, I stopped ignoring it.

I couldn't say what flipped the switch. Maybe watching Sophie and Max chase their passions reminded me to chase mine. The kids turning eleven and thirteen showed me how quickly the time was passing. Or maybe it was Jessica. Her presence, her perspective, her ability to challenge me without even trying. She never pressured me. Never asked what I was waiting for. But something about her made me want to keep moving forward. In life. In love. In all of it.

And yet, something between us still felt like it was idling.

We saw each other at least once a week. Carved out evenings when Lily was with Lucas or my kids were with their grandparents. We made a point to get the kids together occasionally, which felt like a small miracle considering how complicated parenting schedules could be.

I had suggested a weekend getaway once, just the two of us. Some place local. Nothing over the top. But Jessica had hesitated and politely declined. She gave a reasonable excuse at the time. Something about Lily's schedule or wanting to get caught up at work, but I knew there was more to it. She still worried about her presence in Max and Sophie's lives. About what her involvement would mean long-term. I respected that, truly. She was thoughtful, intentional, and deeply aware of the weight that came with blending families.

But I'd be lying if I said I didn't wonder if that wasn't all it was.

We'd said "I love you." And we meant it. That part was never in question. But sometimes love wasn't enough to push things forward.

Lately, it felt like we were just circling each other. Not in a bad way. But we weren't moving either. Not forward. Not back. Just this familiar cycle we'd created. A routine I loved, yes. One that gave me space, connection, and comfort. But it didn't feel like we were building toward anything. Not anymore.

And what confused me most was this: Jessica didn't seem to worry about my role in Lily's life. Not at all.

She'd told me more than once that she appreciated how Lily felt safe with me. That she was glad Lily saw someone treat her mother with love and kindness. And when Jessica told me that Lucas was getting remarried in December, and that she had not only accepted it but supported it, I was stunned.

She'd given Emily her blessing. I couldn't help but contrast it with us.

Jessica didn't flinch at her daughter gaining a stepmom. But she seemed hesitant, maybe even afraid, that my children might achieve something like a stepmom, too.

I didn't need titles. I didn't need a ring on her finger or a wedding or Jessica to wear my last name. But I needed to know she could see a future that looked a little more connected. A little less temporary.

Sometimes I caught her looking at me like she wanted to say something, as if she were about to share a thought that had been sitting in her chest for days. But then she'd smile, lean in, and ask how Sophie's dance showcase had gone or if Max was ready for the next wrestling season coming in the fall.

And I'd let it go because I didn't want to push.

But now, school for both me and the kids was back in session. The leaves on the trees had begun to turn the faintest shade of amber now that fall was quickly approaching, I realized I didn't want this all to have been just a "summer thing." Or a once-a-week kind of relationship.

I wanted the whole damn picture.

I wanted the chaos and the quiet: the Thursday night leftovers and the Sunday mornings in bed. I wanted to wake up with her more than just once every two weeks. I wanted to make coffee for her every morning. I wanted to know that, someday, we could actually do the messy, real-life, every-day-together thing.

But maybe she didn't want that. And maybe, after everything we'd both been through, that was okay.

Still, I knew one thing for sure: I wasn't going to keep circling forever. I was going to talk to her. Not to demand anything. Not to pressure her. But because she deserved my honesty, and I deserved hers, too.

It was time to figure out where we stood. And where we were headed.

59

Jessica

SEPTEMBER HAD CREPT in quietly. But then, suddenly, it was everywhere. Lily had started third grade, and signs that she was back in school were all around me. School updates from her teacher taped to the fridge. New sneakers by the front door. That unmistakable mix of nerves and excitement every time Lily mentioned her new teacher and the kids who were in her class.

This all said, summer had disappeared faster than I'd imagined. Somehow, in the shuffle of split custody, camp pickups, and late-night laundry folding, the days had blurred together. Lucas had Lily every other week, and I had grand plans for those "off" weeks. Time to rest, recharge, maybe even schedule a weekend away. But as it always goes, the calendar filled up fast.

I picked up extra shifts at the hospital when I could. And then there was the new neuro patient. It was a complicated case with a long recovery ahead. I'd been visiting her at a local rehab facility every day. It was fulfilling work, the kind that reminded me why I got into this field in the first place. But it was also draining. Between that, managing Lily's world, and trying to show up as a whole human being for my dad, especially, I was often left wondering if I had anything left to give anyone else.

And still, every week, I saw Will.

It became this unspoken rule between us. No matter how chaotic things got, we carved out space for each other. A walk. A takeout dinner. An hour with no distractions. Sometimes we met up with the kids, like when we took them to the Franconia Sculpture Park up in Scandia. Or that beach day, when Max and Lily buried Will in the sand and Sophie actually smiled as she helped. And of course, Lily had attended Sophie's birthday party at the trampoline and inflatables park; moments like those kept me going. They gave me something soft to land on.

But now, the school year was in full swing, and I could feel the tension in Will every time we talked. He was working on continued lesson plans for his fall classes, studying curriculum updates, juggling open-house schedules, and managing after-school logistics for Max and Sophie. And he was finishing up his exams from his summer master's program. We were both moving at a full sprint, parallel lives racing forward.

I missed him.

Not just the physical presence, though that, too. But I also missed the deep conversations, the laughter that came from nowhere, the feeling that we were slowly building something meaningful.

And yet, we weren't moving.

It wasn't that I didn't love Will. God, I did. I felt it every time he looked at me like I was the center of his universe. Every time he texted to ask how my day was going. Every time he reached for my hand at the exact moment I needed grounding. But something in me was... stuck.

Liz had said it plainly: "You need to figure out what you want with Will."

At the time, I'd told her I wasn't ready to get married. That had surprised her. Maybe even surprised me. Because the truth was, I did want to get married again. I wasn't opposed to love, or commitment, or building a future with someone. I wanted all of that.

I just wasn't sure I could do it with kids who already had someone else as their mother. And not just any mother. Katie. I didn't know her, but I knew of her. And the grief that lingered in Sophie and Max's eyes told me everything I needed to know.

Katie was loved. Deeply. She still is.

I kept going back to that day at the zoo. Sophie was sitting beside me on the bench, watching the otters play while something heavy stirred in her little body. Her words were careful but raw. "I'm starting to forget her," she'd said.

And I had understood her. Far more than I wanted to admit.

At that point, it had barely been a handful of months since my mom died, and already the edges of her voice were starting to fade. I'd had my own breakdown last week when I realized I hadn't remembered to call her at 4 p.m., our old ritual. As if I still could. I'd lost track of the last real conversation we'd had. I'd stopped trying to recreate it. Even the guilt felt duller now, like a familiar pain I no longer flinched at.

So, what would it mean for Sophie if I were to marry her father? What would it mean for Max?

I wasn't afraid of being a stepmother. I was scared of becoming the wrong kind of one.

I couldn't replace Katie. I didn't want to replace her. But I also wasn't sure where that left me. Somewhere in the middle, I guess. Never quite belonging to them, but never really separate either. And then there was Lily. She was already learning what it meant to share a parent. How would she feel sharing me?

I wanted to have this conversation with Will. I needed to. But every time I saw his face, so full of belief in us, I couldn't bear to say, *I'm scared*. I mean, he knew I was scared because I'd already told him as much. But that fear wasn't really going away. And I wasn't sure what it would take for me to feel completely at ease.

I didn't want him to think I was doubting him, or doubting us. Because I wasn't. I was doubting myself.

60

Will

FRIDAY NIGHTS FELT DIFFERENT once school started back up again. The chaos of summer camps, schedules, road trips, and last-minute sleepovers had settled into a more familiar, if hectic, rhythm. Lunches were packed, homework was creeping in, and Max had already forgotten his gym shoes twice.

I was standing at the bathroom mirror, smoothing down my hair and giving myself a pep talk. We were going out. Not just Jessica and me, but Liz and Matt as well. Yes, my Matt. My buddy. A double date. At the W Hotel's Prohibition Bar, no less.

The last time Jessica and I had gone there... well, let's just say our dessert became something other than a chocolate cake.

The memory tugged a grin across my face. I adjusted my collar and walked back into the living room, where Max was watching TV and Sophie sat curled up with a book. Our babysitter, Ella from next door, would be over soon. Max had rolled his eyes at the idea of needing a sitter, even a casual one, now that he was thirteen and Sophie was eleven, but I wasn't taking chances. Especially not when Matt's kids were joining the party.

"Dad," Max called out. "We're fine. Seriously. I don't need help watching Sophie."

I raised a brow. "And if the blender explodes or someone wants popcorn and the bag sets off the smoke alarm?"

He groaned. "One time."

Sophie looked up. "I like Ella."

"You like anyone who braids your hair," Max shot back.

I held up a hand to cut off the usual sibling bickering. "She'll be here for a few hours. Be nice. Pizza is in the oven. You've got the emergency numbers."

As if on cue, the doorbell rang. Ella appeared with a confident wave and an oversized tote bag that probably had everything from board games to a fire extinguisher.

"I'm good," Ella assured me as I stepped aside to let her in. "I've got this."

God bless responsible teenage girls.

Matt was due any minute to drop his kids off at my place before we headed downtown together. He texted that he was five minutes out. I made sure Ella had everything she needed, including the wifi password, snacks, and emergency numbers, and gave

Max and Sophie one last pep talk before Matt's knock sounded on the door.

"Hey, man," he greeted, two backpacks slung over his shoulder and his kids trailing behind him. "You ready?"

"Just about," I said, grabbing my keys and giving Ella a thumbs-up. "Thanks again," I told her as Matt and I stepped outside.

We were headed to Prohibition Bar at the W. Jessica and Liz were already downtown. Apparently, they'd met up earlier for pedicures at a spa not far from the hotel. Jessica had texted just as we pulled onto 8th Street: *We're grabbing a table now. You'll know us. We're the loud ones with great toes.*

I smiled at my phone. I already couldn't wait to see her.

Prohibition Bar's moody lighting and plush couches give it an an old Hollywood vibe. As promised, Jessica and Liz were already there, drinks in hand. Liz was holding court, naturally, probably mid-story about one of her clients or, knowing her, her latest dating app fiasco that somehow turned into a free dinner and a new contact for her network.

"Look what the late-September wind blew in," Liz called out when she spotted us, rising from her seat with a dramatic flourish.

She threw her arms around me. "You clean up well, Will. Still got those teacher-of-the-year vibes."

I laughed and hugged her back. "Good to see you too, Liz."

Jessica smiled from her seat, her eyes catching mine. She looked incredible in a deep burgundy dress that hugged her in all the right places. It was the kind of look that made me forget there were other people in the room. She gave me that familiar smile. I could get lost in that smile. I was lost in that smile.

Matt stepped forward and extended his hand. "Hey, Jess," he said with an easy grin. "Good to see you again."

"Matt," Jessica nodded. "You, too."

Matt and I had been friends since elementary school. The kind of friendship built on years of inside jokes, sleepovers, basketball games, and shared high school heartbreaks. He was still the same guy, taller than me by an inch, with that dad-who-plays-pickup-on-Saturdays vibe. Confident. Chill. Dependable. And though his heart had been broken when his wife had been killed in that horrific car accident, he'd picked up the pieces and found a way to move on—two little kids in tow.

We ordered drinks. Jessica went with a bold glass of red, contrary to the typical buttery Chardonnay that she preferred; Liz had something botanical and gin-heavy, while Matt and I stuck to a solid local IPA.

The four of us sank into the low couch seating situated by the tall windows, the skyline glittering behind us like a live-action postcard.

Prohibition was relaxed, almost deceptively so. Jessica slipped her hand into mine, and I gave it a squeeze.

"So," Matt said, nudging me with a grin. "Still molding young minds?"

I grinned back. "Gotta love high school history."

Liz leaned in, curious, turning her attention toward Matt. "What do you do?"

"Accountant," Matt said with a shrug. "Mostly small business clients. Some tax work. Nothing glamorous, but it keeps me busy."

"Stable and smart," Liz said, raising an eyebrow approvingly. "A rare combination."

"Flattery already?" Matt teased. "We just met."

Jessica laughed, and I added, "He's underselling himself. He's been running his own firm for years."

"Play nice," Jessica said, elbowing me.

"Oh, I am," I said with a wink.

Conversation flowed easily. Matt was sharp but down-to-earth, the kind of guy who asked thoughtful questions and listened with genuine interest. For a first date, he carried himself with quiet confidence, not trying to impress so much as connect.

Liz, true to form, didn't hold back. She threw in a few irreverent dating stories, but also lit up when the conversation shifted to work. When she found out Matt owned his own accounting firm, her eyes widened with interest. "Well, look at that," she said. "I spend my days teaching financial literacy to people who don't have access to accountants like you."

Matt grinned. "Then maybe we're on the same team." They traded philosophies on budgeting tools and credit education while Jessica and I exchanged amused glances. And when Jessica brought up Lily or I mentioned Max's recent NHL obsession, Matt didn't miss a beat. He didn't just listen. He leaned in, like someone who knew that falling for someone meant signing on for their whole story, not just the highlight reel.

It felt good. Natural. Easy.

Then Liz shifted in her seat, her drink swirling with more intent than necessary.

"So, Jessica," she said, her voice bright with faux-casual energy. "Do you think you'll ever get married again?"

Jessica blinked. I felt her whole body tense beside me.

"That's... a topic shift," she said, forcing a laugh that didn't quite land.

Liz missed the cue. Or maybe she ignored it. "No, really. I mean, you and Will are clearly into each other. And we're not in our twenties anymore. It's not like we need to date for five years to know if it's a fit."

Jessica set her glass down slowly. "I think I need to use the restroom."

She stood up too quickly, her heels clicking against the wood floor as she made her exit.

Liz's mouth opened, then closed. I gave her a look that said *Let it go*, and after a quick beat, I slipped out of my seat to follow Jessica.

I found her in the hallway outside the women's restroom, leaning against the wall, arms crossed. Her eyes flicked up to meet mine.

"I didn't mean to make a scene," she said quietly.

"You didn't," I assured her. "Want to take a walk?"

She nodded, and we wandered down the hallway, past the velvet ropes and gold-framed mirrors, until we found a quiet alcove near the oversized windows that overlooked downtown Minneapolis. We stopped there, the view below glowing in the twilight haze of city lights and Friday night traffic.

"She caught me off guard," Jessica said finally. "And I can't believe she would bring that up. In front of you."

"She caught me off guard, too," I admitted. "I wasn't expecting that."

She turned to me, her eyes reflecting the shimmer of headlights below. "Will, I love you. You know that, right?"

"I do," I said, brushing a hand along her arm. "And I love you. There's no schedule I'm trying to stick to. I'm here, Jess. That's it. That's the point."

Her eyes welled up. "I've just been thinking. A lot. About your kids. About Lily. About everything, this means. What it might look like... in the long term."

I nodded. "And?"

She hesitated. "I'm scared. Scared I won't measure up. That I'll mess something up for Sophie or Max, they've already had enough loss."

Her voice cracked slightly, and I felt her vulnerability ripple out in waves.

I let the silence hold steady and open before responding.

"Jess. Katie will always be their mom. I won't ever try to rewrite that part of their lives. But they don't need you to replace her. They need someone present. Who listens. Who loves them? You already do that."

She looked down at her hands. "But what if I can't be enough?"

"You already are," I said. "And you don't have to carry it alone. That's what this is, right? Being in it together?"

Jessica gave me a wavering smile and let out a breath. "I'm not saying no to the idea of marriage. I'm just saying I need time to figure out what it would look like in this version of my life."

I reached out and cupped her cheek, drawing her a little closer. "I'm not asking you to marry me tonight. Or tomorrow. I'm asking you to come back to that table, finish your wine, and laugh at Liz's ridiculous stories. And c'mon, you have to see that there's a bit of a spark between those two, right?"

That earned me a real laugh. "Deal," she responded. "And yes, there's definitely something up with those two."

We returned to the table, and the mood, thankfully, had softened. Jessica sat down with grace and lightness, and when Liz opened her mouth to apologize, Jess waved her off with a grin.

"You were being you," she said. "Just maybe hold the life-planning questions until round two."

Matt raised his glass. "Cheers to that."

The rest of the evening was lighter. We debated the best pizza (Fat Lorenzo's) and burgers (a tie between Matt's Bar and the 5-8 Club) in the Twin Cities, swapped stories from our own awkward middle school dances, and made tentative plans for a backyard BBQ before the first frost hit.

When the night wrapped up, we stepped out onto the sidewalk together. The fall air had that crisp, just-right bite to it. Not cold. Just enough to make Jessica lean a little closer as we strolled toward her car. The city buzzed around us. Headlights sliced through the darkness, laughter drifted down from an open rooftop, and the faint scent of dough sneaking in from a late-night bakery down the block.

Jessica stopped by her car and turned to me. "Thanks for tonight," she said, her voice soft. "I wish we could extend the evening, but I have an early appointment at the hospital tomorrow with my new patient. She's had some setbacks."

I smiled with understanding. "I know—no need to apologize. We'll make it happen. Next time."

She leaned in, and I met her with a kiss. Slow, lingering, a moment neither of us rushed. When we finally broke apart, she let her forehead rest lightly against mine.

"I'll call you when I get home," she said.

"I'll be up," I promised.

As she got in and pulled away, I stood there for a moment, hands in my pockets, watching her taillights blend into the night. The sidewalk felt still for once, even with the city pulsing around me. No pressure. No second-guessing. Just a certainty settling into my chest like a stone in a calm river.

Whatever this was, whatever Jessica and I were becoming, it wasn't a finish line. It was a beginning. Our beginning. But I knew I needed to help her overcome her fears. Sophie and Max would be fine. They needed Jessica to be Jessica. Nothing more. Nothing less.

I turned and made my way back to where Matt had parked a block over. The night air was cooler now, and I tugged my jacket tighter as I rounded the corner. The glow of the streetlamp stretched across the hood of Matt's SUV, and that's when I saw them.

Matt and Liz.

Leaning against the driver's side, fully immersed in their own little bubble, lips locked like two people who forgot the rest of the world existed. Her hands were in his hair, his resting at her waist like they'd done this a hundred times before.

I stopped a few steps short, unsure if I should clear my throat or just back away slowly and let them finish. But I'd already been spotted. I gave it a beat, then coughed. Loudly.

Matt pulled back like a guilty teenager, and Liz blinked up at me, cheeks flushed, but she didn't look embarrassed—more like... satisfied.

"Well, well," I said, grinning as I walked up. "Do I need to find another ride home?"

Matt laughed and straightened his shirt. "You wish. Get in, loverboy."

Liz gave me a smug little wave before heading off in the opposite direction, calling over her shoulder, "Tell Jessica she's not the only one writing a new chapter or finding her own new beginning."

Matt unlocked the car, and we climbed in.

"So... successful night all around?" I asked.

He glanced at me and smirked. "Yeah. I'd say we're all off to a pretty good start."

61

Jessica

I SLAMMED THE DISHWASHER SHUT harder than I needed to. The sound echoed through my quiet kitchen, but I didn't care.

How dare she? The words kept cycling through my head like a broken record. How. Dare. She.

Liz had always been the bold one. The say-it-without-a-filter friend. But last night? That crossed a line. A big one. *She knew*. She knew I wasn't ready. I had confided in her, just days ago, on her stupid wine-stained couch, baring my thoughts about Will and his kids and this beautifully complicated thing we were building.

And what did she do with that trust? She ambushed me. In public. In front of Will.

I poured myself a cup of coffee I didn't want and leaned against the counter, trying to slow my pulse. Who was she to ask that question? Who was she to press like that?

Liz didn't have kids. She'd never had to consider how her love life would ripple into someone else's. Never had a child look up at her and ask a question they weren't old enough to understand.

And yes, Liz had lost her parents, too. But she was already in her early twenties when it happened. Off to college. Figuring out who she was. Her grief was real, but it was different. She hadn't lost them while still needing them. She hadn't had to bury her childhood and grow up overnight.

She didn't know what it was like to tiptoe around grief, to fall in love with someone who still had ghosts sitting quietly at the dinner table. And she sure as hell didn't know what it meant to try to be something for someone else's children, primarily when that "something" was and still is someone irreplaceable.

I took a sip of coffee and immediately set the mug down. My stomach churned so much that I couldn't keep anything down. I wasn't mad at Will. Not at all. He had handled it graciously, gently, the way he always did. He hadn't pushed. He hadn't taken the bait. When I told him I loved him, there, in the hallway with the skyline behind us, he didn't pressure me for more. He just... stayed.

That's what Will did. He stayed. He showed up. And I loved that about him. I loved *him*. So why did the word 'marriage' make me want to bolt?

Because it wasn't just about *us*. It was about Sophie and Max. And Lily. And Katie, in the way she still hovered just beyond the edges of everything. It was about being asked, expected, to step into a role I wasn't sure I had the right to occupy.

I paced the kitchen. The truth? I *wanted* to marry Will. Someday.

But I also wanted to know what that would look like. I wanted to discuss the difficult aspects. Like what it meant to co-parent his kids in real life, not just on our once-a-month outings. What holidays would look like. Whether Sophie would come to me with her broken heart or if I'd always be just 'Dad's girlfriend'.

I wanted to talk to Will about whether he'd be open to more kids because I had decided I wanted another baby. And getting Lily hadn't been the easiest path. But maybe Will had already closed that chapter. Plus, I wanted to know that Lily would still get enough of *me*. And that I'd still get enough of *me*, too.

I wasn't asking for a roadmap. But I wasn't ready to walk blindfolded into forever, either.

My phone buzzed on the counter.

Liz: *Hey. Can we talk?*

I stared at it. Not yet. Not until I cooled off. Because if I answered now, I'd say something I'd regret. Something like: *Maybe you should try actually raising a kid before telling someone how to love one.*

Instead, I flipped the phone face down and went to check on the laundry.

I kept myself busy the rest of the afternoon, folding laundry that didn't need folding, vacuuming the already clean living room, rearranging the throw pillows on the couch like that would somehow straighten out the ache in my chest. The truth is, I didn't know if I was more hurt or angry. Maybe both.

I'd replayed that moment a dozen times in my mind. The way Liz casually tossed out that comment, like my future was some kind of group decision, hit harder than she probably realized. But that was Liz. Blunt. Loud. Occasionally careless with her words. And still, my best friend.

By early evening, I'd worked myself into a spiral. I'd crafted a dozen different text messages. Some snippy, some sarcastic, one that included a GIF of a woman flipping a table. None of them felt right. None of them sounded like me. Or at least not the version of me I wanted to be.

I sat on the edge of the bed, staring at my phone, thumb hovering over the screen. For a minute, I thought about calling her. Hearing her voice might make it easier. But I wasn't ready for that. Not yet.

Still, letting this sit between us felt worse. So I exhaled, tapped open our thread, and typed:

Me: *I'm not ready to talk about this now, but I know you didn't mean what you said to come off the way it did. I'm just not ready to talk marriage quite yet, okay? So let's just move forward and not talk about it right now.*

I read it three times before hitting send. It wasn't everything I wanted to say, but it was enough, for now.

A few seconds later, the typing bubbles appeared.

Liz: *Okay. I love you, Jess.*

That was it. Five words. But somehow, it was exactly what I needed. I set my phone down, this time screen-up, and crawled under the covers. Whatever tomorrow brought, at least this part didn't have to hurt anymore. And besides, there was so much to look forward to with Will, even if I wasn't ready to put marriage on the table.

62

Will

MID-OCTOBER BROUGHT with it the first hints of real cold. That Minnesota chill that sank into your bones, even when the sun was still out. School was in full swing, the rhythm of the year finally settling into something that felt manageable. Max had joined a club hockey team as though we needed another sport on his roster. Sophie was prepping for the winter recital. And Jessica. Well, Jessica was still saying yes.

To me. To us. I hadn't taken it for granted.

We had our weekly dates. Sometimes we stayed in, cooking something half-decent while the kids took over our respective homes. Sometimes we went out. She even came to Max's recent wrestling meet and cheered like she'd been doing it for years. And when the noise faded and the night got quiet, I could see it in her eyes: she was still holding something back.

But I didn't push. I knew better than to press on grief before it had time to soften its edges.

Matt and Liz were still… whatever they were. From what Matt told me, things were going well. But the way he said it was like someone describing an unseasoned soup. Fine, just fine. I wondered how much of it was real and how much was just good sex. Jessica had her theories, mostly that Liz had never figured out what a real relationship looked like. I wasn't sure Liz would let anyone get close enough to try. And I knew that Jessica still harbored some ill will toward Liz after the night at Prohibition.

But that wasn't my problem. And this weekend was for us.

My parents had finally returned from their six-month retirement tour of Europe, tanned and well-fed and full of opinions about Tuscan vineyards and Parisian croissants. When I told them I wanted to get away for a few days with Jessica, they jumped at the chance to stay with the kids. "Go," my mom had said. "This woman means something to you."

And so I finally talked Jessica into taking a weekend away with me. And to my surprise, she agreed.

We drove up to Lutsen, winding along the North Shore, the trees just past peak color, gold and rust leaves dancing down in sheets every time the wind kicked up. Jessica had her boots propped on the dashboard, her knit cap pulled low, sipping coffee from a travel mug, and humming along with the music.

It was easy. That was what surprised me the most, how easy this kind of quiet could be.

When we got to the cabin, I took the bags while she walked in ahead of me, turning in a slow circle like she was taking it all in—wood-paneled walls, a stone fireplace, a view of Lake Superior right from the deck.

"It's perfect," she said.

"Good," I replied, setting the bags down. "Because I need you to stay put for a sec."

She raised an eyebrow.

I went to my coat pocket and pulled out the envelope. The orange one. The one that had sat in the drawer of my home office desk for several months now. I held it in my hand for a moment, wondering, for the thousandth time, if now was really the right time. But I had promised myself this weekend I would stop wondering.

"I need to tell you something," I said.

Jessica sat on the edge of the couch, watching me. Focused on the envelope in my hand.

"End of the school year, I was clearing out my classroom. You know how I am with clutter. I found this folder at the back of my bottom drawer. Inside... were letters. A whole stack of them. From Katie."

Jessica's breath caught. Her hands folded slowly into her lap.

"I'm still not sure how they got there. Maybe Katie left them on my home desk, and I grabbed them by mistake. I don't know. But they were there. And this one..." I stepped forward and handed her the envelope. "This one's for you."

Jessica looked down at the orange envelope. Written in Katie's looping, careful handwriting, though a bit messy and blurred, it read, To the woman who loves him next. She traced the letters with her thumb. "Will..."

"You don't have to read it now," I said. "You don't have to read it at all if you don't want to. But I think... I think she meant for you to have it."

Jessica's eyes glistened, but no tears fell. She nodded, slid the envelope into her purse, and set it aside.

"I will," she whispered. "When I'm ready."

That night, we sat in front of the fire, tangled on the couch, a half-drunk bottle of Chardonnay forgotten on the table beside us. Jessica wore one of my sweatshirts and nothing else, her bare legs stretched over my lap.

It was different this time. The way she relaxed against me. The way she let herself be comfortable. Not as armor or escape. Just presence. Real.

When she looked up at me, I learned forward and kissed her without waiting, long and deep and slow. She removed her legs from my lap and moved to straddle me. She seemed to like that position until I flipped her over and took charge. But we didn't rush. There was no hurry. No noise. Just breath, just warmth, just the quiet rhythm of hands and mouths and whispered promises in the dark.

Later, in the bedroom, the windows open to the cold lake breeze, she curled into me under the quilt, our bodies bare and relaxed. Her fingers traced slow circles across my chest.

"I'm scared," she whispered.

"I know."

"But I'm here."

"I know."

We didn't talk about the letter again that weekend.

But she didn't hide from it either. The envelope stayed tucked in her purse, always close, like a stone in her pocket—a weight she was learning how to carry.

As we drove back toward home, the sky over Duluth started to snow. Just flurries. Just a hint of what was coming. Jessica reached across the console and laced her fingers with mine. We talked about Lily's upcoming birthday party and Jessica's disbelief that her daughter would soon be nine. We reminisced about our favorite parts of the weekend. And we talked about us.

"Will you wait for me?" she asked.

I squeezed her hand, tight. "Always," I said.

63

Will

THE FIRST SNOW what actually stuck had fallen just days before Emily and Lucas' wedding. Not much, just a light frosting on the lawns and rooftops, enough to make the streets slick and the air carry that unmistakable bite of winter. Emily and Lucas were getting married at a small venue south of the river, and it was perfect for the kind of intimate ceremony they wanted.

Jessica had called Lucas just the night before, asking if I could be her plus-one. I wasn't surprised. Not really. I'd met Lucas back in June, just after Carol passed. He struck me then as a guy who understood that life was complicated and messy and not always what you planned—the kind of man who didn't hold old hurts in clenched fists. So when Emily hijacked the phone from Lucas and pretty much screamed that I was welcome to attend, I had a feeling they meant it.

I wore a charcoal suit, one of the few I still had from back when Katie and I used to attend fundraising galas for her hospital. It still fits, mostly. I adjusted my tie in the rearview mirror before walking around to help Jessica out of the car.

She looked stunning.

Her navy dress hit just below the knee, simple and elegant, with a wrap coat cinched at her waist. She'd curled her hair and worn a pair of pearl earrings I hadn't seen before. She caught me staring and smiled.

"What?" she asked.

"Nothing. Just... damn."

She laughed, looped her arm through mine, and we walked inside.

The ceremony was intimate, maybe thirty people total. Lily was in the back room with the other kids, already dressed in her flower girl dress, spinning slowly in front of a mirror like she couldn't believe she looked that pretty. Jessica helped pin a small clip into Lily's hair, her hands methodical, speaking the words that didn't need saying. Watching her made something in my chest ache in the best way.

She didn't even realize what she was doing, how easily she stepped into moments like this—not replacing anyone and just showing up. Fully. Honestly. Lovingly.

That was the word for her. Loving. Not in grand, performative ways. But in all the little ones.

She caught me watching her and mouthed, "You okay?"

I nodded—more than okay.

The ceremony was beautiful. Simple vows. A few tears. Laughter when Lucas nearly fumbled the ring. And when Lily walked down the aisle, scattering petals with so much finesse that the guests had to stifle a giggle, I glanced over and saw Jessica biting her lip to keep from crying.

"She looks like you," I whispered.

Jessica shook her head but smiled. "She's all Lucas."

After the ceremony, the reception kicked off in all its glory. Once again, I took in the minimalist decor. What a perfect venue for such a lovely new beginning. Jessica and I shared a table with a few of Emily's friends from the writing world. Emily is an author.

Jessica didn't drink much, just a glass of champagne for the toast and water after. She was quieter than usual, her fingers occasionally brushing the small clutch on her lap. I knew what was in it. She hadn't said, but I could tell she'd brought the letter.

Katie's letter.

Later, when the music softened and the cake had been cut, Jessica and I stepped outside. Just for air, she'd said. The cold hit us immediately, but neither of us minded.

"Lily's having the time of her life," I said.

Jessica nodded. "She's growing up so fast."

"She's lucky to have you."

She looked at me then, her eyes reflecting the string lights that wrapped around the patio railing. "You're not bad at this, you know."

"At what?"

"This. Showing up. Making it easy to breathe around you."

I didn't know what to say to that. So I kissed her instead. Just once, softly and slowly, with no agenda behind it.

That night, after the last dance and a dozen heartfelt goodbyes, we helped Lily out of her flower girl dress and back into leggings and a hoodie, her curls a mess around her face. She was half-asleep in the back seat by the time we pulled up to Jessica's place. I helped carry her to her room, tucked her into bed while Jessica turned on her nightlight, then stepped out into the hallway to give them a moment.

Once Lily was settled, Jessica joined me on the couch in the living room. It had been a good day, and we were beat. I turned to Jessica and asked her how she was feeling. I didn't want to belittle the fact that we had just attended her ex-husband's wedding.

"I'm good," she said. "Lucas is happy. Emily is great. It just feels like they were meant to be," she responded.

I felt that we were meant to be, too. And Jessica was getting closer to understanding that.

We didn't talk about the letter. Not that night. We kissed slowly, like we had all the time in the world. Like nothing needed fixing, only feeling. And then we made love. It was unhurried, encompassing everything we hadn't said aloud.

In the quiet that followed, we lay tangled in the sheets, her head on my chest, my hand resting on the soft curve of her hip. The weight of the past still lingered, but it didn't feel so heavy now.

The next morning, just as the light was beginning to stretch across the room, we heard the sound of little feet pattering down the hall. Lily barreled into the bedroom without knocking, still in her leggings and hoodie from the night before.

She climbed right onto the bed, wedging herself between us like she'd done it a hundred times.

"Hi, Will," she said casually, like it was the most normal thing in the world for me to be lying there beside her mom.

Jessica froze for half a second before letting out a soft laugh, and I couldn't help but smile. It was quite a different reception than what had happened at my house with Sophie.

"Hi, Lily," I said, brushing a strand of hair from her forehead. She grinned and flopped back against the pillows.

That was the moment I knew. I'd been falling for Jessica for months, but this, this was the life I wanted: the mess, the mornings, the unexpected moments of being right where I was meant to be.

We hadn't talked about the future yet. But it was already unfolding. I knew that our new beginning was just around the corner.

Epilogue

Jessica

IT WAS LATE MORNING by the time I finally poured my second cup of coffee and sat down at the kitchen table. The sun streamed through the windows in soft golden patches, warming the hardwood floor. Somewhere down the hall, Lily was humming to herself, immersed in her stuffed animals or her markers, no doubt orchestrating a story only she fully understood.

Will had left earlier, smiling as he kissed me goodbye, ready to trade the peace of my place for the chaos waiting at home. He'd texted not long after: *Sophie's already yelling at Max for hiding the remote. All is right with the world.*

I'd smiled at the message. At how normal it felt. How easy.

But it hadn't always been.

My thoughts drifted back to the day before, when I watched Lucas marry Emily. Watching Lily toss petals down the aisle with that serious little face she makes when she's trying not to smile.

Watching Lucas beam with a joy I once thought I'd never see on his face again.

And I'd felt something unexpected: peace. Not loss. Not envy. Just... quiet resolution.

That was what I'd needed, wasn't it? Not a proposal or a promise. Not even a roadmap. I'd needed to see Lucas happy. To know he'd found someone who could love him the way I once did, in a way I no longer could. I needed to know Lily was good, that she could thrive in this new chapter of all our lives.

And this morning, when she'd jumped into bed beside me and Will with that sleepy grin and a "Hi, Will," like it was the most natural thing in the world. That was my answer.

She was good. We all were.

I walked over to my purse and extracted the orange envelope. I stared at Katie's handwriting, wondering what the letter would say. I held it in my hands for a long moment before opening it.

Then, with a breath, I unfolded the letter and began to read.

To the Woman Who Loves Him Next,

If you're holding this letter, it means Will has chosen you, and knowing him, that's a significant gesture.

It means you're kind. It means you're patient. It means you probably love books and are quietly strong in the ways he needs most. It means you didn't run when you realized how deeply he still aches that he didn't scare you away with his endless dad jokes or his habit of organizing everything down to the hour. (Yes, I'm aware of the color-coded calendar. I started it. Sorry.)

I don't know your name. I don't know what your story looks like. But I do know this:

You are walking into a family that knows loss. A family that has seen the worst days and made it through. But you're also walking into a family that loves harder because of it.

Will is the love of my life. And I don't say that to haunt you or to cling to something that isn't mine anymore. I say it because he's worth it. He's thoughtful and loyal and frustratingly stubborn. Yet, he loves with his whole heart. And if he loves you, it's because you've earned a place in that heart. Don't take that lightly. And don't be afraid of it either.

As for my children, my beautiful Sophie and Max, please love them. Please don't try to replace me. They don't need another mom. They just need someone who will show up. Someone who will listen. Someone who will cheer the loudest at their recitals, wrestling matches, dance recitals, and school plays. Someone who will sit quietly with them when they miss me, and not try to fix it. Just be with them.

You will get it wrong sometimes. That's okay. I did too. But if you lead with love, they will know. They will feel it.

Please help them remember me. No, not in some grand, pedestal way, but in the small things. Let Sophie keep the necklace she likes to wear that was mine. Let Max tell the same story he always does about the time we got locked out of the house and had to crawl through the doggy door that we had, even though we didn't have a dog. I do hope that one day, they'll get a dog.

Laugh with them. Cry with them. Let them be exactly who they are. And let yourself be who you are, too.

You don't need to be me. You don't need to carry my shadow.

You're there now. You're the one showing up in the morning. You're the one making their world feel safe again.

Thank you for loving him. For loving them. And for giving them a future that still has joy in it.

With more gratitude than I can put into words,

Katie

I folded the letter slowly, a tear slipping down my cheek. It wasn't out of sadness, but out of something more sacred. Grace.

I held the envelope in my hands and brought it to my face. I could smell the mustiness of the envelope. Then, I looked toward the hallway, where Lily had just started singing again.

And for the first time, I didn't feel like I was standing on borrowed ground. I felt like I knew the path that had been set out for me. Despite the loss of my mother. Despite the loss of Sophie and

Max's mother. And because of my intense love for Will. I rested my hand on my belly. This was my new beginning. Our new beginning.

Acknowledgments

WHEN I FIRST SAT DOWN to write *Emily's Next Chapter,* I thought it would be a one-and-done kind of story. A standalone novel about love, loss, and second chances, but as I wrote, I realized there was more to tell. There were more layers to the people I'd created and the lives they were rebuilding.

Jessica's story, in particular, stayed with me. Her voice kept nudging me, asking for space to speak. And so, *Jessica's New Beginning* was born. What started as a single story has evolved into what I now lovingly call my *Starting Over Trilogy*. It's a series about finding strength in the aftermath, choosing love again, and believing in new chapters, no matter how life unfolds.

Much of this book is imagined. But its foundation, what it feels like to start over, to carry the weight of a past while hoping for a better future, that's real. If you've experienced divorce, heartache, or the ache of wondering what's next, I hope this story speaks to you. I hope it reminds you that healing doesn't follow a straight line, and that love, true, imperfect love, can find its way back to you, even if it arrives wrapped in uncertainty.

This book was written during a season of profound change. I became a grandmother for the first time and discovered a new kind of love, one that expands the heart in ways I never imagined. I watched my mother fight a health battle that she eventually lost. In fact, she lost her fight just four days after I finished writing this book. And I was reminded, again and again, that starting over isn't the end of something; it's a new beginning. Sometimes, it's the best kind of beginning, and sometimes it is simply different than what we had planned.

I have so many people to thank, and I know I won't name everyone who deserves it. But if you've been part of my life, if you've supported me, listened to me, or simply cheered me on, please know I'm grateful.

To my husband, Scott: You are my second chance, my safe place, and my forever. Thank you for building this life with me.

To my children, Cate and Zach: Watching you grow into the people you are continues to be one of my life's greatest honors. You make me proud every single day.

To my son-in-law, Nathan: Thank you for being such a solid, kind presence. I'm so thankful you're part of our family.

To my stepdaughter, Faith: You are my chosen love. Your laughter, your hugs, and your heart bring so much joy to my world.

To my dad and sister: Thank you for giving me a foundation of love and resilience. I am endlessly grateful for the support you've offered me, especially in the most trying seasons. And to my mom, I miss you and I love you so much. Thank you for sharing your love of reading with me. Without that passion for words, I wouldn't be the writer I am today.

To my best friend, Kirsten: You are my person. The bestest bestie a girl could have. Always. There are no words strong enough, but I'll keep trying anyway.

To the Classy Bs: Thank you for being my constants. I hope I'm half the friend to you that you've been to me.

To Missy, Shelley, Jackie, Julie, Erin, Robin, Karen, and all the amazing women who put up with me clicking away on my laptop while you're trying to craft, thank you for the laughs, the love, and the weekends that fill my soul.

To Jennie, Aimee, Kirsten, and Marge: You made this neighborhood feel like home. Thank you for every walk, every porch chat, every tear, and glass of wine shared.

To the entire Schreiber family: Thank you for opening your hearts to me and my children, for cheering on our new chapter, and for your unwavering love.

Life rarely goes the way we think it will. But sometimes, it leads us somewhere even better.

And now, to my readers, thank you for reading *Jessica's New Beginning*. I hope, in some small way, it helps you believe in your own.

Last but definitely not least, thank you to the team at Fox Pointe Publishing. Thank you for helping me through this fourth book, which, we now know, will turn into a fifth. Kiersten, thank you for your leadership, guidance, and, most importantly, your belief in me and for helping me share my thoughts with the world.

To Scotty, thank you for designing the most amazing book covers that help reflect who I am and the stories I have to tell. Your covers are so inspiring, and I am so appreciative of everything you do in bringing my stories to life.

www.ingramcontent.com/pod-product-compliance
Lightning Source LLC
LaVergne TN
LVHW050028080526
838202LV00070B/6962